# Killer Scarecrow

## THE APEX ALGORITHM

A NOVEL

# Joseph Basile

Suite 300 - 990 Fort St
Victoria, BC, V8V 3K2
Canada

www.friesenpress.com

**Copyright © 2017 by Joseph Basile**
First Edition — 2017

All rights reserved.

No part of this publication may be reproduced in any form, or by any means, electronic or mechanical, including photocopying, recording, or any information browsing, storage, or retrieval system, without permission in writing from FriesenPress.

ISBN
978-1-5255-0140-1 (Hardcover)
978-1-5255-0141-8 (Paperback)
978-1-5255-0142-5 (eBook)

*1. FICTION, MYSTERY & DETECTIVE*

Distributed to the trade by The Ingram Book Company

*For Joan*

# INTRODUCTION

**THE SPIRIT OF** Saint Louis played on a black and white television console, a biographical film starring James Stewart as Charles Lindbergh. This movie was the start of many that had captivated the imagination of a young boy. I was eleven years old, enthralled in Lindbergh's historic nonstop solo flight across the Atlantic. I wanted nothing more than to do the same – design, build and fly a record setting airplane.

The fascination in aviation was the first revelation that year in 1973. The second was the tendency for waking up abruptly before it was time. I'd be panting and exhausted as if I had run the Boston marathon. Hearing my parents moving about I presumed they caused me to fall out of slumber. It was momentary though because as fast as I awoke, I had fallen back to sleep.

Unclear if this had gone on for days or weeks however, one particular morning my mysterious wakeup call was witnessed by another. Certain its discovery would end the peculiar behaviour of mine. It was on the day my mother heard noises coming from my room, puzzled why I would be jumping on the bed 5am in the morning. Placing her hand on the door knob the noise had ceased. Upon entering my room she found me non-responsive, tense and rigid as oak. Her words not mine. Obviously, my phenomenon witnessed was no closer to being understood. Multiple doctors prodded, probed, tested, interviewed me with and without my parents but the diagnosis and resultant prognosis took months to decide.

During this period of uncertainty, the condition continued roughly the same time every morning. Later, the occurrences transitioned to any time of the day that enabled everyone to observe the disorder. This isn't true but the sympathy factor I received seemed as if they all had. The few that actually experienced the full spectrum of my disorder had helped piece together a diagnosis – epilepsy. The treatment – 400 milli-grams of dilantin and 50 milli-grams of phenobarbital. Years later, the phenobarbital was discontinued.

A daily dosage of dilantin has kept me seizure free for more than forty-years. The epileptic disorder has taught me that half measures do not solve problems and just as important, do not take anything for granted. Flying the contraptions I designed and built didn't materialize because of the medical requirements for a pilot's license. While one door closed on my entrepreneurial and aviator record setting aspirations, another door opened. Instead of building and flying, it led me down a path to maintain and repair transport category aircraft. I started turning wrenches on airplanes that began eighty years following the Wright brothers' first powered flight; or, fourteen years after man's first lunar landing. Though a career in the airline industry wasn't my first passion, the new path I had taken never had a dull moment, always challenging and rewarding.

More than three decades spent in this industry, I witnessed why it's no coincidence that air travel is safer than any other means of transportation. It is a reflection of the combined efforts of the regulatory authorities, manufacturers and airline companies. Generally speaking, the high level of safety is due to enhanced aircraft design, new materials, better navigational equipment, maintenance and above all, the higher standards. I will not bore you with statistics to quantify airline travel is safe. Needless to say, the leading causes of death published by Canadian, European and United States government agencies are irrefutable. Your chances of dying are exponentially greater behind a wheel of a car than soaring thirty-five thousand feet in the air.

\* \* \*

My first novel is a fictional story about an up and coming airline stationed in Charlottesville, Virginia. In a saturated market, Virginia Airlines established their base of operations in a rural area that prospered by connecting isolated communities to major cities. The business plan conceived by Alexander Cooper, the airline's cofounder and CEO had never anticipated the level of success. Considering every financial institution had refused to back his venture and declared the investment nothing more than a foolhardy gamble. If it were not for private investors, Alexander's business endeavor would never have taken flight in the mid-1960s.

The Virginia Airlines glorified by the Washington Post for being in the forefront of safety innovation, excellent service and on-time performance. Leading newspapers in every city and town along the eastern coast wrote similar articles. From Maine to Florida and as far west as Mississippi, provided the best advertisement money couldn't buy and made Alexander's airline a household name. Prompted by the David and Goliath headlines, New Englanders and southerners all read with interest how the major airlines failed to compete against a small rural airline.

In business for nearly ten years without a mishap, Virginia Airlines' highly modified Fairlane airplanes held a pristine safety record. The most technologically advanced aircraft received its first safety blemish on August 17, 1974, shortly after take-off, the airline's flagship airplane experienced the unthinkable - a dual engine failure.

As in all incident or accident investigations, the ultimate goal is to prevent another occurrence. There are a myriad of plausible factors labeled as human error, mechanical failure, weather, and sabotage, may occur singularly or a culmination of these factors. Human error is the leading contributor and whatever the person's reason for being indecisive or taking an inappropriate action, blaming that individual will not introduce the necessary change to prevent reoccurrence. The remedy is typically corrected by dealing with the chain of events leading to such an error. Fixing this issue may consist of lessening the workload or modifying procedures to reduce a series of actions required to accomplish a task.

Another solution is the adaptation of an aid. The creation of a checklist is one example prompted by a Boeing Model 299 bomber. In 1935, the airplane stalled after take-off and crashed, then exploded into a ball of fire. Two out of five crew members later died from their injuries, including a very experienced pilot. The investigation implicated pilot error because the pilot had forgotten to remove the elevator control locking mechanism prior to flight. The lesson learned here is the acknowledgment that this new complex and sophisticated airplane can not rely on human memory. With the aid of a checklist, pilots went on to fly the Model 299 designated as the B17 bomber, nearly two million miles without an accident.

Mechanical failures rank second. Understandably, over the decades a lot of effort has been exhausted to understand the predictive failure and analysis, improved quality control, better materials, inspection intervals, manufacturing and design process. These measures increased reliability, on-board computers and the inclusion of redundant aircraft systems had significantly enhanced safety.

Inspecting Virginia Airlines crash site, an investigator found evidence of a bird strike. The first clue deemed as an act of God that may have attributed to the crash. As rare as it may be however, wildlife hazards is a known variable. The first recorded bird strike event involved Wilbur Wright in 1905, just two years after their first and earth-shattering man powered flight. However, Calbraith Perry Rodgers, in 1912 was the first to die because of a bird strike. In 1960, the first commercial airline disaster occurred at Boston's Logan Airport. Hundreds of European Starlings flew into the airplane's path caused three out of the four engines to shutdown.

The NTSB led the crash investigation with the FAA's participation. While substantiating or disproving each significant finding, their combined efforts have unearthed information requiring the FBI's involvement. Three collaborating agencies driven by their own agendas sift through the body of evidence. Their initial findings seemed self evident on the surface until they delved into and immersed themselves into the data. It gave credence to the old adage that 'nothing is what it seems'.

# CHAPTER 1

**THOMAS B. WRIGHT** penciled his comments into his night shift log, pausing at times to take a bite out of his tuna sandwich. Of late, working through his lunch hour had become a habit to stay one-step ahead of the maintenance activities. Employed with Virginia Airlines as the shift duty manager, responsible to ensure his crew work the aircraft in a safe, efficient, and timely fashion.

The airline's aggressive growth, however, was outpacing the infrastructure's ability to support it adequately. While the fleet expansion had ceased at twenty-five airplanes, for the moment anyway, their daily utilization continued to grow. Planes flying more each day have reaped its reward, profiting on the newly introduced calculated route structure.

Passenger loads were consistently above the break-even mark, meaning Virginia Airlines was basking in profits after years of operating in the red. However, sustaining the current level of success afforded minimal time to maintain the airplanes. Aircraft technicians predominately comprised of ex-military personnel, all doing their part to step up while additional staff are hired and trained.

He pushed the remaining portion of the sandwich into his mouth. The bread stuck to the roof of his mouth, so he used the last bit of coffee to wash it down.

He tossed the wrapper like a basketball into the waste bin against the wall. His watch indicated he was running six minutes behind schedule. He quickened his pace to clear off his desk and restore it from a cluttered lunchroom table to an orderly state. He returned the thermos to his lunch box and tucked it away in the lower desk drawer.

He grabbed the night shift log sheet and slipped it into his clipboard. It listed the outstanding tasks prioritized by criticality that could jeopardize aircraft readiness. He felt a slight rush of air as he opened the door and crossed the threshold into the hangar. The two large hangar doors on the opposite side of the building were wide open. He could clearly see three out of the five aircraft were outside with both engines running.

"Perfect," Thomas murmured.

It was his last day on shift before vacation, a needed leave for the first time in ten years. Olivia Cooper, the acting president and CEO of Virginia Airlines, extended it to a compulsory four weeks in Fiji. It was a goodwill gesture to recognize his efforts, and just as important, to get him as far away as possible. It was an orchestrated measure to ensure he didn't pull the same stunt as other years, opting out of vacation under some false pretense.

Thomas stood at the hangar's threshold and gazed into the eastern sky. He could make out the horizon, *it's dawn - the shift will end soon*, he thought. The clipboard tapped against his thigh, a nervous tick, as he waited for the clear signal from each aircraft. The roar of the 645 engines wound down to an idle speed.

"Come on, let me have it," Thomas muttered. He rubbed his head in a circular motion. "Don't keep me waiting."

Thomas coached his staff to use the landing lights to convey aircraft status. Lights turned on, then off, signify the operational test had passed. When they're illuminated for an extended period meant a failed test. That would prompt every able body to rush the aircraft and brainstorm the problem. As a unified team, their joint efforts increased the odds of a quick resolution.

Aircraft 645 flashed their landing lights. "Yes! There it is." Thomas acknowledged it with an extended thumb held high in the air.

The crews in the other two aircraft watched his reaction to 645's status and quickly communicated their test results. Aircraft 660's lights burst on then off and taxied away, following 645 to the terminal. The technicians in the third aircraft, 667, flickered the lights repeatedly for a strobe effect. Thomas grinned, appreciating the sentiment and waved his clipboard to say knock it off.

The three airplanes completed ahead of schedule had the largest work packages. His satisfaction was short lived when he directed his attention at the two remaining airplanes. They had the least amount of work required, but to his disappointment, they had fallen behind schedule.

He stared at the hangar's interior and saw no one present. The aircraft technicians should have cleared the area by now in preparation to tow their planes out. *Have they lost their minds?* He thought.

Leonard entered the hangar through the main hallway doors. On his own, without the support of his crew, he pulled one toolbox while pushing another. He cleared them away from his airplane.

"Leonard!" Thomas called. "What's the status of your bird?"

"Thomas B. Wright be right, my brother." Leonard laughed.

"I'm not your brother," Thomas snapped. "Your bird should have been the first one out the door. So what do you have for me?"

Leonard refrained from responding. He acknowledged Thomas's serious demeanor. It would have been futile to state the obvious and contradict his supervisor. Barricaded by another aircraft, he could not have brought his airplane out first. However, the light work package should have rendered his aircraft ready before the others.

"Well? Is you aircraft ready?" Thomas pressed.

"Indeed."

"What fixed the pilot discrepancy?"

"You were correct," Leonard began. "The number two hydraulic system had a lot of air. Bleeding the system took longer than expected. We needed to crack open additional fittings up in the tail section to release the trapped air. For the rest of the work package..."

"That's fine," Thomas interrupted. It was redundant to revisit the tasks he had monitored throughout the night. He agreed the simplest of tasks became problematic but it did not excuse why the crew abandoned their workstations. An extended break taken minutes prior to head start was unacceptable, even careless. "All tasks are signed off?"

Leonard held up his clipboard. "Yes sir. She's ready to go."

"Not until we clear the equipment."

Emma Ferraro, a competent lead mechanic with short jet-black hair joined Thomas and Leonard. She sensed the tension. In a direct tone, she asked, "Shouldn't this plane be out of the hangar by now?"

Thomas rubbed his shaved head. "Get your crew to help Leonard get his aircraft out."

Without hesitation, Emma complied. She put both index fingers into her mouth and blew a sharp piercing whistle to grab her crew's attention. Like a baseball coach, she gestured with her hands and arms to her crew. They jumped into action, executing the request without uttering a word. A well-coordinated crew exercised their roles with great precision.

Thomas placed his left hand on Leonard's shoulder. "It's all right, son. You are new to the position of lead mechanic. However, your crew are well-seasoned technicians and they should have known better. They left you holding the bag. They're testing your leadership skills."

"Yes, sir."

"You need to deal with them." Thomas held his clip board against his chest. "Not with an iron fist. Always convey clear direction and expectations. Offer praise for a job well done and, just as important, challenge them when a task veers off course. That is how you will earn their respect."

"Yes, Mister T."

"Mister T, my ass." Thomas smiled. "You'll be all right. Go on, Emma will bite your head off if you let her crew do all the work."

Leonard joined Emma. "I appreciate the help," he said. "Are we a go?"

"We will be after you get your ass into the cockpit," Emma said.

"Okay." There was no reason to argue why he should perform this menial task. He had no leverage to push back on a fellow lead mechanic, especially one who was bailing him out of a difficult predicament.

The main hallway door creaked opened as Nathan Aschan entered the hangar. Seeing Thomas in the hangar meant he had misjudged the time. Nathan could feel his face heat up and kept his eyes glued to the floor. Thomas held out his left arm and stopped the youth in his tracks.

"Nathan."

"Eh, Mister T."

"Is everything all right, son?"

"Oh, yeah," Nathan said with a forced smile.

"What is the status of your aircraft?"

"Oh, it's all done, or so I'm told."

"So you were told?" Thomas repeated, throwing his head back. "You know that we deal in absolutes. A non-definitive response does not give me the confidence this bird is ready to fly."

"Yes sir."

"Who mentioned the aircraft is ready?"

"Ah, Mike."

"Mike advised your crew's airplane is ready and he's not around." The young technician did not respond. Thomas referred to his clipboard. "Engine oil and fuel filter replacements need an engine run and leak check."

"That's right," Nathan confirmed. "Once we complete the runs, she's good to go."

"Well then, since you're all alone, I'll get Emma and her crew to assist you."

Thomas curled his tongue and whistled. Emma heard it while parking the tug. Scanning the hangar floor, she set her sights on Thomas. He was too far to talk, so she waited for the series of hand gestures.

He pointed to the aircraft in the hangar, then motioned outward with a fist with the thumb extended like a hitchhiker. He made a circle with his finger and pointed to himself.

She acknowledged the instructions with an extended thumb up.

Leonard sat in the tug next to her. "What did he say?"

"We need to get aircraft 641 out of the barn. For whatever reason, he will personally perform the engine runs."

"He said all that?"

"No. He also said to get the idiot in the passenger seat to help as well." Emma smiled. "Well!" She looked at his dumbfounded face. "Help Nathan clear the area while I drive the tug over."

Thomas met the rest of Diego's crew in the corridor. Brian and Zac walked back to the hangar. They avoided eye contact, acting coy like nothing was wrong.

"There's work to be done, gentleman," Thomas said without taking his sight off the building's entrance doors.

Zac glimpsed at Thomas, who was heading for the exit. "If you're looking for Michael, he has gone to the terminal to catch a flight."

"Terminal?" Thomas remembered a request of some sort. Referring to his clipboard, he found Michael's request to leave early approved a week prior. He turned to Zac. "We have work to do."

"On it, Mister T."

"You better hurry if you don't want Emma to tear you apart."

"Sir?"

"Her crew is working your aircraft."

"Shit." Zac quickened his pace.

Everyone stood by the nose of aircraft 641 positioned on the tarmac in front of the hangar. It's prepped and ready for Thomas to carry out the engine run. Thomas glanced at Emma. "We have twenty minutes to get the runs done and towed to the terminal."

"Better yet, we'll taxi it," she said. "It will be quicker."

"Get Nathan please. I want him to join me alone in the cockpit."

She replied with a nod.

In the cockpit, Nathan searched behind his seat, on the glare shield, then in his side pocket. "What are you doing?" Thomas asked.

"I can't find the checklist," Nathan replied.

"Don't worry about that," Thomas said as he began the pre-start checklist from memory. "I need you to tell me what is going on."

"What do you mean?"

He looked Nathan in the eye. "Really? Don't play coy. You know what I mean." Thomas held up two fingers by the front windshield.

Emma received the signal and prior to giving the go ahead to start the number two engine, she confirmed the area was clear of personnel. She pointed to the engine with one hand and made a circular motion with the other.

"We're cleared to start?" Thomas asked.

"What?" Nathan said. He noticed Thomas's finger tapping the starter button. He realized he was required to perform his duties in the right seat. "Oh, right." He looked out the window and verified the area was clear.

Thomas depressed the starter button and confirmed engine rotation. At the predetermined speed, he selected the fuel on. The engine sped up to a self-sustaining speed and the start sequence ended on cue. He gave the engine a few seconds to stabilize and signaled to Emma that he was ready to start the number one engine.

Within minutes, Thomas and Nathan were satisfied both engines were operating at the manufacturer's specifications. They advanced the throttles to seventy-five percent power. The gusting crosswind caused the aircraft to rock. Now and then, they glanced out the windows to assure the area remained clear while two twelve-foot diameter propellers spun at 925 rpm.

"Do you agree this setting held for ten minutes is sufficient for a leak check?" Thomas asked.

"I think so," Nathan responded.

"Good." Thomas signaled Emma with a tap to his watch then held up ten fingers. "This will give you enough time to tell me what the hell is going on."

Nathan gulped, rubbed his palms together, and spewed all he knew.

# CHAPTER 2

"**WHAT ARE YOU** looking at?" Emma said while pressing a sequence of buttons to unlock the gate.

"Quiet," Thomas whispered. Standing on the path that leads to the parking lot, he worried her intrusion will unsettle his new and bizarre companion.

"What is it?" Emma asked, closing the gate behind her.

"There she is." Thomas signaled with his head. "Isn't she beautiful?"

Emma scanned the horizon. "What am I looking for?"

"Quiet!" Thomas said. "Over there, at the base of the tree."

"Holy shit!" She could not believe her eyes. She placed her hand on his shoulder. "Is this the bird you rescued two weeks ago?"

"Yup," he said. "Isn't she incredible?"

"Yeah."

The peregrine falcon standing at the base of the tree spread her wings, flapped gently, and took flight. Bells rang as she flew away. She circled above Thomas and Emma, gaining altitude with little effort while drifting over the airport. "Did you hear bells?" Emma asked.

"I'm sure there's a disappointed falconer missing an expensive bird," he said. "These falcons migrate thousands of miles."

"Should she ever come back, maybe we could see her tags."

"She's not a dog." Thomas giggled.

Arriving at their cars, she watched Thomas remove the ragtop off his restored 1939 Morgan roadster. He was leaving for a month-long vacation, but they hadn't been apart for more than a week in a long time. They were no longer a couple, but her feelings for him remained strong.

Emma unlocked her car door and glared at the empty bench seat of her Ford pickup. It triggered an empty feeling in the pit of her gut, an emotion she felt on and off since they mutually decided to give their relationship a break. Against her better judgement, she gave in to her emotions. "Need company before you head off on vacation?"

Thomas placed his lunch box on the passenger seat and straightened up. He rubbed his head.

Emma knew it meant he needed a second to consider an appropriate response. "That's fine," she said. She felt vulnerable. To ease the awkwardness she said, "You're probably busy packing and all."

"Emma, it's..."

"No, that's fine," she interrupted. "Have fun and..."

"Emma!" He was planning to go to Luray, Virginia, to visit his wife's grave. His hesitation wasn't a reflection on how best to let her down, but rather how to express that his deceased wife had more priority. "I'm heading north."

Emma knew what that meant. Of all the excuses he could have come up with, this is the only one she considered acceptable. "I understand."

"What if I take you out for dinner tonight?" Thomas said.

Emma hopped into her pickup truck, closed the door behind her, and rolled down her window. "Better yet," she shouted over the sound of her revving engine, "I'll cook for you." She winked and flashed a smile, then drove off, tires squealing.

\* \* \*

Now in their twilight years, Edgar and Millie Brooks were childhood sweethearts. They were born, raised, and lived their lives in Winston-Salem, North Carolina. Like most residents, they spent their careers working for the RJ Reynolds Tobacco Company. They held prominent positions and the high wages they earned gave them a comfortable lifestyle.

"This is the best idea you have ever had," Millie said, tipping the thermos to pour herself a cup of coffee. "Would you like a refill?"

"Sure," Edgar replied, holding up his cup. "I never thought retirement would be this fun. I wish we had done this trip sooner. I've always wanted to see the rest of the country, but I must confess, it's time to go home and stay put for a while."

Stretched out in lawn chairs, they watched the sunrise from their Winnebago's rooftop. They were parked at Charlottesville Airport, where they had spent the night to rest up. They needed a good night sleep before completing the last leg of their trip home.

"Considering this will be our last day on the road, why don't we take it slow?" Millie suggested, "Let's enjoy the remaining hours we have together."

"You sound like we're going our separate ways." Edgar laughed.

"You know what I mean." Millie grinned. "We worked forty-five years building our careers at the same company, under the same roof, and we saw so little of each other." She looked across the airfield lit by the sun peering over the horizon. "I would be remiss if I did not mention how much it meant to have you all to myself."

"Not to worry, dear," Edgar said. "We're now retired. We'll be spending plenty of time alone together, with the kids, and the grandkids, and..."

"Oh stop." She tapped his wrist.

"I relish the thought of sleeping in our bed again, but we can take it slow. We have been away for two years; what's another day?"

She squeezed his arm in appreciation. "Oh look, they're bringing the airplanes from the hangar to the terminal. I'll make us breakfast and we can watch them take off while we eat."

Edgar noticed an eagle, or maybe a hawk, he was not sure. It was slowly circling, riding a thermal as it gained altitude without beating its wings. "Let me have the binoculars for a second."

"What's up?"

"There's a bird of prey to the north and about five hundred feet in the air," he said. Holding the binoculars to his eyes, he adjusted the thumbwheel to sharpen the fuzzy image. "It's a peregrine falcon and she's climbing fast."

Millie tugged on his shirt. "Let me have a look."

He hesitated at first, then relented and passed her the binoculars. "She's over there."

Millie scanned the sky, unable to spot the falcon. She checked around and soon found it. "There it is. I see it now."

Emptying the contents of the thermos into his cup, Edgar said, "We're out of coffee."

"That's fine," Millie responded without taking her eyes off the soaring apex predator. "Take mine. I've had my fill."

The majestic bird's wings were held out, allowing the air to flow over them. Millie noticed the falcon's head move side to side, scanning the sky and landscape, searching for food. Floating on a layer of air, it entered a circular flight pattern, riding another thermal and soaring without exhausting any energy.

She traced the rise in engine noise to Virginia Airline's hangar. Adjusting the focus, a vision of a muscular woman with spiked black hair came into view. A fire extinguisher sat by her right foot while aircraft's engines ran at high power. Hangar doors wide opened gave Millie a glimpse into the brightly lit facility.

Setting her binoculars on her lap, she searched for the falcon with her naked eye, but it was gone. Her stomach growling reminded her she needed to get motivated and start cooking breakfast. "Would you like an omelette, scrambled, or fried eggs?" she asked.

"Scrambled will be fine," Edgar said with one eye open.

"Don't fall asleep," she said. "I will only be a minute."

"Mm hmm."

Millie shimmied down the ladder, rounded the corner, and stepped into the rectangular mobile home. She stumbled, startled by an unexpected presence in the kitchen.

"Kak kak kak kak," the peregrine falcon called out in distress. The bird picked up a twitching mouse from the counter then flew across the aisle to the kitchen table. It plopped the mouse on the table and cried out again, "Kak kak kak."

"Shoo, shoo," Millie said, waving her hands then reached for the broom.

"Kak kak," the falcon countered. Its body swayed side to side and bells jingled as she stomped her feet. "Kak kak kak."

The falcon reared its head while Millie shook a broomstick at it. The feathered intruder sidestepped across the table toward the opened window.

"Shoo, shoo," Millie repeated.

The falcon exited the Winnebago, leaving the mouse Edgar had failed to trap over the past week. The bird flapped furiously as it flew off into the distance. Relieved, Millie returned the broom to the closet, draped the mouse with a napkin and started on breakfast.

As she placed the dishes on the food tray, the airport activity intensified with engine sounds. She poured one glass with orange juice and another with Edgar's favorite, grape juice. With the food tray in hand, she quickened her step and hurried out the door. Plane watching to serve as their last activity of their two year trek and she didn't wish to miss a second of it. Balancing the tray on one hand, she grabs the run of the ladder with the other. "Coming up." She climbed to the top of the Winnebago where Edgar greeted her.

* * *

Odessa Clarke, Charlottesville's station manager, was forced to work behind the counter. Two of her staff called in sick just minutes before starting their shift. This was the third weekend in three months the same two ticket agents, Jena and Candice, didn't show up for work on a Saturday morning.

She had just enough time to call in reinforcements and was grateful her staff seldom refused overtime. The first two employees she contacted agreed to come in as fast as they could. Until the cavalry arrived, she returned to the counter to tend to the passengers.

Odessa was born and raised in Charlottesville, Virginia. She was a full-figured woman, black, twenty-six years old, and the first person to receive a scholarship from Virginia Airlines. She majored in finance and after graduating with honors, she worked for the airline. Working with spreadsheets was not her cup of tea. Within the year, she transferred out of finance to the airport division, where she excelled.

Michael arrived at the terminal and approached the counter at the gate. With folded arms, he leaned on the counter. "Did you get demoted?"

"Good morning, Michael," she said while reviewing a telex highlighting the Richmond flight manifest.

"Call me, Mike."

"Okay, Mike." The pleasantry made Odessa cringe.

"What are you doing out here?"

"I'm sorry," she said. "I can't chat right now. I need to get ready for this flight to Richmond."

"Excellent. That's where I'm headed. I don't have an assigned seat though. I'm listed as standby."

"Honey, I received a telex from reservations and the manifest shows this flight is full." She reached behind the counter to receive another telex comprised of several pages.

"Is that an updated manifest?" Michael asked.

"No," Odessa replied, "it's the flight release and weather report for the flight crew."

"I can tell your hands are full," Michael said, knocking twice on the counter. "I guess I can stick around for a while. Let me know when you get your head above water."

"Yes, of course," she sighed. "Should there be a no-show, you are next in line for a seat assignment. There's a party of three connecting from Miami and the flight is running late."

"You think I have a good..." he paused, staring over Odessa's shoulder and through the large terminal windows, fixated on the aircraft towed to the gate. It was the airplane he had worked on the night before that was now headed to Richmond.

"Michael?"

He snapped out of his trance. "That's aircraft 641."

She looked over her shoulder and confirmed the aircraft's designator. Six hundred and forty-one painted in black across the nose section. "So it is, what of it?"

Michael checked his watch. "I have twenty minutes," he said grimly. He took a moment to weigh his options. "Odessa, please take me off the standby list."

"We'll know for certain in a few minutes. You'll never know, you may have a chance."

Michael took a step back away from the counter and said. "Not with my luck, I prefer to drive to Richmond after all."

# CHAPTER 3

**PHILIP SCHMIDT FLASHED** his badge as he slipped through airport security. Dressed in a dark navy blue uniform, each jacket sleeve wrapped with four gold stripes. Silver wings were pinned to his chest and hat. Eyes hidden behind the green tinted Ray-Ban aviator glasses, he strolled through the terminal with an air of confidence. Philip tipped his hat at the folks working behind the concession stands. Lugging his flight bag loaded with various manuals and aviation charts, he approached the lounge at Gate 3.

"You're late," Odessa said.

Philip removed his hat and planted a kiss on her cheek. "How is my favorite ebony gal?"

"Honey, I'm too much woman for you to handle." She giggled. "Anyway, you better get your scrawny white ass on the plane; we're boarding in five minutes." She put one hand on her hip and the other on the counter. "I thought you were taking the day off to be with my cuz."

"I tried to get the day off but there's no one to cover for me. We have a number of pilots off on sick leave."

"Oh Philip, today is the seventeenth."

"You don't need to remind me. I, more than anyone, know how much this day means to him. I'll make it up to him, we're getting together tomorrow."

"You need to get going," she said, handing him the flight release.

"Send me off with a kiss then," he said with his cheek turned to her.

"You're incorrigible." She nudged him gently. "Now get going, Ace, before I put you over my knee."

He put on his hat and picked up his flight bag. "I like it when you talk dirty to me."

While Odessa enjoyed the cat and mouse routine, she needed to return to work to avoid taking a delay. She had just picked up the microphone to start the boarding announcement when the cavalry arrived. "You two are a sight for sore eyes," she sighed.

Alice and Ellie relieved her of the gate agent duties without missing a beat. Alice took the microphone from Odessa's hand. "Is flight 1001 ready to board?" Alice asked.

"Yes, dear," Odessa said.

"Good morning, ladies and gentlemen," Alice began. "This is the pre-boarding announcement for flight 1001 to Richmond. We are now inviting those passengers with small children, and any passengers requiring special assistance, to begin boarding at this time."

Ellie rubbed Odessa's back. "It must have been a hectic morning."

"The last minute sick calls didn't help," Odessa declared. "I don't normally work on the weekends, but when I saw Jena and Candice were scheduled to work this morning, well, let's just say I had a bad feeling."

"They're young and immature," Ellie said.

"Right," Odessa frowned, not wanting to say anything further she may regret later. She retrieved her purse, walkie-talkie, and the clipboard from the counter. "I appreciate you two coming in. We'll chat later."

Philip placed his flight bag in the cockpit between the side console and his seat. He removed his jacket and hung it on the hook on the flight deck's bulkhead.

"Hey mister, you're cutting it close again," Eva Muller, the first officer said.

"Don't I know it," he replied. He extended his lanky leg over his cockpit seat. "The car battery died and I had to knock on several doors until I found someone with booster cables."

"Uh huh. Wasn't it the transmission the month before and the carburetor the month before that? Maybe it's time for a new car."

"Trade in my '54 Oldsmobile Ninety-Eight Starfire?" He snickered as he secured his five-point harness. "Are you mad?" He raised an eyebrow. "She's twenty years old. A classic I tell you."

"Whatever." Eva laughed.

"And what do you drive, missy, a Volkswagen Beetle?"

"No," she growled. "My baby is a BMW 2002."

"The hell you say. On your salary?"

Eva tucked her long blonde hair behind her ears. "I'm daddy's little girl," she replied with an exaggerated grin.

Philip reached behind the center pedestal.

"If you're looking for the logbook, it's by my side." She passed him the logbook. "I haven't completed the entries. I'm waiting on the passenger load and baggage count."

"That's fine. I didn't intend to check your weight and balance calculations, I'm just curious on this aircraft's history. It's been a while since I flown this bird." He flipped through the pages, familiarizing himself to the plane's discrepancies sustained over the last couple of days. He paid particular attention to the maintenance accomplished that previous night, for good measure, should there be anything worth noting for the day's flying. "During your walk around did you take a good look at the engines?"

"Yeah, they're pristine," Eva replied. "You can tell they had washed the aircraft last night. Is there something wrong?"

"No, just curious." Philip smiled when he noticed the signature beside the engine run entry. "My good buddy Thomas had carried out the operational checks. We have nothing to fear." He returned the logbook to Eva. "Let's get started on the pre-start check list."

Gabriela Ramirez, the lead flight attendant, poked her head in the cockpit and held out a piece of paper. "Here's the flight manifest. We have a full load minus two no-show passengers."

"Gabby," Philip said. "How's my favorite gal?"

"I'm doing fine Ace," Gabriela replied. "Do you guys need anything before we get going?"

"I'm fine," Eva replied, retrieving the slip of paper. The manifest displayed the flight attendant's passenger count broken down into male, female, and children. In addition, the inclusion of the baggage count placed in the forward and aft cargo compartments. She plugged the numbers into her weight and balance calculations.

"I'll have a coffee, black, once we're at cruising altitude."

"Roger that," Gabriela said cheerfully.

\*\*\*

Edgar laid his empty dish on the foldable table, then grabbed a piece of toast from Millie's plate.

"You're still hungry? We have bacon and tomato. I can make you a BLT."

"Nah, I'm fine."

Unfolding her napkin, she exposed his nemesis - the mouse. "What about a small snack?"

He laughed. "Yes! We finally caught him."

"We didn't catch a thing, mister. It was a feathered creature."

Edgar winced. "What are you saying?"

"Our feathered friend - the falcon," she started, "came through the kitchen window and did our bidding."

He shook his head. Looking up, he noticed the falcon soaring, climbing higher. "Speak of the devil."

Millie reached for the binoculars.

"I can barely see her," Edgar said.

"She's milking that thermal." Millie held her breath, then said, "Oh my God."

"What's going on?"

"The falcon narrowed her tail, tucked in her feet, and went into a dive when she folded her wings," Millie said, bouncing in her seat. "She went into a dive!"

With his naked eye, Edgar followed the falcon falling out of the sky. At that moment, he noticed two Canadian geese flying a hundred feet up, not far from them. "She's after those geese."

She didn't respond and continued to follow the falcon in its teardrop shape, aerodynamically formed to reduce the amount of drag to achieve maximum velocity. Millie continued to watch with amazement. She noticed the falcon pull out of the dive and with balled up feet struck the trailing goose. A split second before impact, the goose changed course, which caused the predator to miss the deadly blow to the head and instead struck the left wing. Millie covered her mouth to muffle her squeal.

"Damn!" Edgar said. "Man oh man. Did you see that?"

"That's awful," Millie said. "The poor geese were minding their own business."

"Look!" Edgar pointed to the injured goose, struggling to stay aloft.

Twenty feet away from their Winnebago, they observed the goose try to regain stability. It landed firmly, causing the legs to buckle. The extended wings kept the goose upright as it slid across the manicured lawn.

"Poor thing," Millie said. "It's injured. Edgar, we should help it."

"I'm not sure about that," he replied. "Wild animals are more resilient than you think. Let's give it a minute."

"Look, it's stumbling around."

"Probably stunned by the fall," Edgar said.

At that moment, the falcon pounced on the goose's back and bit firmly at its neck. Millie zoomed in on the peregrine's bloody beak. The second bite seemed to awaken the Canadian goose. It fought back with erratic movements, wings flapping frantically, and knocked the falcon off its feet.

"That's one tough bird," Edgar said.

"She's putting up a good fight," Millie said. "I hope she makes it."

Survival instincts caused the goose to take flight. It moved as fast as it could to distance itself from the predator.

The falcon was dazed, but quickly recovered. It took a step back, one-step forward, and shook. It then looked eagerly in the direction of its prey, flying southwest.

"Your bird may have a chance after all," Edgar said, pouring his wife's coffee into his cup. "Anyway, we need to pack up and get going."

The falcon took chase.

\* \* \*

Air Traffic Control provided take-off clearance. Philip, seated in the left seat in the cockpit, advanced the power levers gradually, taking care not to exceed the engines' temperature and horsepower limitations. Increasing power levers too quick can cause an auto-feather if it's above 65 degrees before the engine thrust reached a positive 500 pounds.

Philip released the toe brakes as the engines accelerated. The aircraft rolled down the runway, picking up speed to generate lift from the air passing over and under the wings.

Eva placed her left hand on her own controls. Once Philip, the pilot-in-command, set the approximate engine power, she would complete the adjustment to the proper take-off setting. While barreling down the runway, the captain's main concern was to control the aircraft.

The takeoff criteria predicated on two engine power parameters, halting the throttle advancement whenever the maximum allowable turbine inlet temperature or shaft horsepower setting occurs first. On the morning of August 17, the engine's turbine inlet temperature reached its limit at 932 Celsius.

Eva glanced to her left at the annunciator panel, which housed a group of indicator lights for each aircraft system on the center console. No system had a light illuminated, meaning all was normal. Then she reaffirmed her dashboard instruments were operative by validating that no mechanical red flags were in view. Next, she set her sights on the airspeed indicator.

The aircraft continued to race down the runway as it passed through 90 knots. Philip eased his force, pushing against the column to permit the elevator surface to assume a neutral flying position. At 108 knots, she called out "V ONE," signalling that they have achieved their decision speed.

Eva's V1 call out triggered Philip to peek at his onside airspeed indicator, a second pair of eyes reaffirming they had achieved rotation speed. For good measure, he waited until the plane's airspeed exceeded V1 by two to three knots before he applied back pressure on the column. The rearward movement of the column pitched the elevator surface up to push the tail section down. This caused the nose gear to lift off the runway at VR.

The airplane pointed into the sky. The two main gears followed suit and separated from the runway. It defied the laws of gravity from the lift generated by the wings. Philip angled the plane to maintain an eight-degree pitch up attitude. They ascend into the air at a V2 speed of 111 knots.

The plane entered into a positive climb. Philip called out "Gear up" to give Eva the cue to retract the gear and streamline the aircraft.

She moved the gear handle to the up position, caused the three gears to unlock. The hydraulic pressure routed to the retract actuators draw each respective gear into their wheel well.

Bang.

"What was that?" Eva asked.

Phillip thought it had something to do with the landing gear being stowed. Instinctively, he scanned the engine instrument panel and noticed the right engine had lost thrust. "It's the number two engine."

Philip fought the inclination to use the ailerons to straighten the aircraft. Instead, he used the rudder to stay on its current flight path. "Max power," he said.

Eva pushed the power levers forward. She glanced at Phillip and felt her nervousness subside through his calmness and sense of control. He showed no concern, treating this event as another ordinary flight. She felt her confidence build, her nervousness forgotten. Her piloting skills kicked in as she reached for the engine shutdown checklist.

"It sounded like the engine let go."

"I was thinking the same," she said.

"Whatever happened, we're in good shape. I'll stay on this heading. There is no need to go into a bank until we get more space between us and the ground. Get the engine shutdown checklist."

"I'm already on it. We should pull the T-handle."

"We don't have an engine fire. Is that necessary?"

"It wouldn't hurt."

Phillip shrugged. The purpose of activating the T-handle during an engine fire is to stop the flow of flammable fluids to a burning engine. Separating the engine from the airframe systems is the first step in extinguishing a fire. He did not see the harm in taking the added precaution.

Eva needed Phillip's concurrence to deviate from procedure was in their best interest. She reached up for the number two engine's T-handle. Before pulling it, she realized she was holding the wrong engine's handle. Realizing she nearly shut down the only serviceable engine made her quiver. She yanked the right handle and activated all the corresponding electrical switches.

The left hand engine shut down.

The plane pointed upward in a climb and, without its engines, quickly lost airspeed. Phillip struggled to maintain control. The flight controls felt sluggish and unresponsive. His effort to get the nose down, increase airspeed, and avoid a stall was faltering. The stall warning horn sounded and soon the ground proximity warning system activated. A recorded voice repeated, "Pull up, pull up."

*** 

Minutes earlier...

Engines roar as aircraft 641 sped down the runway. The wildlife activity nearly caused them to miss the last Virginia Airline's plane departure. While Edgar monitored the runway, Millie kept a watchful eye on the sprinting waterfowl.

"She is giving all she has," Millie said. "It may not be enough." She paused, taking a moment to assess. "The gap is closing."

Edgar took his eyes away from the ascending airplane. "The goose isn't letting up?"

"She's maintaining speed but it won't be enough. The falcon is right on her tail."

"Where are they?" Edgar asked, looking up.

"They're ahead and to the right of the aircraft."

The goose snapped to the left and dove toward the runway. The maneuver helped and it provided an edge. Her acceleration had widened the gap from the determined and unrelenting predator. The ascending aircraft passed several feet below the falcon. Turbulent winds trailing behind the plane tossed the bird of prey around, putting a halt to the chase while it regained stability.

The goose continued on its flight path with the same vigor and determination, unaware of the collision course with the iron bird. The right engine swallowed the goose; two identities fused together in a seamless and instant transformation as one distinct object.

Smoke exiting from the right hand engine's exhaust as its propeller slowed to a complete stop. Aircraft 641 continued to climb.

"What a nightmare," Millie said, dropping the binoculars to her side. "What a horrible day this is turning into."

Edgar folded his chair without taking his eye off the airplane. "What are the odds?" he smirked. "Surely, the plane will have to return to the airport."

"No doubt," she agreed.

Millie watched Edgar carry his chair to the edge of the Winnebago, standing beside the ladder to descend from the rooftop. "I got the hint. I'm right behind you." With her back to the runway, she screwed the cap on the thermos. Startled by the sound of his chair crashing against the rooftop, she spun around to see him staring in the distance. "What's wrong?"

"The other engine shutdown," Edgar replied.

"What do you mean?" Millie said.

He slowly moved along the length of the Winnebago. "It's going down."

"How can that happen?"

He shook his head. "I don't know."

Millie grabbed Edgar's arm and without uttering a word, they watched an airplane full of passengers roll on its side. Time slowed as the plane collided with a church. They gasped when the left wing tore up the rafters while it sliced through the roof. The fuselage slammed against the stone walls.

Millie covered her mouth with one hand and dug her nails in Edgar's arm with the other. Eyes glued to the unfolding spectacle that had started by an unpredictable chain of events. Mindful of those on board, she thought of the children, business travellers, vacationers, students, and retirees. She moved her trembling body against Edgar, pressing her head against his chest, and began to sob.

Sirens sounded in every direction.

# CHAPTER 4

**THIRTY MINUTES EARLIER...**

Olivia Cooper started her day at the office with a cup of coffee and three financial newspapers spread across the large oak desk. She buzzed her secretary on the intercom. "Beatrice, Mister Longhorn will be arriving any time now. Whatever you do, don't let him into my office until I give you the word."

"Yes, ma'am," Beatrice replied. "Should I prepare the coffee for his arrival?"

"No. He prefers tea." She glanced at her flight ticket on the left corner of her desk. "And Beatrice, please cancel my flight to Richmond."

"You're not meeting with the governor today?"

"We spoke last night; he will be coming to Charlottesville instead."

"I'll take care of it," Beatrice said.

Olivia removed her high-heeled shoes, leaned back into her leather chair, and planted her feet on the desk. Her elbows rested on the armrests and she held her cup of coffee by her fingertips. She took a sip.

Facing the window extending the length of the office, she watched the activity at Charlotte's airport, monopolized by Virginia Airlines. Four Model VA980 Fairlanes lined up wing tip to wing tip at their respective terminal gates. They were prepped and ready to start their operational day. The fifth and last aircraft was being towed to Gate 3, making it to the terminal just in time for its scheduled departure.

"You're the man, Thomas," she whispered.

Olivia reached for the nearest newspaper, then rifled through the pages of the Wall Street Journal. She scanned the articles for news of her competition and sought out opportunities that may require her airline's services. Then rifling through the business section of the New York Times and Washington Post, she circled several prospects in red.

Two seafood restaurants announced grand openings. Olivia found it intriguing and wondered how they received the catch of the day. How was it transported from Chesapeake Bay to inland locations? She made a note in her journal - fish markets, fisheries, and distribution. She retraced the word distribution several times for emphasis.

"Mister Longhorn is here to see you, ma'am," Beatrice announced over the intercom.

Olivia stood. She collected the relevant newspaper sections, folded them into quarters, and inserted them into an expandable accordion folder, secured with a flap and elastic cord. She placed it at the edge of her desk.

"Ma'am, Mister Longhorn," Beatrice said.

"Let him in," Olivia replied. She put her feet on top of the oak desk, sipping her coffee. Beatrice led Mister Longhorn into the office and closed the door behind him.

"Feet on the desk? Really? I'm beginning to think you do that just to annoy me."

"Relax, Cecil!" Olivia said. "Don't be such a tight ass."

"A tight ass I'm not," he said as he admired the office. The walls were lined with dark stained mahogany paneling and the ceilings were detailed with fine intricate molding. "I see you kept your father's office as he left it."

Olivia kicked her feet off the desk and reached for her shoes while Cecil walked to a painting hung above a French provincial sofa. "Is this a new addition?"

She placed her left hand on his right shoulder then leaned in to press her cheek against his, kissing the air so not to smudge her lipstick.

Cecil took his gaze off the painting just long enough to give her a peck on her cheek, a customary greeting between a godfather and godchild.

Olivia picked up a 1920s USSR wooden, hand-carved cigarette box from the coffee table and offered one to Cecil. He shook his head.

"You still roll your own?" she asked before lighting her cigarette with a silver-plated Ronson Queen Anne table lighter.

"It helps me cut down," Cecil replied, still gazing at the painting. "The intricacy and detailing of the Sabre F86 pursuing the MiG 15, it's nearly photographic." He paused and brushed his goatee with his thumb and index finger. "The gray and cloudy back drop reminds me of the first day your father and I were flying in MiG Alley." He turned to Olivia. "Your father and I served together in two wars."

"Yes, I'm aware," she said, rolling her eyes. "I have been told on more than one occasion."

He smirked. "Of course you have."

She did not bother to respond, took a drag from the cigarette, and exhaled forcefully. The smoke exited through her nostrils and pursed lips.

"I have seen him among follow airmen and when pressed hard, and I mean hard pressed, he begrudgingly mentions a tiny insight on his contribution to the war effort. I, on the other hand, would exercise my bragging rights if I held his rank and was a two-time ace pilot."

Olivia tilted her head. "And why not?" Cecil's continual pursuit for undeserving recognition was clear, but hearing him say it directly was surprising. "The painting is called First Kill, painted by an airman in your squadron."

Cecil leaned in to read the brass plate attached to the frame. "I don't recognize the name. Anyway, this painting is inaccurate."

"Why is that?"

"I was your father's wing man. This is historically incorrect."

"Right," Olivia agreed, humouring him. There was no point arguing about the past. She didn't bother mentioning that he was lost in the clouds when her father engaged the faster MiG on his own.

Beatrice entered the office and placed the tea tray at the end of the coffee table. Handling the china tea set with care, she turned to Mister Longhorn. "Do you still take two lumps and a drop of milk?"

"You remembered," Cecil said.

Beatrice smiled as she raised the china teapot, adhering to proper tea serving etiquette.

Olivia was eager to get to the core of why she had asked Cecil Longhorn to her office. "Thank you, Beatrice. That will be all."

"Ma'am?"

"I can serve myself, thank you."

She nodded. "As you wish."

Olivia unlocked her top desk drawer with the gold plated key she pulled out of her bra. Taking a red folder, she waved it in the air. "This is why I called you here today."

Cecil leafed through the pages. "A business proposal?"

"More like a business strategy," Olivia said, lighting another cigarette.

"You smoke too much."

"Tell me something I don't know." She took one drag and smashed the cigarette into the ashtray.

Cecil placed the folder down and slid it across the coffee table. "You want to expand the fleet?"

"I do."

"This is the same proposal the board of directors rejected," Cecil said. He unbuttoned his jacket and sat on the edge of the sofa. "Virginia Airlines' continual expansion, no thanks to your father, has over extended the organization. I applaud the board's efforts to keep his ambition in check."

Her demeanor remained neutral, not to betray her true feelings. Cognizant of Cecil's reluctance to support an organization her father had founded she went against her instincts. She gave Cecil, her father's long-time friend, first dibs to take part in the next phase of the airline's expansion. Out of respect and love for her father, she blindly carried out his bidding. It was bitter sweet to have foreseen the outcome, his unwillingness to push Virginia Airlines to the next level. "I understand how you feel. Thank you for coming in. I appreciate you taking the time to speak with me."

"I don't understand."

"Cecil," Olivia said, picking up the red folder and returning it to her desk. "I know you too well."

"And what is that supposed to mean?"

"You like a sure thing," Olivia lied.

Cecil stood. "My dear, managing risk and return on investments is my business." He buttoned his jacket. "Though I must confess that your father's stubbornness to start an airline in a rural area had served him well."

"You being so close to the family and all, I thought I would give you first dibs." Olivia opened the office door to let him out. "But the risk is too high, I get it."

He took a breath. "Well then, I guess that's it."

They shared an awkward stare until Beatrice said through the intercom, "Ma'am, Albert Casey is on line one."

Olivia poked her head around the door. "Tell him I'll be a second."

"The new president and CEO of American Airlines?" Cecil asked.

"He's also the chairman of the board," Olivia replied. "I really need to take this call."

"Okay, I'm leaving." He turned around at the threshold to face his godchild. "You're thinking of selling the airline?"

She could see his mind at work. Brokering a deal to sell Virginia Airlines to American would be a money making proposition. Selling would be preferable to the risky prospect of continuing the airline's expansion into unchartered territory. The commission for negotiating such a deal would be in the millions.

"No!" Olivia said. "It's just an investor willing to take a chance on us."

"Hear him out but don't agree to anything," Cecil said. "Let me get back to you. I may have an alternative to American Airlines."

Olivia assured him with a nod and closed the door behind him. Back in her chair, she kicked off her shoes and plopped her feet back on the desk.

Beatrice stormed through the door to retrieve the tea set and tray. "Ma'am, would you like another cup of tea before I take it away?"

"Yes, please."

She handed Olivia her cup. "Did it help?"

"Did what help?"

"The line about Albert Casey."

"I believe he has taken the bait," Olivia said. "Will he run with it or spit it out, it's too soon to tell."

Suddenly, the floor trembled, windows rattled, teacups clanged, desk picture frames toppled, and paintings tilted.

"It's an earthquake," Beatrice said.

"I wish it was," Olivia said, stepping to the window. Aviators Baptist Church was ablaze with shooting flames piercing through and behind the black dense smoke, mushrooming into the sky. As far as she could tell, an airplane had crashed, and it could be no other than one of her own.

Olivia flinched at a second explosion, as fierce as the first. She had difficulty catching her breath and then swallowed hard to suppress her emotions. *Why today?* She thought. Just when things are in the balance. Wiping a tear away from the corner of her eyes, she stomped her foot, straightened her posture, and spun around. "Beatrice, connect me to dispatch. Now!"

\* \* \*

Dave Steadman turned on to Interstate 64, leaving the city of Williamsburg, Virginia, behind after spending a weekend with his daughter Grace. Upon completing her first year at William and Mary Law School, she remained in Williamsburg for the summer. She worked several jobs to keep her head above water, and the six-day work week kept her away from home.

It had been nearly five months since Dave saw his only child. After repeated requests to spend the weekend at home in Georgetown came to no avail, he made it a point to go to her instead. Their time together exceeded his expectations.

He turned on the radio. A Baptist preacher yelled about how god is good and the devil is bad. He listened for a minute or two, then decided audible static was preferable to the gospel's misinterpreted intent. Dave was a god-fearing man and had little patience for a ranting pastor instilling fear rather than teaching the word of God. Pastors, he thought, are like government employees; you have good ones as well as bad. He turned the dial to a local country music radio station playing Jolene.

He drummed to the music on the steering wheel, head swaying, and mouthed the lyrics. He pressed the accelerator on his Chevrolet Nova to overtake a slow vehicle. Returning to the right lane, Dave continued to drive ten miles over the limit.

The DJ chimed in before the song ended. "That was Jolene, written and performed by Dolly Parton. We are WMCM broadcasting live on AM820 from the Williamsburg Inn, where you'll find plenty of activities for kids of all ages, low priced meals in the diner, and a whole lot more."

The promo segment continued at great length and segued into a news flash. "The total number of fatalities has climbed to eight," the DJ said. "It is presently unclear what caused the airplane to crash after taking off from Charlottesville Airport. We have been told a Virginia Airlines spokesman will issue a press release later this afternoon." A song began to play in the background. "The temperature is 81 degrees on this gorgeous day. You are listening to WMCM broadcasting live from the Williamsburg Inn. This is Back Home Again by John Denver."

Dave Steadman was a Federal Aviation Administration inspector, specializing in aircraft accident and incident investigations out of the Washington D.C. office. He usually stayed near his home when it was his turn to be on-call. There had been no activity over the last several months and he had let his guard down. Disappointed he had neglected to provide his whereabouts, he stopped at the nearest pay phone and dialed the office. "Shirley, is that you?"

"You have great timing. I..."

"I've just heard about a crash at Charlottesville Airport," David interrupted. "It was just broadcasted over the radio."

"It happened this morning," Shirley said. "I had received the notification an hour ago, approximately three hours after the fact. The delay, I can only presume was due to everyone actively dealing with the issue." She paused. "Grace said you two had a great time this weekend."

"We did. When did you speak to her?"

"I have her on hold on the other line." She chuckled. "Clare gave me her number. I can tell she hasn't adjusted to the empty nest syndrome the way she was carrying on about Grace."

"We knew the time would come when our only child will go off on her own," Dave said. "The separation anxiety was unexpected at first. She's much better now. So, am I neck dip in trouble for being M.I.A?"

"I don't understand what you mean. You are on route to Charlottesville. Traffic must have held you up."

"I appreciate you covering for me. I'm on Interstate 64 and I can be there in two hours."

"That's fine. Our higher ups haven't called so I don't think anyone is aware."

"What do we have so far about the accident?"

"Nothing really," Shirley said, looking at her notes. "We're still waiting on the passenger manifest. The airport manager, I didn't get his name, indicated both engines were not rotating prior to the crash. Last fatality count is ten and climbing." She leafed through the pages. "Yeah, that's about it right now."

"What about the weather?"

"Not an issue."

"Have we spoken to the airline?"

"I finally got a hold of a spokesman. He was avoiding me, thinking I was the local press." Shirley tapped her pencil against her notepad. "I told the receptionist that I would shut the airline down if someone in authority did not call me back in five minutes." Shirley said proudly.

"You're bad," Dave said in disbelief, but he admired her guts. "I certainly don't want to get on your bad side."

"You will be if you don't get moving. Call me after your preliminary assessment." There was a long pause.

"Shirley, you're still there?"

"Your precious daughter hung up. I guess the little princess couldn't hold on for a second longer." She laughed. "I'll call her back. Drive safe."

# CHAPTER 5

**THOMAS WRIGHT DID** not bother to go home and shower, or even sleep for a few hours after being awake for the last thirty-four. Instead, he finished his midnight shift and drove north for an hour and a half to Page County. He parked on an unpaved road accessible from Compton Hollow. A concealed entrance covered by shrubs and tall grass obscured the road, known only to a few long-time residents.

The half-mile hike through the woods lead him to Shenandoah National Park's backcountry and a hidden cemetery. It was one of over a hundred cemeteries in the park, but this one was special. This one held his wife, laid to rest among her ancestors in a long forgotten place.

The segregated cemetery was split between family, local residents, and unmarked graves. Thomas went to work on the list of mandatory chores before he paid his respects to his wife, Sarah Jenkins.

Tucked away among the trees stood a small shed Thomas had built several years ago to store garden tools and maintenance equipment. He pulled out the reel mower and rubbed his thumbnail against the five curved blades. Their dull edge reminded him of the last and exhaustive visit. He exerted needless energy mowing the grass and he did not intend to strain himself again. He started to sharpen the blades, which took him nearly an hour and caused him to sweat heavily in the tiny shed.

Thomas repeated the monotonous process of pushing and pulling the blades against the sharpener. He felt a welcoming breeze rush past him and closed his eyes to enjoy it. Another breeze passed through the small opening in the woods and swirled around him.

"You're tired," a voice whispered.

The voice's familiarity made him smile. "I'm always tired after working the night shift," Thomas said.

"You're sleeping standing up. You should be in bed."

"I'm not sleeping, just resting my eyes," Thomas replied.

A presence stood in front of him. "You look good. A little thinner though. Are you eating?"

A vivid image of Sarah appeared, dressed in a white cotton dress, the one she wore around the house during hot summer days.

She ran her fingertips across his jaw line.

"You always say that," he said.

"Because it's true. You're not taking care of yourself. Not to mention, you should not be coming here on your own. What would happen should you get hurt? There's no one around for miles."

"You're watching over me. I'll be fine."

The long pause caused Thomas to open his eyes. He was alone. He was disappointed he had only seen her for a moment, but in the end, it did not matter. It was better than not seeing her at all. Time spent maintaining this holy ground was the only opportunity he had to feel Sarah's presence. He cherished every minute he spent with her. It only happened once a month, on the seventeenth day, the day she passed away over five years before.

He closed his eyes again, hoping she would return, but heard only the birds chirping in the trees and a rustle in the tall grass. He opened his eyes and focused on a moving tree branch slithering between his feet. His eyes adjusted to the bright sunlight and he realized it wasn't a branch but a lethal copperhead snake.

He reached into the tool shed for anything that could serve as a weapon. He grabbed a spade, planning to thrust it at the snake to sever its head. It was just out of his reach. Stretching a little more, his fingertips brushed against the handle. He glanced at the snake, which was now wrapped around his right ankle.

With extreme care, he wiped the sweat from his brow and stretched and nudged the spade. It slid off the nails holding it against the shed's wall and struck the wooden flooring, causing other tools to tumble. The crashing sounds scared off the venomous snake. He let out an exasperated breath, fortunate that Sarah wasn't around to say, 'I told you so.'

Thomas washed off the grinding compound from the blades and cutting bar with a wet rag, reconfigured the gears back to their original positions and began to mow the grass. Before racking and bagging the grass clippings, he grabbed the clippers from the tool shed and snipped away the weeds around the tombstones. Two unmarked graves sat at the edge of the clearing. He left them for last.

He returned the equipment to the tool shed and laid down on the six-foot bench that faced Sarah's grave.

"You will fall asleep and get a sun burn."

Thomas opened his eyes. Sarah blocked out the sun, though he could only make out her silhouette. "What do you suggest?"

"Sit up," she said. "I'll give you a massage before you drive home."

"Now you're talking," Thomas said. Sitting up, he folded his legs on the bench seat and placed his hands on his knees.

Sarah's hands pushed on his shoulders, thumbs pressing against his back in a circular motion.

"Oh, that feels good."

"You are really tense. But not to worry; I will have you back in tip top shape."

"That's the can-do attitude I need," Thomas said, grinning as he imagined her fingertips press against his shoulder.

He recalled the first time when he felt her soft touch when they met on Langley Air Force Base, not long after he had returned from the Korean War. He noticed Sarah staring at a map as she walked. He steered alongside her and offered to help. Impressed with the uniform lined with ribbons and stripes, she accepted.

After spending the day visiting her brother, who was also in the air force, she joined Thomas that evening for dinner. Their stroll through the park was his favourite part of the date. While seated on a park bench, Sarah rubbed his ailing back. The unsolicited gesture had shown a side of her warmth, sincerity, and caring personality. Her touch was magical.

"That feels good," Thomas said.

"Quiet," she whispered.

"I miss you."

"I know you do." Sarah rubbed her palms up and down along his back. "You should get back together with Emma."

"Where did that come from?"

"She is good for you. You too need each other."

"You think so?"

"I know so." She moved her palms in a circular motion. "Tonight's dinner would be a good start to let her back in."

"Emma's a little too passionate. At times, possessive. Ouch! What was that for?"

"Don't be critical of her. It is her way and she really cares about you. Anyway, she isn't possessive, you're just stubborn."

Thomas felt her arms wrap around him with her head resting against his. "I suppose."

Sarah kissed him on the neck. "You need to let me go and start focusing on Emma. Coming here every month, rain or shine, isn't helping."

"I promised you I would."

"You were by my side when I needed you most. You did your part." She then whispered in his ear, "I release you of your promise. Now wake up, Thomas. Wake up!"

Emma gave him a gentle nudge, then another, "Thomas. Wake up."

"Emma?" Thomas said, shielding his eyes from the sun. He could see something was wrong. Whatever it was, it was important enough for her to drive all this way and couldn't wait until they met for dinner. "Is everything okay?"

"One of our birds crashed." She hugged him. "Olivia asked everyone to report back to work."

"When did this happen?"

"This morning," she said. "When it took off from Charlottesville." She held him tight. "Thomas, it was 641."

\* \* \*

Explosions from the airplane's fuel tanks blew out the Aviators Baptist Church roof rafters, cupola, and stained glass windows. Spectators, emergency responders, reporters, and the parishioners watched the flames engulf the house of worship. The fire shot out through the window openings, doors, and collapsed roof.

The first two fire trucks on the scene wasted no time to setup the hoses and begin their battle. One of the trucks parked in the church's lot. It faced the north side of the building, closest to the airplane.

The mid portion of the plane's fuselage rested on top of the north and west walls, held in placed by the left wing, which was burrowed through the church's roof. Only a small segment of the right wing remained after the explosion torn it away. The front end of the fuselage was partially sheared aft of the cockpit's bulkhead, which caused the nose to peer over the west wall toward the ground. The tail and aft fuselage were detached behind the wing, which had proven most fortunate. All the passengers seated in the last eleven rows survived.

A black Cadillac Fleetwood approached the crash site. Cecil's personal driver parked the car at a distance, not to attract attention. Seated in the backseat, Cecil reached into the brown paper bag and offered Carlos a coverall. "Wear this."

"What's this for?" Carlos asked.

"It's the aircraft technician's uniform. It will help you fit in when you approach the wreckage."

"The Virginia Airlines logo will make me stick out like a sore thumb," Carlos said. "Look out there, it's chaos. I'll be inconspicuous without it. I'll be fine."

"Very well, get going and be quick about it."

A fire fighter stood on the aerial ladder extended above the church. Water was directed through an opening in the rooftop. Thousands of gallons spilled on the blaze, making a small dent in it until the second fire truck joined the effort. A third truck helped to subdue the raging blaze after a few hours.

A firefighter glanced at the torn fuselage resting on the north wall. He could not determine why the image, now vivid in his mind, had not registered earlier. He stared at the charred body, bent over with arms extended across the aisle, gripping the armrest on a neighbouring seat. He rested his chin on the ladder's top run and closed his eyes in prayer.

"Are you alright?" A voice from the ground shouted.

He lifted his head off the ladder's run, looked at the ground, and shouted, "Yes. I'm just tired."

"Let's go!" his co-worker insisted. "We'll need to clear our equipment to give the recovery crew access to the site."

"Is he alright?" The police officer looking on asked the firefighter.

"Up high, you'll get a better appreciation of the carnage. He'll be alright. He's a firefighter."

"I just arrived on the scene," the police officer said. "I suppose everyone on board perished?"

"No, a number of passengers were taken away to the hospital." The firefighter paused and pointed behind the officer. "I don't believe that person belongs here."

"Excuse me, sir," a police officer called. "This area is off limits. You need to get back behind the yellow tape."

"I worked for Virginia Airlines," Carlos Ramirez said, looking up at the police officer patrolling the crash site. "I can be of some assistance."

Ignoring the officer's instructions, Ramirez started into a jog toward the crash site. He was quickly tackled to the ground, causing his face to slam against the concrete sidewalk. With a knee driven into his back, he relented. His hands cuffed behind his back and he yelped when the police officer lifted him to his feet.

"Do you understand English?" The officer asked. "Look at me! Do you understand English?"

"Yes!" Ramirez answered. Experiencing excruciating pain in his arms he added, "You're hurting me!"

"Sir, have you been drinking?"

"Of course not," Ramirez whimpered.

"Then what the hell were you thinking? I can arrest you for failing to obey a police officer, resisting, and obstruction. I'll find something else if you continue to piss me off." Blood ran down Ramirez's nose. The police officer pulled out a handkerchief and wiped it away. "Tilt your head back."

A large sedan pulled into the lot behind the firetrucks and Cecil Longhorn jumped out. "Officer, I know this man."

"Stop right there, sir. Do not come any closer." The officer released Ramirez's arm and placed his hand over his holster.

"My name is Cecil Longhorn. I'm on Virginia Airline's board of directors."

The officer eyed the gentleman in the pinned striped suit, bell bottom pants, and the cane with an ivory snakehead handle.

"I also own and operate Longhorn Investment Brokerage," Cecil added.

"That's the firm that manages our pension fund."

"That's correct." Cecil sighed. "This man was acting on my behalf. I apologize if his overzealousness to comply with my request may have overstepped your authority."

The police officer removed the handcuffs. "As a favour to you, sir, I'll cut him a break."

"Thank you, officer. That's much appreciated."

Stepping towards the car, Cecil glanced back at the officer who returned to his crowd control duties. "What the hell were you thinking?"

"I couldn't reason with him."

"Don't say a word," Cecil said. "I saw the whole thing." He opened the rear car door. "Anyway, I'm leaving you here to keep an eye on the cargo. I'll have someone join you shortly."

Carlos nodded.

Cecil passed him a handkerchief. "Your nose is bleeding again."

"Thanks."

"For our well being," Cecil began, "no one can know what's on board that airplane."

"Have you spoken to Juan Pablo?"

"Don't worry about him. Just be invisible and don't do anything stupid. We'll take care of our problem this evening when there's no one around."

# CHAPTER 6

**AS INSTRUCTED BY** corporate office, maintenance staff closed the large hangar doors. The intent was to avoid drawing unnecessary attention to the gathering onlookers, as per Olivia Cooper's request. Just as important, it would prevent reporters from dropping into Virginia Airlines' affairs.

To compensate for the warm hangar temperatures and aid in ventilation, eight three-foot diameter fans were positioned throughout the hangar. The staff began to arrive as early as an hour prior to the commencement of the meeting. Ticket agents, pilots, flight attendants, ramp attendants, A&P mechanics, non-essential personnel, and everyone else employed at the airline gathered in unexpected numbers. The two coffee machines in the small lunchroom brewed pot after pot.

The fans did little to cool the growing crowd. Propped opened emergency doors on the north and south side of the building didn't help either. Everyone made themselves at home while they waited for their president to arrive.

The mood was somber. No one spoke of the incomprehensible tragedy, as if it had not occurred. They focused their thoughts to the well-being of the flight crew and the passengers. Hope fueled by eyewitness reports communicated on radio and local television stations indicated a large number of survivors had walked away from the plane. The media, however, cautioned that the police, airport management, the FAA, hospital staff, or airline representatives did not substantiate the eyewitness accounts.

Olivia stood at the threshold at the emergency door held opened on the north side. The immense crowd clamored by the doorways for the light breeze that was preferable to the stifled air inside the maintenance facility. The employees noticed her standing with her management team behind her. The chatter stopped and the only audible sound was the buzzing of the fans. The people nearest to Olivia stepped aside, clearing a path, and the rest followed suit all the way to the podium.

Olivia took a deep breath before stepping into the hangar. She recognized some by not others. They gave sombre looks and she reciprocated with a gentle nod. Standing by the podium, she waited for her management team to join her.

She started with the introductions when a comment from the back of the crowd shouted that they couldn't hear. A megaphone was retrieved from a fire kit used for emergencies.

"Can everyone hear me now?" She said through the megaphone. "Good. Let me start by saying I appreciate everyone for coming down on a Saturday. For most of you, this is your day off and I wish we were here under better circumstances." Olivia scanned the crowd, making direct eye contact with her employees. "As you are aware, aircraft 641, the flagship my dad helped redesign and fly under the Virginia Airlines banner, crashed after take-off."

Olivia looked up from her notes and spoke in a soft but direct tone. She swallowed and continued reading her statement. "It departed this morning on its first flight of the day from runway 21. The fire department claims the right engine has evidence of blood and feathers on the intake belonging to a Canadian goose. The FAA inspector's initial assessment confirmed that observation. The media's reporting has sensationalized the circumstances of the crash, which is why I had called this meeting. The media has suggested a flock of geese flew across the plane's flight path. Eyewitness accounts indicate both engines were not rotating before it fell onto Aviators Baptist Church. Though this has some validity, I need to caution everyone."

Olivia took a sip of water and placed the glass back onto the podium. "Although the evidence suggests a freak of nature may have induced this tragedy, do not speak to the press."

She shifted her weight to her left foot. "The press will be persistent. They will befriend you and prod for any information. You may feel obliged to defend our organization. No matter what good intentions you may have to set the record straight, they will twist your words around. For those of you dealing directly with the public, the press will have easier access to you. It's best to not say a word and simply direct them to call our hotline. I can't stress this enough. Do not continue to propel this speculation until the authorities have an opportunity to complete their investigation. Maintenance, I need you to keep working on the other planes, but stay away from anything that might be of use in the investigation."

"There have been eighteen fatalities. The names will be released once the families are notified. Our incredible flight crew on board..." She paused. She walked to the side of the podium, ignoring the notes prepared by Virginia Airlines' attorneys. "Two of the four crew members are no longer with us."

The news that two of their own had died caused a wave of emotion. The majority welled up while the few wept aloud. "I'll be sure to release their names as soon as I possibly can." She regained her composure as the worst of what needed to be said was out of the way. "I know I can count on you all to ensure we remain as this country's best airline. We are professionals." She paused for a second and added. "We shall persevere."

"Yes we will," someone shouted from the back of the hangar. Laughter ensued and transitioned into applause.

Olivia left the podium and joined her employees. She greeted Odessa with a hug.

"Philip piloted the aircraft," Odessa whispered.

"I know," Olivia replied.

"I don't think our sweet Philip had made it," Odessa struggled to get the words out.

Olivia released her embrace. She didn't wish to confirm Odessa's intuition. "Everything will be alright."

\* \* \*

Curled up in the back seat, Thomas was sound asleep as Emma drove back from Page County. Turning onto the Airport Service Road, she steered toward the maintenance hangar. There were an unprecedented number of cars parked on both sides along the length of the road. Cars were parked in designated and non-designated areas, even double-parked on the lawn. Pressing the accelerator, she continued to the end of the street to the only available spot next to a fire hydrant.

Emma placed the gear in neutral, applied the emergency brake, and gave Thomas a nudge. "We're here." After removing the key from the ignition, she gave him another nudge. "Hey! Wake up, sleepy head."

"Okay, okay, I'm up." Thomas stretched. "I wish the ride back was longer."

"No wonder, you have been up for nearly thirty-four hours. We'll do a quick meet and greet, then I promise I'll take you home."

Thomas noticed the cars. "Jesus, is the entire town here?"

Amused by the observation, she glanced up at the sky and saw the falcon they bumped into earlier that day. She could not be sure since the bird of prey flew too high to listen for the bells strapped to its legs. Thomas on the other hand paid no attention as he walked with determination. No doubt, his mind is swirling around on what had transpired to our flagship airplane in his care hours earlier.

Appreciating there is an army of technicians inspecting, servicing and addressing the overall airworthiness state; it is no surprise that air travel is the safest means of transportation. Regardless the odds are greater of dying from an automobile accident, firearm assault, exposure to smoke or fire, it offered no comfort. It is concerning, especially when fatalities occurred on our aircraft. Entering the hangar from the north side, they watched Olivia and the management team mingling with the staff. They figured the meeting had ended.

"We missed the meeting," Thomas said, relieved. "I can get briefed after I get a good night sleep." He rubbed his eyes and let out a sigh. "While we're here, there is something I can look up."

"Where are you going?"

"To my office," he mumbled.

Emma sensed his sleep deprivation is affecting his state of mind and decided to stay with him at all times. She had experienced long hours working without sleep in Vietnam while serving in the Army Nurse Corps. Stationed at Cu Chi with the 7th Surgical Hospital near a combat zone, she spent long shifts attending to the wounded soldiers. Bandage them up to a satisfactory condition to send them off to an evacuation hospital.

The unlucky ones sustained minor injuries and once stitched up, they would return to their unit. Before leaving Emma's care and heading off to the combat zone, they receive the best word of advice a nurse can offer: "The next time you visit, be sure to shoot yourself in the foot."

\* \* \*

Mingling among the employees, Olivia thanked them. The pages containing her statement were folded in half and she used them to fan her face. "Leonard," she shook his hand. "I appreciate you coming in. How are you holding up?"

"A little shocked," he said. "I would never have thought given our high standards and attention to detail, this could ever happen to us. You know?"

"I do. We all share the same sentiment." She placed her hand on his arm. "Our maintenance team is the very best so keep it up, we're counting on you guys."

"Thank you, ma'am."

"Ms Cooper," Jean Martin said, a newly hired pilot.

"I'm sorry," Olivia replied. "I don't believe we met."

"That's right. I'm new with the company, just shy of four months."

"It's too bad we met under these circumstances," she said. "I do however appreciate you coming in."

"It's important for all of us to be here," he replied. "There's a lot of conflicting reports as you know. Everyone is anxious to know what really happened and not knowing has some of us concerned. So we value you for setting the record straight - it helped."

"I glad to hear you say that."

Two other pilots joined Jean and Olivia's discussion. She saw Thomas enter the hangar and watched him walk along the wall to go undetected toward the maintenance office. Stuck talking with the three pilots, she had difficulty excusing herself. The pilots were determined to share their near miss experiences with geese. Such occurrences were not frequent at Charlottesville. However, the Washington D.C. International Airport has runways surrounded by water and parklands - a waterfowl haven.

"Considering what occurred this morning," Jean Martin began, "There's an aviation magazine article that offer ideas and measures to lower bird strike risk."

"I would definitely like to read that article," Olivia said. She smiled and tried to leave the discussion, but a gentle tug on her arm halted the retreat. "I need to go gents."

"Sorry ma'am," Jean said, releasing his grip from the crook of her elbow.

"It's Olivia." She stepped in the direction of the maintenance office. It is imperative she speak to Thomas about his dearest and closest friend had died. "Jean I will see you in my office next week. I would like to hear more about wildlife hazards. Regardless what findings and recommendations may come from the NTSB's investigation, if there's any mitigation action we can proactively execute, I don't see why we should procrastinate." With her back to the group she added, "We have a lot of work to do."

# CHAPTER 7

**OLIVIA KNOCKED TWICE** on the shift duty manager's door and stepped right into the office without waiting for permission. She noticed Thomas sitting behind the desk, rummaging through the shift logs. He looked different, thinner, with dark sunken eyes. She realized it had been some time since she set eyes on him.

Emma Ferraro stood by his side, one hand resting on the desk and other on the backrest where Thomas sat. While looking over his shoulder, she was distracted when the door creaked and closed behind Olivia.

"Hello, Thomas," Olivia said.

"Olivia," he replied. "How are you doing?" He flashed a lazy wave hello. "That was a stupid question. I'm sorry."

"It's okay," Olivia said. "Setting aside why I asked you all here today, I was doing well." She took a step forward and added, "It is good to see you." She glanced at Emma and returned her gaze back to him.

"I should leave you two alone," Emma said. "I'm sure you have a lot to discuss." Without thinking, she gave Thomas a peck on the cheek. "I'll be waiting outside." She eyed Olivia up and down. "Miss Cooper."

"Oh, of course." Olivia stepped away from the door. "It's good to see you again, Emma."

Emma did not respond. She simply extended her muscular arm for the doorknob and left.

"That was awkward," Olivia said.

"Don't mind her," Thomas replied. "It's her way."

They approached one another. Standing in the center of the room and they hugged. The hardy embrace held for several seconds.

"It's been a while since dad and I have seen you at the house," Olivia whispered in his ear.

Thomas broke up the embrace and went to the coffee maker sitting on the credenza. "Do you want a cup?"

"Sure. How are you feeling?" Olivia sat in one of the chairs angled in front of his desk.

"You should be worried about the families that lost their loved ones. I'm still here - tired, but still here."

"We're all thinking of the passengers and the..." She stopped short of mentioning the crew. She wasn't ready to talk about Philip. "Right now, I'm concerned about you." Olivia rose from her seat. "I've known you for a long time and you are aware how I feel about you."

"Sit down," Thomas said, passing her a cup of coffee. "You still take it black?"

"That's fine," she said.

"I must confess I was shaken up," he said. "When I first heard 641 had gone down, I needed to verify the work completed last night. As I suspected and based on what is known, our efforts could not have contributed to its crash." He took a sip of coffee. "I was told it was a flock of geese. There's nothing anyone could have done to prevent it."

"We won't know for certain until the NTSB complete their investigation." She lit a cigarette and inhaled. "Blood and feathers in the right engine's intake suggest it but it isn't conclusive."

"What about the left engine?"

"It's charred from the explosion," Olivia said. Failing to find an ashtray, she flicked her ashes into her coffee cup. "The FAA inspector at the scene is confident that is the case. He participated in the Eastern Airlines crash on October…"

"October 4th, 1960," Thomas said. "I remember it like it was yesterday."

"You know about it? That's a surprise."

"It shouldn't be. All seasoned airmen do. We're all aware of the damage airplanes incur and the mounting repair costs sustained from bird strikes." Thomas leaned back in his chair. "We share the skies with the feathered creatures and when they take down an aircraft, it's unsettling."

"I can't get over the fact that small birds can inflict a devastating blow to a large piece of machinery. I get that a small private plane is susceptible but the Fairlane 980 is built like a brick shit house."

"And the Lockheed L-188 Electra is built like a tank. Still, little starlings crippled it."

"It's inconceivable," Olivia said.

"Granted, the risk is low, but in October of 1960," Thomas straightened in his seat, "Six or seven seconds after the Electra had taken off from Logan Airport, hundreds of starlings flew into its path. Three out of the four engines shut down after ingesting countless birds. Though the aircraft crashed almost vertically from an altitude of three hundred feet, ten passengers survived. I heard more than half survived 641's crash. Is it true?" Before she could respond, Thomas placed his coffee cup and elbows on the desk. "Do you know who the crew members were? Did they make it?"

Olivia thought about the need to mention Philip's passing. If she told him, he'd lose even more sleep. They served in the same squadron during the Korean War and remained close friends ever since. "I'll let you know when I receive confirmation."

"You don't know?"

"It's been a crazy day. Get some sleep and come over to the house in the morning for breakfast." She walked to the door. "I'm sure dad would love to see you. It has been a while and he worries about you."

"It's been a hectic couple of years," Thomas said. He had purposefully stayed away from all acquaintances he and Sarah knew. Spending every moment in the company of friends recounting and reminiscing about her was like a thousand daggers pushed into his heart. At the best of times, it only felt like salt poured into an open wound.

"Well then, get some sleep," Olivia said. "I'll see you tomorrow."

Olivia went to the hangar to see her management team. She almost collided with Emma, who was leaning against the wall by the office door.

"I need to take him home," Emma said, squeezing by her.

"Yes, that's a good idea," Olivia said. "Olivia wanted to tell her that Thomas didn't leave Emma for her, but it wasn't the time. Seeing them together made her relieved that he would have someone to lean on through all of this."

\* \* \*

Olivia pressed the button to open the gate to her property. Turning off the road into the driveway, she slowed and squeezed her Mercedes through. The gate closed behind her as she continued down the half-mile path lined with dogwood trees on either side. Entering the circular driveway at Cooper's Manor, she steered toward the three-car garage on the right, pressing another button to open the middle garage door. Gary Pinkerton, a resident at the estate employed as the stable master, approached with Buddy in tow, a Hanoverian gilding standing seventeen hands tall.

"Missy can you leave the door open?" Gary asked.

"What are you two up to so late at night?"

Gary, an African American in his late sixties, small in stature with a medium build, removed his Boston Sox cap. "You know, he has not been himself," he said with a southern drawl.

Olivia's concern for the well-being of her horse of twenty-three years was short lived when Buddy rested his chin on Gary's head. She laughed. Stretching her arms out caused Buddy to nudge Gary out of his way so he could approach Olivia. He lowered his head and placed his forehead against her tummy. She leaned in and wrapped her arms around his neck. "Not feeling well, buddy?" The horse pushed his muzzle against her twice in response.

"You're such a good boy," Olivia said, rubbing his neck.

Gary looked on, pleased to see the two carrying on the way they do. He marveled at her ability to turn a 1,300 pound animal into a little puppy dog. It was evident from the onset when the two met for the first time. Everyone could see they were meant for each other. They were a perfect match, competitive partners and companions since she was twelve and he was five years old.

"What's with the hair loss?" Olivia asked

Gary pulled on the lead line attached to Buddy's rope halter. "You shouldn't concern yourself about this; I'm taking care of it. Anyway, you have more important matters to deal with." Gary grimaced, "I heard about this morning's incident."

"Yeah," she said, nearly inaudible. "We lost a lot of good people today."

"I'll tend to Buddy. You should go to the house. Your father has been waiting all day for you."

"How's he doing?"

"He's holding up as best as he can I guess," he replied. "He's just worried about you and wished he could have stood by your side today."

# CHAPTER 8

**OLIVIA FOLLOWED THE** interlocking brick pathway from the garage to the mansion, an enormous home, her father had built for a family of three. The pathways throughout the property totaled eight miles and varied in construction methods. The cobble stone driveway was the oldest path, constructed with stones collected from the property. It ended at the staircase leading to a roof-covered veranda supported by four concrete columns.

The grand house was built where their ranch house had once stood. Fourteen years ago, the original home measured eleven hundred square feet. The cramped accommodations did not concern Olivia, who spent most of her time outdoors.

What first attracted Alexander Cooper to this property so many years before was the acreage. Once a thriving horse race training facility in the 1840's, it was carefully designed to provide the ultimate privacy with the dense woodland. It was the solitude Alexander preferred and convinced Hannah, by which she had agreed to purchase the property with one caveat, he build her a bigger house. It took two decades to make good on his promise. Where the tiny ranch house once stood now replaced by a grand veranda, and then built the dwelling ten times larger than the first humble residence.

A mansion wasn't what Hannah had in mind. She only asked for something a little larger and more practical. The house grandeur however was a reflection and a product of Alexander's guilt. When he served as a pilot in his military and civilian life had kept him away from his family for far too often.

Olivia walked to the house, where the exterior chandelier shined bright. She noticed Henry Wilkins, the estate manager, exited through the front door accompanied by six women outfitted in maid uniforms. The women were all Mexican of various ages, the youngest in her teens and the eldest in her fifties.

They walked single file on to the veranda, forming a line shoulder to shoulder. Each of them thanked Henry upon receiving a small brown envelope. A handsome pay, Olivia knew, not just for house cleaning services but a little extra her dad called, 'incentive pay to keep them honest.' Over the years, these women had proven to be loyal, dedicated, and hard working.

Two taxis arrived near the steps leading to the mansion. The women descended the stone steps while the eldest woman remained behind, as she always did, to express her appreciation to Henry. "Gracias, señor. We will be back, same day, and we won't be late next week. Okay?"

"Thank you, Teresa," Henry said. "Today's tardiness is understandable given the unique circumstances. Not to worry."

Olivia waved to the women. "Hello ladies."

"Buenas noches, Miss Cooper," they replied as they climbed into the taxi.

Olivia recognized the taxi driver and offered him a Victorian wave, a stiff hand pivoting side-to-side on the wrist. The taxi driver tipped his cap in recognition. She ascended to the midpoint of the staircase, where Teresa greeted her with a kiss on each cheek and a hug.

"Careful," Olivia said as she tried not to lose her balance.

"You are so kind. I will not fall," Teresa said.

Olivia was worried more about herself in high heels on a narrow step. She placed her hands on Teresa's shoulders for support to wiggle herself free from the embrace.

Teresa's facial expression showed concern. "I am so sorry, Miss Cooper. I do not know what to say that would be appropriate." Mindful that English was not her first language, she chose her words carefully. "It seemed Mother Nature has turned on us in a cruel twist of fate. Those poor souls - just the thought it upsets me." She pulled a tissue out of her bra to wipe the tears trickling down her cheeks. She paused to blow her nose. "No, Mother Nature did not have a hand at this. She's not that cruel. It is the devil's work, I tell you. Who else can it be? To take people's lives while setting a house of worship ablaze. It is a terrible thing."

Olivia rubbed her hand along Teresa's arm. "Don't believe everything you hear," she said. "We don't know what happened, but we will make certain it will never happen again."

Teresa collected herself. "Yes, of course. I believe God will guide you through this terrible tragedy. We shall persevere, yes?"

"Yes, we shall." Olivia smiled and kissed Teresa on her cheek.

Teresa went down the remaining steps and looked at Olivia again before stepping into the taxi.

By the mansion's entrance, Henry lifted Olivia's attaché from her shoulder. "You'll need to see your father right away. He is expecting you on the terrace."

"Thank you, Henry."

"I'll put something together in the kitchen and bring it out to you."

"That won't be necessary. I had something to eat earlier today," Olivia said.

"That's a lie," Henry replied without batting an eye.

"I appreciate the thought, Henry, but as I said, I ate earlier." It wasn't a lie, but a small exaggeration. Breakfast was the only meal she had eaten all day. She enjoyed her slim physique and had no intention of working out to burn off the calories of a late dinner.

"Very well, ma'am."

The terrace faced southeast toward Charlottesville Airport less than two miles away. Alexander Cooper was seated with a cigar in one hand and holding a glass of brandy in the other. Watching the airplanes arrive and depart was his favourite pass time. At this distance and late hour, the planes were visible by their navigation lights on the wing tips, tail, and fuselage.

"Dad! You're smoking a cigar?"

"You sound like your mother," he replied. He waved the cigar at her. "It's not lit."

"I'm glad you're listening to your doctor, Daddy."

"Why would I listen to that crack pot? He diagnosed my angina attacks as heartburn!"

"Oh, what the hell," she said. "If you want to light up, go ahead. You are your own man."

"That's my gal." Alexander pulled a Zippo lighter out of his pocket and lit it. He positioned the cigar between his lips and raised the flame an inch away, but it reminded him of the pressure in his chest. He flipped the lighter's lid to extinguish the flame. He pulled the unlit cigar away from his lips and sighed. "Your mother will kill me."

"You got that right." Olivia chuckled.

"You shouldn't laugh," Alexander said. "I'll single you out as the temptress daughter wanting me dead for my inheritance."

They gazed at one another and both let out a belly laugh.

"Your mother would see right through the bullshit."

"Damn right she would." After the laughter died down, she asked, "Where's Mom?"

"She retired early. Not pleased with me being on the phone all day. She kept saying you were taking care of business and to leave well enough alone." He poured her a glass of brandy.

"Here, have some of this."

Olivia lit a cigarette and exhaled forcefully. She dropped into a lawn chair. "I can honestly say today is the worse day I have ever experienced." She reached for the glass and took a sip. "But this is really good."

"Given the day you had, I asked Henry to retrieve the best brandy we had on hand."

They enjoyed each other's company in silence. Staring into a distance, they watched the last departure of the day.

"Are you going to tell me?" Olivia said, breaking the silence.

"Several board members have called and it's not what you think."

"I'm sure they had something to complain about my poor handling of the day's events."

"On the contrary," Alexander said. "They contacted me to express their satisfaction on how well you managed the media and press statements."

Olivia crushed her half-smoked cigarette in the large glass ashtray and leaned back into her chair, cupping the brandy glass with both hands.

"I have the highest level of confidence in your abilities and time after time, you continue to exceed my expectations. Now, I'm not just saying this because I am your father, but you are running the company better than I ever did." He paused to pour himself another drink.

"There are two kinds of people in our business, airline employees and airline people..."

"I know the saying, Daddy," she said.

"Well, let me finish. Airline employees are great at executing procedures. We have the best team working together to deliver a consistent and reliable product. Airline people, however, are a different breed. They are bred for this industry with an instinct not just to think outside the box, but they're unaware a box even exists. This makes their reach into innovation, safety, cost effectiveness, and efficiencies limitless." He swirled his brandy, glass held at chin level to breath in its aroma before taking a sip. "Honey, you have proven to be an airline person and instinctively taken our organization to the next level. How you come up with some of your ideas, I'll never know."

"It's easy to improve upon a product. You give me too much credit. I don't have the guts to do what you did to risk it all, to start a company in a saturated market and make it into a success."

Alexander noticed her voice crack in her attempt to put up a good front. To undermine his meaningful and heartfelt recognition was unbecoming of her character. "What's on your mind, honey?"

"Nothing, Daddy, I'm just tired." She lit another cigarette. "It's been a long day."

"If you're worried today's incident will tarnish our reputation or your ability to run the company, that's just..."

"That hadn't crossed my mind at all," she interrupted.

"Then what's troubling you?"

"Why bother?" She rolled her eyes. "It won't change anything. What's the point?"

"It would be good to get it off your chest," he said. In a brief moment of silence, Olivia's drag from her cigarette and vigorous exhale were amplified. "You're mother has served as my sounding board over the years and it has helped me think things through. Sometimes saying it out loud helped to put things in perspective."

"I feel ashamed," Olivia whispered.

"What on earth do you have to be ashamed of?"

"Philip Schmidt survived the crashed. Did you know that?" she asked.

"No, I understood he was killed by the impact."

"He survived the impact. The explosion killed him just as he was climbing out of the aircraft."

"That's most unfortunate. Philip was a good man."

"He was a great man," she said. "The fire fighters on the scene even called him a hero. They say Philip assisted the co-pilot out of her seat and out his window." She took a drag and exhaled through her nose. "While all this was happening, all I could think of was thank God I missed the flight." She took a mouthful of brandy.

"Honey, you're just being hard on yourself."

"It gets better." She exhaled. "When I heard the news that a flock of geese had collided into 641, I felt relieved." She wiped a tear away from the corner of her eyes, careful not to smear her mascara. "I don't know what has got into me."

"It's just your coping mechanism," he said. "You'll be surprised how one's mental state and capacity handles such a traumatic event. It affects everyone differently. Nonetheless, your defense mechanism is nothing to be ashamed of."

"You're sweet." Olivia managed a smile. "I appreciate the kind words but it doesn't change the way I feel."

"One thing is for certain, once the smoke clears, your emotions will unravel and hit you hard. You may even suffer from survivor's guilt. You should speak to someone like Doc Peterson."

"Our neighbor?" she asked. "Why would I do that when I have Doc Cooper to take care of me?"

# CHAPTER 9

**MICHAEL HALL FACED** the television set seated in his favourite chair. One hand gripped a beer bottle, the other reached into a propped up bag of potato chips. It was 8:45am and Sunday's cartoon hour had 15 minutes of play remaining before the evangelists started occupying the airwaves. He kept the TV on to serve as background noise and to dampen the sense of being home alone.

He focused on the framed photo taken in 1947 of his parents and him at ten years old. It was the only image to have survived the fire, which killed his parents and prompted the home's demolition and reconstruction. The black-and-white photo portrayed the three of them in Brooklyn, New York, in their Sunday best standing beside a loaded station wagon before moving to Virginia. It was a simpler time.

His legs crossed on the coffee table and wedged underneath his feet was the morning's daily newspaper. The front-page photo showed Virginia Airlines' plane 641, broken up in several sections at Aviators Baptist Church. Depicting the devastation, Samaritans aiding the injured, and the roaring fire filled the backdrop. The photo captured the event after the aircraft's wing fuel tanks had ignited and before the first responders arrived on the scene.

Michael ignored the knock at his front door. His gaze drifted to the newspaper, partly covered by his pant leg, and caused him to look away. He bit into a potato chip and washed it down with beer. Another unanswered knock was accompanied by a familiar voice.

"Hello? Mike?"

He stuffed another potato chip into his mouth.

"Hey Mikey, it's me, Nathan."

Michael leaned his head back and closed his eyes. He had no intentions of seeing anyone, especially now while he was struggling with his premonition of 641's fate. More than a feeling, he knew his actions conducted in isolation would have serious consequences. Replaying the what-ifs, he acknowledged it was only a matter of time. The National Transportation Safety Board investigators will connect the dots leading straight to him.

Nathan entered the living room. He exercised care while he stepped across the littered floor through the unsettling number of empty beer bottles. "Hey Mikey, are you asleep?"

Mike's head was tilted back, eyes closed, a beer bottle resting on his knee on the verge of toppling over. Nathan reached over to pluck the bottle out of his friend's loose grip.

"What are you doing?" Michael groaned.

"The bottle was about to..."

"What the hell are you doing here?" Michael said. "Don't you have anything better to do?"

"I was just checking in. See how you're making out."

"I'm still alive. Now go."

Nathan took a step back, startled. He was disappointed in Michael, particularly because he had welcomed him into the crew when the others shunned him. Nathan had stood by him even when Thomas Wright and Diego Gomez had questioned Michael's reputation, claiming that he had performed unexplained and undocumented maintenance on the aircraft.

Nathan gave him the benefit of the doubt for the unusual disposition and attributed it to trauma or survivor's guilt. With that in mind, he ignored Michael's temperament and sat on the sofa. "You mentioned you were heading to Richmond. I wasn't sure if you had made the flight."

Michael drank what was left in his bottle and tossed it on the floor, adding to the litter of glass and torn paper.

"You know the plane to Richmond crashed on take-off?" Nathan asked.

"No fucking shit, Einstein," Michael said. He picked up the newspaper, threw it at his co-worker, and went to the kitchen.

Nathan threw his hands up to shield his face and managed to catch the newspaper. Some of the pages fell to the floor but the front-page stuck out. From the striking headline to the numbing photo, his eyes glued to the sight of his airplane. He felt a knot in the pit of his gut that swelled into a sharp piercing pain.

Michael returned from the kitchen, placed a beer bottle on the coffee table meant for Nathan, and sat back down in his chair.

I guess he doesn't want me to leave after all, Nathan thought.

Michael guzzled his beer and stared off into space. His feet, planted on the coffee table, exposed a torn piece of paper, damp from spilt beer, stuck to the bottom of his shoe. Nathan noticed a familiarity in the cursive writing, so distinct it can only belong to Thomas. Based on the paper grade, line spacing, and handwriting, this is a page from the duty managers' shift log. Nathan knew these logs were treated as the holy gospel, with access limited to the few among the management staff.

The torn shift log wasn't as pressing as his co-worker's strange behaviour. Nathan had a sense that he should leave, but wasn't sure how to do so without offending Michael.

"You're beer is getting warm," Michael said, breaking the silence.

"Oh," Nathan said, thinking it was probably a good time to make his getaway. "Appreciate the beer, Mikey," he said. "I just wanted to drop in, see how you were doing before I head to the hangar." He got up and inched away, resisting the impulse to hasten his pace. Approaching the front door, he said, "I need to pick up some tools for a plumbing job at home."

"Go then!" Michael said.

"Okay. Good to see you're still with us."

"Get the fuck out!" Michael shouted as he jumped to his feet. He tossed his beer bottle, spraying its contents as it flew through the air before striking against the wall.

Nathan leaned forward as if to lunge, instead he refrained himself and stared back. The initial fear turned into defensive mode for self-preservation. Ready to pounce and fight back should Michael leap toward him. A moment of the posturing ended when Nathan walked away without saying a word.

The screen door slammed behind him as Nathan ran across the porch, where he met Leonard. He grabbed Leonard by the arm and pulled him away.

"Hey, what is going on?" Leonard asked, while he was hauled to the side of the road. "What's gotten into you?"

"Michael has come unglued. I'm guessing it's about 641."

"Unglued? That's unlike him. I heard from Odessa that he didn't get on flight 1001. He is one lucky son of a bitch."

"You'll never know it by speaking to him," Nathan said. "He's not in a good frame of mind. I would leave him alone if you know what's good for you."

"Survivor's guilt?"

"Perhaps, but I'm not certain," Nathan said, looking at his boots. What would the odds be? He wondered. Checking the sole of his boots and under his breath he said, "Yes!" He peeled away two overlapping pieces of paper.

"Isn't that Thomas's handwriting?"

"Yup," Nathan said. "I have an idea. Let's go to the hangar."

\* \* \*

It was Sunday morning, August 18, 1974, the day after the incomprehensible and senseless accident. For a moment, Thomas had no recollection of it while he lay half asleep in bed. He tried to roll over and put his back to the sunlight seeping through the horizontal blinds. His left arm felt weighted down from the lack of circulation.

With his eyelids held shut, the right hand reached over to grab his left wrist to help bring it back to life. Instead, his only mobile hand rested on what felt like someone's waist. He continued to feel his way up to a shoulder and with little difficulty found his hand cupped over a breast. Squinting, he waited for his eyes to adjust to the light to notice Emma asleep by his side.

Fully clothed under a light blanket, she lay on his arm, solving the mystery of its dormancy. He moved toward the edge of the bed and pulled his arm free away without waking her.

Thomas had no recollection of how he had made it home and into bed with his ex. His last memory was his discussion with Olivia in his office, but he could not recall how he had driven home. There was no way Emma had picked up his sorry ass out of the car. Yet, there he was, at his home with a woman with whom he had once shared a bed.

Feeling light-headed, he sat up and pressed his legs against his chest. He steadied his head on his knees, hoping it would stop the room from spinning.

"Morning," Emma said, stretching her arms and legs. "How are you feeling?"

"I'm up but I don't feel rested."

"Lie back down. It's the first day of your vacation. You deserve to sleep in."

Thomas unbuttoned his shirt and pulled it over his head. He folded it into a ball and tossed it to a chair next to the bed.

"Now you're talking." Emma growled like a tiger.

"I need to shower. I reek of body odor," he said.

"I don't know what you mean," she replied with a noticeable change in the tone of her voice.

He noticed she had pinched her nose. "Smart ass!"

She laughed and continued to hold her nose. "You don't think this voice is sexy?"

"It's a definite improvement." He laid himself back down with his back to her.

"Shut up." She nudged him with her foot. "It feels good to lie next to you again."

"Uh-huh."

"Are you falling back to sleep?"

"I will if the room stops moving long enough," he murmured.

"Thomas?"

"Mm-hmm."

"I always wanted to tell you something but never had the nerve. When we decided to go our separate ways, I had to contend with several unresolved issues. In no way was it a reflection of what you said or did. That applies to me without saying. It was just, well, I had no one to confide in besides you. It dawned on me I have plenty of acquaintances but no one I can call a..." She rolled her eyes on how trifle it sounded. "I just want to apologize if I was distant or behaved inappropriately after our breakup. Whatever I had going on in my head is no excuse for my behavior, and I am sorry."

Emma grinned at the sound of Thomas's breathing. He hadn't heard a single word. She eased herself off the bed, stepped to the window, and turned the wooden wand to close the horizontal blinds.

* * *

Leonard jogged to catch up to Nathan's speed walking across the hangar floor. There were no aircraft present, which was a good thing. It meant all the planes were serviceable and generating revenue. As a result, the aircraft technicians working the day shift were all assembled at the ready room, a small maintenance office at the terminal. Situated near the gates where the aircraft are parked, they serve as a Formula One pit crew, able to jump into action to repair the aircraft at a moments notice. Nathan hoped for an easy shift so no one would see what he was about to do.

He approached the shift duty manager's desk and opened each drawer, searching for the shift logs.

"What are we doing here?" Leonard asked.

"We're here for the shift logs."

"The Shift Logs the Duty Managers maintain?"

"Yeah. Help me look," Nathan said.

"Was it something Michael said?" Leonard walked to the credenza and opened the cupboard door. "Here they are."

"Holy shit. How many are there?" Nathan asked. He pulled out several shift logbooks and placed them on the desk. "There must be over a hundred."

Leonard, take a few and go through them. Note anything done on aircraft 641." He passed him a pen and notepad. "Let's be quick. We can't be found rifling through the logs. That's all we need to trigger rumours that my crew had contributed to 641's accident."

"What am I looking for?" Leonard asked.

"There were eye witness reports that both engines failed after take-off. Look for anything common to both systems. It can't be that hard."

Leafing through dozens of shift logs, Leonard said, "The entries made by the shift duty managers are minimal compared to Thomas. Maybe the problem wasn't documented."

"I wondered the same, but we have to look." He flipped through another book. "Each manager documents the work accomplished. Compared to the entries made by Thomas, they lack specifics and from what I can tell, it's all here."

"There's nothing in these logs." Leonard said. He felt like they were chasing a ghost. "You heard what Miss Cooper said; a flock of geese brought the aircraft down. The auto-feather was armed, but bird ingestion can make the propeller thrust decay and feather the propeller automatically."

"I suppose," Nathan said.

"Engines ingesting geese is common to both sides. It's fucked up when you think about it. The auto-feather system operated correctly. It sensed propellers producing less than five hundred pounds of positive thrust and boom, both engines shut down and the propeller blades feathered."

"So if 641 really did fly into a flock of geese, the only way the flight crew could have prevented the crash is to disarm the auto-feather system."

"Yup. Pretty fucked up, right?" Leonard ran through the auto-feather system description and operation in his mind. "Actually, that's not right. The auto-feather system would never shut down both engines. It's part of the fail-safe design. When one side is activated, the logic circuits will lock out the opposite engine to prevent it from shutting down as well."

Nathan did not respond and focused on a single page. "Look at this." He passed the shift log to Leonard, opened to the page dated December 20, 1973.

Leonard shrugged. "I don't see aircraft 641 listed."

"Take a closer look." Nathan sorted the hard cover logs and hurried their return to their rightful place.

"I'm not getting it. What do you see here?"

Nathan closed the door panels to the credenza. "Look at the entry dates and the page numbers."

"December 20 and December 22," Leonard read aloud.

"What happened on December 21?" Nathan asked. "Entries made in error have a line drawn diagonally across the page. What would possess a shift duty manager to tear out a page when it's contrary to procedure?"

"That doesn't mean anything," Leonard said.

Nathan reached into his shirt pocket and held up the piece of paper his boot picked up from Michael's floor. "I wasn't sure at first but I'm certain this piece belongs to this logbook." He placed the portion of the tattered paper to the corner of the page Leonard held opened.

They stared at the bold blue forty-two imprinted on the torn piece of paper. It was the number of the missing page.

Leonard picked up the ragged piece of paper. "Whose writing is this?"

"Block lettering written in pencil can only be Logan."

"The shift duty manager that accused Michael of suspicious work practices and tried to get him fired?"

"That's him," Nathan said.

"So the rumours are true," Leonard said. "There's no logical explanation why Michael would have the shift log page in his possession, unless he had something to hide."

"Yeah." Nathan reluctantly agreed. "In all likelihood, the shift log page can prove he did undocumented maintenance on our aircraft."

"Don't let this get you down," Leonard offered.

"It's not," Nathan snapped. "I was just thinking we should take this to Thomas. I wouldn't mind getting his opinion. All we have is circumstantial evidence and we're probably blowing this out of proportion."

Leonard glanced at the shift log book, flipped through several pages and slammed it shut. "I suggest we confront Michael. He has been preaching to us how the shift duty managers have mistreated him. How it's in our best interest to unionize for our own protection." Leonard shook his head in disappointment. "He played us." Waving the log book in the air he added, "Knowing what we know, let's take him to task."

"As much as I like him, I'm aware he is full of himself," Nathan confessed. "In his present condition, however, taking him to task will serve no purpose. You weren't there, he is not in the right frame of mind."

There was a moment of silence. "What's that?"

Nathan stepped to the window looking into the hangar. "The hangar door is opening. They're bringing in an aircraft."

"Turn off the lights. We need to get out of here - now!" Leonard tucked the logbook in his windbreaker as they left the office.

# CHAPTER 10

**EMMA WASHED THE** dishes and put them away. It was 10:35am. Thomas had fallen back to sleep three hours earlier and there was no need to wake him until he was fully rested.

His only appointment of the day was to meet with Virginia Airlines' president for breakfast, but Emma rescheduled it. With a brief telephone call to Cooper's manor, she learned why Olivia needed to see Thomas. She agreed without question; Thomas needed to hear that his closest friend had died by none other than Alexander Cooper, the person he held the highest respect and admiration.

Emma poured herself a fresh cup of coffee. On the kitchen table she noticed a book titled 'Tinker, Tailor, Soldier, Spy' by British author John LeCarre. Another spy novel. She smiled at Thomas's infatuation with espionage and the British Secret Intelligence Service. Leafing through the book, she found a photograph serving as a bookmark tucked between the pages near the end of the novel.

It was of her and Thomas on the tarmac at Key West International Airport. They were on an aircraft recovery mission to repair an engine oil leak. It happened to be the 641 aircraft. On the photo's backside was the date February 24, 1970, written in blue ink. It captured the time they spent working together away from home, which led into their first intimate episode later that evening.

Emma fanned her face with the photograph as she recalled the vulnerability, the unparalleled passion and intimacy of that night. It was unlike anything she had ever experienced. They continued to see each other and the sexual interludes persisted upon returning to Virginia. Their relationship evolved and became serious for over twelve months. She knew no one was to blame but herself for the separation. It was all because of what she considered his obsession over a dead woman.

It was idiotic, she now conceded, unwilling to accept his compulsive behaviour. Come hell or high water, he paid his respects to his wife Sarah. On days leading up to and following the seventeenth day of every month, his persona would change. It was subtle at first. He would be less attentive to her needs, until the quick ramp up to his total disengagement. Emma was treated as if she did not exist. Thomas became himself a day or two later, ignorant of the fact he had been distant.

His painstaking willingness had maintained the holy ground where Sarah was laid to rest. It was a promise he made on her deathbed and held true years after. When Emma deemed his preoccupation unhealthy, she made calculated efforts to keep him away from Sarah's grave. She purposely organized functions on the seventeenth day but he went anyway, and his absence enraged her.

The last three months of their relationship was full of intense arguments and rehashed comments. It ended when Emma uttered the ultimatum: her or me. His silence spoke volumes and caused Emma to walk away. That remained her biggest regret. Today, however, she was determined to remedy it - if Thomas was willing.

Placing the photograph back in the book, she heard the sound of running water from the shower. She took a deep breath, stood, and began to unbutton her blouse. Moving across the living room floor, the blouse fell off her shoulders and dropped to the floor. She unzipped her blue jeans and yanked her legs out. Standing outside the bathroom door, she unhooked her bra and pulled down her panties.

She took another deep breath to build up the courage but accepted whatever consequence may be in store for her.

She entered the bathroom filled with steam spilling over the drawn shower curtain. Her heart was racing as she approached the shower, and she paused before pushing the curtain to one side. It was empty. She felt a touch on her back that startled her. Thomas was standing inches away with only a towel wrapped around his waist. They looked at each other and Emma tugged on his towel, letting it fall to the floor.

They embraced and kissed with the same intensity they once shared. Their breathing intensified while Thomas pressed himself against her and she reciprocated. Emma felt his arousal on her abdomen.

She reached down for his manhood and he pulled away, whispering, "I need to wash up."

"You're fine the way you are," she said.

"I will only be a second." He kissed her on the lips and darted behind the shower curtain.

Emma followed and reached for the bar of soap. She put it under the running water and then dragged it across his shoulder blades, lathering him up. He responded in kind, lathering and caressing her.

Her left hand grasped the back of his neck to draw him near. Planting her mouth firmly against his, she plunged her tongue in. While their tongues twirled, she felt a rush when their wet soapy flesh touched. Their bodies pulsated together in a slow and rhythmic motion.

An advancing car sounding its horn interrupted them. "Who can that be?"

"Who cares," Emma whispered. "Ignore it, whoever they are will go away." Noticing his enthusiasm fade, she reached down to revive it.

"The front door is open with the screen door unlocked."

"I'll get rid of them," she said tugging on his male appendage. "Don't go anywhere." She yanked the bathrobe off the hook and covered herself to meet the unwelcomed guests. To her surprise, Leonard and Nathan stood on the porch. "What are you guys doing here?" she asked the technicians.

"We could ask the same about you," Nathan said.

"Really," Emma said exposing her dragon lady demeanour. "It's Sunday, boys, and Thomas is off duty for a month. Anyway, he didn't mention you two were coming over."

"We need to speak to Thomas," Leonard said. "It's about 641 and…"

"We just need to speak to him and get his thoughts on something. That is all," Nathan said.

"Uh huh," she replied with a raised brow. Something in the background caught her attention and she looked past them.

The men spun on their heels to see a peregrine falcon fly by. It held a prey clutched in its talons and was travelling westward toward Turk Mountain.

"You don't see that every day," Leonard said.

"That's pretty neat," Nathan said. "Did you hear bells?"

"Yeah, I did," Emma said. "I've seen that falcon before."

She had no idea about falconry but considered the peregrine falcon another tool in her toolbox. A raptor kept at the airport would be a sophisticated scarecrow. No doubt, if they had one, it could have prevented 641's accident. "That's the same falcon Thomas had spoken about several weeks ago."

The falcon flew beyond the mountain ridge and went out of view. "The show is over guys," she said. "You might as well come in since you're here. I'll get you boys a cold drink."

Leonard and Nathan each took a seat at the kitchen table while she reached into the refrigerator for two Miller beers. "You take it in a glass?" she asked.

"It's still morning," Nathan said.

"It's happy hour somewhere in the world." She laughed.

"I'll drink it straight from the bottle," Leonard said.

"Boys," Thomas said, walking in. "What are you up to on a Sunday morning besides drinking my beer?"

Nathan stood. "We need your advice on something."

Leonard leaned forward in his seat. "It's about 641 and..."

"Yeah," Nathan interrupted, holding out his hand. He wanted to tread lightly. The evidence they had pieced together was damaging and their suspicions warranted careful scrutiny. "We need your take on something, but it's a bit out there."

Thomas grabbed the ends of the towel around his neck and leaned against the kitchen counter. "I guess it must be important to come all the way from Charlottesville." He eyed Leonard and then switched to Nathan. "It couldn't wait?"

"No sir," Nathan said.

"Well then, let me get dressed and we'll talk. In the meantime, drink up. I'll only be a couple of minutes."

"You need to be quick," Emma said, chasing after Thomas to the living room. "She needs to speak to you right away."

"Who?"

"Olivia."

"I seem to be a popular guy for someone that's supposed to be on vacation. It can't wait?"

"No, you were supposed to have breakfast with her, remember? I called and canceled to let you sleep in. I promised you would see her right away."

He glanced at the kitchen where Leonard and Nathan were sitting and sighed. "They came all this way, so I'll hear them out and then head out to Cooper's Manor."

\* \* \*

Thomas removed the cover draped over his Indian 1950 Chief Black Hawk motorcycle. He was folding the cover in haste and stuffing it into the leather saddlebag when a translucent image of Sarah appeared. In her white cotton dress, barefoot, she straddled the motorcycle with her hands gripping the handlebars. "You promised today you would teach me how to ride this beast," she said, smiling.

Her long blonde hair tucked behind her ears and striking blue eyes faded, replaced by a vivid image of a person dressed all in black leather. Assuming the same stance as Sarah, the black visor flipped up on the full-face helmet exposed Emma's chestnut eyes. "You need to get going," she said in a firm tone. Then she was gone.

Thomas rolled the motorcycle out of the barn. Checking the ignition and fuel was off, he kicked the engine over twice to prime it with oil. He moved the fuel valve, choke, and ignition switch to the on position, and then slowly depressed the kick-lever to find the compression stroke. He twisted the throttle twice and after the third snap kick, the eighty cubic inch engine started. Revving the engine cleared the black smoke exiting the exhaust as it warmed up then selected the choke off. He zipped up his leather jacket, strapped on his half helmet, and with the last addition of aviator sunglasses, he departed for Cooper's Manor on his pride and joy.

Riding along the cobblestone driveway, he noticed Olivia mount Buddy. The sound of the Indian Chief's roaring engine and exhaust system had a tendency to unsettle horses. As a courtesy, he turned off the engine and glided toward her. Helmet removed and placed on the handlebar, the bike rested on its side stand.

"You kept me waiting all day," Olivia said, tugging on the reins to keep Buddy from stepping in Thomas's direction.

"I slept in."

"So I heard."

He shifted his attention to Gary Pinkerton, who held the reins of a gray thoroughbred strapped with a Western Saddle, a preference of Thomas. "You are looking well, Gary."

"I'm feeling good, Mister Wright."

"You don't need to be formal and all. You can call me by my first name."

"It certainly has been a long time."

"Yes it has," Thomas replied. "I suppose you saddled this horse up for me."

"Yes sir, just like old times."

"I thought it would be a good idea to build up an appetite for lunch," Olivia said. "As Gary said, it's just like old times."

Rubbing his head, Thomas eyed the mare, then Gary, who wore a wide grin. "So what's her name?"

"Lightning. She's a mighty fast horse," Gary said with a grin.

"You're enjoying this."

"Yes sir. I know how much you love horses."

"I don't."

Gary laughed. "Don't I know it."

"Quit stalling," Olivia said with a laugh. "I'll race you to the old oak tree." She commanded Buddy to canter away and took the path behind the garage.

"Hold her steady, Gary," Thomas said.

"Don't bother yourself worrying about me. I will do my part."

Lightning sidestepped as Thomas placed his left foot into the stirrup. He hopped on his right foot until he mounted the horse. "Great job, Gary."

"Stop you're whining," Gary said. "Go on, Olivia has a good lead on you."

Thomas squeezed his left leg and made several smooch sounds to enter into a trot, but the horse's lack of response needed a persuasive nudge from his heels. Nearing the path that would take him to the old oak tree, he squeezed with his right leg to transition into a canter gait. Lightning responded, but they were too far behind to consider it a fair race. His competitive instincts forced him to consider a shorter yet rugged path through the woods.

Olivia looked over her shoulder and noticed him rounding the garage. To keep up with appearances, she pressed Buddy into a gallop.

Without a whip, Thomas swung the long reins to tap Lightning's right and left hind legs. It signaled the mare to dart towards an opening leading to a narrow path in the woods.

Olivia doglegged to the right, galloped along the tree line. Rounding the bend exposed the view of the old oak tree half a mile away. Slowing Buddy to a canter, she glanced around, but there was no sign of Thomas. Approaching the overlook, the halfway mark to their destination, Buddy slowed to a walk. Thomas exited the woods beside her, Lightning running full bore toward the finish line.

"You're such a cheater!" Olivia shouted. She kicked her heels and Buddy obliged, pushing off his hind legs, and lunged into a run. The sound of Buddy's heavy breathing and hooves pounding the ground drowned out Olivia's encouraging words. "You can do this, boy."

The gap narrowed slightly but Thomas's lead and Lightning's strength was no match. First to reach the old oak tree, Thomas galloped around it to claim his win. "I play to win," he said, pulling alongside Olivia.

"You are a cheat," she scorned.

"When it comes to winning," he grinned, "I have a tendency to exhaust all my options. Anyway, you had one hell of a head start. I had to improvise."

Olivia spun her horse around. "It's good to see you haven't changed."

"Second place isn't an option," Thomas said. "If it's worth exerting my energy and time, I'm conditioned to win. It's in my blood."

"Your absence is felt here," Olivia said, changing the subject. She was pleased to have him back at Cooper's Manor. It was once his second home - until Sarah came into the picture. She always hoped they were more than just friends, yet she couldn't deny Sarah was good to him and he cherished her. They were perfect for each other. They lived their life on Mid Mountain, a homestead that had been in Sarah's family for more than two centuries. "More so for Daddy, but he knew you needed time after her passing." She paused. "Mom often asked how you were doing."

"Your folks are good people," Thomas said. "They have always supported me in every way. I must confess that Sarah's passing threw me into a tailspin. I went through a rough patch. It was a painful time and I couldn't be around people that knew her. Discussing the good old times may help some people, but I simply wasn't ready to reminisce."

"We figured that," Olivia said. "Your absence was often a topic of discussion at the dinner table."

"Thanks."

"Don't be that way," she said, swatting at a fly. "We worried about you."

"As I said, Alexander and Hannah are good people."

"It was good seeing you behind your desk yesterday," Olivia said. "It reminded me of the good old days. I noticed you and Emma were acting chummy. So what is going on between you two?"

"Why would that matter?"

"Beside the fact she can't stand the sight of me," Olivia said. "I see how you light up when she's near."

"She's a loyal friend."

"I thought she was more than that," she said. "Sarah would have approved of Emma."

"I know she does."

Olivia puzzled by the present tense response, she decided to ignore it. "You still haven't answered my question."

"Have you asked me here to discuss my relationship status or was there a more pressing issue?" He asked.

She looked at him for a moment and smiled. "Come on, let's go have lunch."

Olivia cantered ahead and Thomas followed.

# CHAPTER 11

**COLONEL ALEXANDER COOPER** reached out to his friends serving at Langley U.S. Air Force Base for support. An Aircraft Recovery Team was assembled and sent to Charlottesville in a matter of hours. It was comprised of fourteen technicians, trained and motivated to deal with such matters. They arrived in a C-130 Hercules aircraft with equipment and tools needed to disassemble 641.

The broken sections of the fuselage, detached wings, engines, gears, and remaining parts were placed on three flatbed trucks. Within thirty-six hours of the accident, the crash site was cleared and the items taken to a privately owned hangar at Charlottesville Airport. No remnants of an airplane remained at Aviators Baptist Church. Alexander hoped the wreckage would be shipped to Washington D.C. so as not to serve as a constant reminder to the local residents.

Its presence had also attracted a great number of souvenir seekers. Their failed attempts to walk away with a piece of memorabilia prompted the need for a professional security agency. The battered airplane needed a guard to ensure it remained sterile until it underwent a thorough inspection.

David Steadman used Virginia Airlines technicians on a limited basis, predominately serving as consultants. Their expertise helped the recovery team navigate around the airplane. The fire department gave David the green light to recover the black boxes, which in this case were bright orange.

One box was the flight data recorder, which documented five flight parameters: heading, airspeed, altitude, vertical acceleration, and time, all scribed on a metal foil. The other box recorded thirty minutes of audio, called the cockpit voice recorder. These units could endure severe g-forces, high temperatures, and were installed in the tail section to increase survivability. The information they stored was invaluable to any incident or accident investigation. David had overseen their prompt removal under his strict supervision.

Diego Gomez, Thomas's most valued lead mechanic helped on the crash site. "What do you want me to do with the FDR and CVR?"

"We need to box them up and load them into my car," David said. "I am heading back to D.C. now that the wreckage is secured."

Diego signaled to Andy Blair, another lead mechanic, to fetch the shipping containers from the hangar. "The FDR will not be of any use to you," he said to David. "The recorded parameters are very limited. It won't offer a hint why both engines had failed."

"You're probably right, but it's more information than we have now," David said. "It's all a jigsaw puzzle." He stopped himself from saying anything specific about the ongoing investigation.

"It's odd," Diego said.

"Excuse me?" David said.

"The speculation about the flock of geese."

"Go on."

Diego looked at David. "Other than the goose's blood and feathers found on the right engine, there's no other evidence of a bird strike. The left engine was charred by the fire and won't tell us anything until it's taken apart, but the nose section..."

"What about it?" David asked.

"It's clean as a whistle. There's not a mark on it."

David was impressed with the lead mechanic's keen investigative skills. He was a veteran mechanic with broad knowledge and expertise extending beyond turning wrenches. "What else have you noticed?"

"Based on the cockpit's configuration, I can only presume the engine shut-down procedures were carried out on both engines. But if that were the case, they were too close to the ground to restart an engine."

"That's interesting," David said. Without stating outright that his observations were correct, he confirmed Diego's assessment by simply saying, "You're good."

"It's unfortunate, though," Diego said. "If it wasn't for the hydro wires, the flight crew would have been able to land in the open field."

For the moment, David did not consider the hydro wires had played a role in the accident, other than the airplane had plowed through them. He made a mental note of Diego's keen observation none-the-less. The FDR's recorded heading will certainly show a change in direction moments before the impact. He limited his response to, "Maybe."

Andy returned with the shipping containers. The units were installed in their respective box and adhesive tape wrapped around the circumference several times to cover the latches. A general practice, it indicated that the units were not tampered with while in transit. It was unnecessary, since David Steadman, the FAA inspector, would deliver them to Washington personally, but no one bothered to stop Andy.

\* \* \*

Arriving at the stable, Thomas dismounted and noticed Hannah, Olivia's mother, grooming a white Arabian. The horse held in place with cross ties in the alleyway of the six-stall stable nearly rebuilt from scratch. The structure's walls were a combination of a four-foot high stonework with new boards and batten siding extending to the roof. The exterior double doors opened on both ends showed the newly laid brick flooring.

Gary approached and took the reins from Thomas.

"I didn't get thrown off this time," Thomas advised.

"If this becomes a trend, you may love riding horses again." Gary chuckled.

"Let's not push it."

"Tommy," Hannah said with her arms extended.

They embraced. Thomas gently held her in his arms while Hannah's grip was as fierce as a wrestler's bear hug.

She whispered in his ear, "It has been far too long." She held Thomas at arm's length. "Let me look at you." She pulled him back in for another hug.

Olivia carried her saddle to the tack room. "Mother, if you continue to carry on that way, people will talk."

"Let them talk," Hannah said. "They're just jealous they don't have a man like Tommy in their family."

Hannah was the only person he allowed to refer to him as Tommy or Tom. On occasion, she would also refer to him as her son. The bond he had built with Colonel Alexander Cooper during the Korean War included Hannah. Orphaned since birth, she had played a mother figure in his young adult life.

"I'll tell Daddy you're having an affair," Olivia said, returning from the tack room.

"She's bad," Hannah said to Thomas. "Give me a hand with Wanda." She pointed to the stall. "Hold the door while I put her away."

Hannah approached Wanda to connect the lead rope to the halter before she could disconnect the crossties. The 15.2 hand white Arabian moved his head up and down in protest. Showing no fear, Hannah made hushing sounds while gently pulling on one of the cross ties to calm the gilding. She rubbed his neck with a mothering touch and with a slow transition, she grabbed the lead off her shoulder and attached it to the halter's loop. She disconnected the cross ties and her clicking sounds persuaded the horse to follow her into the stall.

"You have a magic touch," Thomas said as he closed the stall door.

"It's all about trust and earning their respect." She glimpsed at him while removing her leather gloves. "Are you ready for lunch?"

Olivia joined them and said, "I'm famished. Let's eat."

Hannah wrapped her arm around Thomas's waist and he put his hand on her shoulder.

"The rebuilt stable looks really good," he said.

"That was all my doing," Hannah replied. "But don't say a word to Alexander. He would flip his wig if he found out how much I spent on the renovation."

They all laughed. Hannah reached for Olivia's hand and the three of them held one another as they walked to the mansion.

Seated at the table on the terrace, beneath the umbrella shielded from the high noon sun, they watched Henry wheel over the serving table. It was customary, the guest was served first and Thomas received his silver plate. Henry removed the silver dome cover and revealed green salad surrounding three beef kabobs on a mound of white rice.

"It's a pleasure seeing you again, Mister Wright," Henry said, laying a napkin on Thomas's lap.

"The feeling is mutual, Henry."

"Do you prefer water, ice tea, or red wine with your lunch?"

"Ice tea will be fine, thank you."

"I will have the red wine," Hannah said.

"I as well," said Olivia.

"Don't wait on us, Thomas, go ahead please." Hannah gazed at him. "I won't gush over you. Lord only knows I have every right to do so, but I won't." She picked up one of the stainless steel skewers and a fork to pull the first beef square free. "You need to promise me that this visit is a start of many more."

Thomas felt he owed them an explanation for his absence, or at least an apology. If there were a time to do so, it would certainly be now, since he had finally come to terms with Sarah's death. Sarah and Thomas had no surviving parents and no family nearby. Hannah's relentlessly kind, uninhibited, and welcoming treatment had never wavered. She helped Sarah at home and at the hospital. She tended to her every need, from the bedpan, feedings, bathing, and more, to care for her. She did more than any family member would have. To his dismay, no blood relative had bothered to visit from the west coast.

"I haven't been myself."

"Hush," Hannah said. "You don't have to say a word. Alexander and I know very well what you were going through. I wished I could have done more."

"What you did for Sarah... There are no words to express my gratitude."

"Thank you. That means a great deal to me. Please eat, don't let your lunch get cold."

"Mom," Olivia said, "Thomas and I will discuss business after lunch."

"I get the hint," Hannah said. "I'm sure you two have a lot to discuss about yesterday's tragic event."

"I supposed you heard about Philip. He was a real hero, right to the end." Thomas said.

"You knew?" Olivia asked.

"Just this morning. Nathan Aschan's mother is close with Eva's mom."

"How is Eva doing? I planned to go to the hospital today to see her."

"She's doing well. Suffered a broken leg and dislocated her shoulder from the fall."

"You're taking Philip's death pretty well," Olivia said.

"Oh, don't let me fool you. I had my time to reflect. It is comforting to know his piloting skills minimized the outcome. We could have lost everyone on-board."

"Excuse me," Hannah said. She dropped her napkin on her seat and hurried away.

"Was it something I said?" Thomas asked. He stood, wanting to chase after her.

"No, not at all," Olivia said. "Sit down, she will be alright. It's too soon."

"I know how she feels. I miss him already."

Olivia nodded. Pushing her plate aside, she lit up a cigarette. They sat there in silence while Thomas cleaned off his plate.

A light breeze passed carrying Hannah's muffled voice. Thomas glanced at the open door leading to the kitchen. He could see her speaking on the telephone.

"She's probably talking to Daddy," Olivia said. "He wanted to be here but he needed to meet with some of the board members informally. He's hopeful he can persuade them to vote in favour of our strategic plan."

"Can I ask what that is about?" Thomas asked. Based on his experience with Virginia Airlines, a strategic plan could only mean growth. This would be an excellent opportunity to impress upon his dear friend, the president and CEO, the importance of building a sound infrastructure first. The need for additional equipment and staff are required to undertake and adequately support the fleet expansion.

She took a drag from her cigarette, exhaled through her nostrils, and flicked the ashes. "Discretion?" Olivia asked.

"Discussions about our organization are always held in the strictest of confidence."

"We are seeking to expand our routes."

"Expanding routes does not need the board's approval." Thomas sipped his ice tea. "You're buying more airplanes."

"That is the intent," Olivia said. "Fairlane Aerospace advised us that four VA980s became available when an undisclosed airline defaulted on payment. The price is too good to pass up. As it so happens, we're in the market to purchase more aircraft."

Thomas fidgeted in his seat. He crossed his legs, then planted both feet back on the ground. Rubbed his head and suggested, "It would be best to hold off. Wait until the NTSB and FAA have completed their investigation."

"What would make you say that?" Olivia said, alarmed.

"I'm not sure we can wash our hands of 641's accident," Thomas said. "I am slowly collecting circumstantial evidence and it suggests the bird strike was just a catalyst. It may not have been the main reason both engines quit on take-off."

"And where is this evidence?" Olivia asked.

"It's not physical. To be honest it's just speculation, but it's based on damning circumstantial evidence."

She chuckled. "Oh my god, you almost had me. What a relief. I was at the crash site last night and witnessed the blood-covered engine for myself. The FAA is exercising their due diligence. They will formally announce that it was caused by a bird - a very large bird."

Thomas sat up straight, guzzled his ice tea, and placed his empty glass on the table. "I hope you're right."

"Let the FAA do their job so we can start putting this behind us. Bury the unsubstantiated speculation and enjoy your vacation."

"I'll try. I need to get going, Emma is waiting for me."

"I hate to do this, but it would be best you stick around in case the FAA needs to speak to you. I can have Beatrice cancel your trip to Fiji."

"Agreed. I planned to anyway. My crew were the last ones to work the aircraft so there is no doubt, we will all be questioned."

"I don't want you to cancel your vacation. You need the time off. Just stay nearby in case you need to return quickly." She gave him a hug. "I will make it up to you."

Thomas descended the steps and approached his motorcycle. He noticed Olivia leaning up against the railing and watched him strap on his helmet. As he unfolded the arms on his sunglasses he is reminded. "You need to make me a promise about the fleet expansion."

Olivia spread her hands apart on the railing to lean forward. "And what would that be?"

Thomas mounted his motorcycle. "The front line staff are burnt out. Before we bring in additional aircraft, let's do it right and staff up accordingly."

"I'll do my best."

He started his motorcycle and revived the engine. "That's not good enough. Let's do it right Olivia, we need to set them up for success."

She stared at him, shook her then smiled. "I take care of it."

"I can't hear you," he shouted so to be heard over the engine noise.

"I will take care of it."

He cupped his hand over his ear.

"I promise!" She said.

# CHAPTER 12

**ODESSA CLARKE ARRIVED** at Stanford Hill, a recently erected high-end apartment complex. A location favoured by many pilots lived on Madison Avenue. She rapped three times on the door numbered 606 in large gold-plated steel.

"Coming," a voice said from within the apartment.

A handsome woman in her fifties peered through Eva Muller's apartment door. It wasn't difficult for Odessa to identify the stranger as Eva's mother. The likeness was uncanny and she could easily be mistaken for Eva's sister. "Hi, I'm Odessa, here to see Eva."

"This is not a good time," the woman said. "For crying out loud, there must be other things you reporters could write about."

"Mom!" Eva shouted from the bedroom. "Let her in. She's not a reporter."

The door closed to remove the chain then swung wide open. Embarrassed, the woman's guarded behaviour changed. "I'm sorry. Please come in."

"Can I presume you are Eva's mother?" Odessa asked.

"You presumed correctly, dear. I'm Eleanor. Please forgive me; it's been a hard couple of days."

"Reporters giving you a hard time?"

"They can be so rude," Eleanor said. "After I had disconnected the phone, they started knocking on the front door at all hours of the day and late into the evening. They don't accept no for an answer."

"I'm sorry to hear that. I guess they would do anything to get a story."

"You got that right," Eleanor said. "I know they have a job to do but it doesn't excuse their rudeness. We have our own way of dealing with disrespecting folks, it's unfortunate we are not in Texas. Follow me, hon. She's in her bedroom."

Eva lying on the bed, her left leg wrapped in a cast and propped up on several pillows. A sling supported her left arm and above it, a bag of ice sat on her shoulder. She looked worn out and exhausted. Considering what she had gone through, she looked better than expected. It's a miracle she's still alive, Odessa told herself.

"Are you going to stand by the door all day or are you coming in?" Eva groaned, struggling to sit up.

Odessa rushed the bed. "Wait. Let me help you." She lifted Eva against the head board stacked with pillows. The bag of ice slipped off Eva's shoulder in the process and toppled on to the bed. "Let me fix that as well. Raise your arm." She repositioned the ice bag underneath the sling for added security. "That should help keep it in place. How does that feel?"

"That's fine. Thanks."

Odessa placed a pillow behind Eva's head. "I tried to see you at the hospital yesterday but was refused entry. I was told only family members were permitted."

"You should have told them you're my sister."

"Yeah, right." Odessa giggled. "It's Virginia, honey, they'd have be swinging from a tree for suggesting such a thing."

"Don't be silly." Eva smiled. "Anyhow, I was in no shape to see anyone. I balled for hours until I dried up. I retraced every aspect of the flight in my mind until I couldn't think any more." She looked at Odessa with red swollen eyes and whispered, "I wish I could have stopped it from happening."

She took Eva's hand. "I want to hold you but I'm afraid I'll hurt you."

The co-pilot's eyes welled up. She leaned her face into the crook of Odessa's neck and began to sob. They shared an embrace. Eleanor stepped away from the doorway and pressed her back against the wall. Outside her daughter's bedroom, she broke down and cried in silence.

"I'm sorry, I don't know what has gotten into me," Eva said, reaching for a tissue. "I didn't think I had it in me for another water works session." She blew her nose. "The guilt can be overwhelming."

"Eva, I'm not going to pretend I know what you are going through," Odessa said. "You can't blame yourself. No one could have predicted a flock of geese would have flown across your path." She crawled on to the bed and cradled Eva in her arms. "No one is to blame. It was a freak of nature."

"Who said that?" Eva asked.

Odessa paused. "That seems to be the consensus."

"What are you talking about?"

"It's all over the news," Odessa said. She brushed Eva's hair away from her face. "The aircraft sustained one or more bird strikes." She noticed Eva's puzzled look. "Olivia Cooper also mentioned it in her meeting that the FAA confirmed evidence that a large bird struck the engine."

"Mom!" Eva called. "Please bring today's newspaper."

Eleanor walked into the bedroom with papers from that day and the last. "I held on to them," Eleanor said. "Until you were good and ready."

Eva fixated on the headline: 'Geese Downed Virginia Airlines Flight 1001'. Ignoring the front-page photo of aircraft 641 broken up and smouldering, she turned the page and started reading. The article identified the correct aircraft and location, but the other facts were foreign to her.

"Honey, are you okay?" Eleanor asked.

"I'm fine," Eva replied.

"You're wincing. Are you taking your medication?"

"Mother please, stop fussing. I've just taken my medication. It hasn't kicked in yet."

Eleanor kissed her daughter on the head. "I'll make us lunch. Odessa, I hope you can join us, I'm making your favourite dish." Her eyes widened. "Fried chicken."

"Um hmm," Odessa responded with a polite smile. She waited until Eleanor left. "What did she mean by that?"

Eva paid no mind and laid the newspaper on her lap. She replayed the flight's chain of events in her head. She mouthed each stage, starting with air traffic control's take-off clearance sounding in her headset. She recalled powering up the engines, rolling down the runway, the V1 call-out, and how the aircraft pitched up to eight degrees. She tapped each sequence with her fingertips on the back of Odessa's hand.

"Eva, is everything okay?"

"Shh." She remembered the bang. Could that have been the time? Was that the moment when the right engine ingested a large Canadian goose. She also wondered if a second goose had caused the left engine to fail too. If that were true, that would have been too coincidental just as I pulled the T-Handle, she thought. "Do me a favour and get me a pen and paper."

Odessa did not ask why. "Where do you keep it?"

"On the desk in the living room."

A sense of liberation rushed over Eva and she welcomed it. Shedding the burden of remorse relieved her of the overwhelming shame that she had caused the crash. Escaping the accident with her life had flooded her with survivor's guilt. Even though she knew nothing could have been done, and yet, there was a gnawing feeling she might have missed something. Especially when considering the flight had turned for the worst just following the impromptu measure - the T-Handle's activation. *That doesn't make any sense,* Eva pondered.

Odessa returned with the pen and paper. Eva frantically wrote down her recollection while it was still fresh in her mind. It would help when the FAA inspectors tried to question her again. Their first attempt was on the day of the accident, but her responses were incoherent because of the morphine. Fortunately, the hospital had the fortitude to end the interview. The FAA's second attempt would require Eva to be flawless, able to recall every relevant fact days or weeks following the incident. Jotting down notes had raised her confidence somewhat. Nearly every aspect, thought, and observation that occurred on flight 1001 was documented to the best of her recollection. She felt comforted that she could stick to the facts she believed, at this minute, rang true. Odessa read the report.

"Well?" Eva asked.

"You should have been a writer," Odessa said. "I'm getting goose bumps just thinking about it." She shook her head at the helplessness Eva felt in the last minutes of the flight. It was like a speeding car hitting a patch of ice, powerless to stop or steer away from oncoming traffic. All the driver can do is brace for impact and hope for the best. "It's a miracle anyone survived."

"Some didn't," Eva whispered.

"There's no mention of flying through a flock of geese," Odessa said, holding the fanned out pages.

"I - I don't remember. If we had seen a flock of geese, we would have turned off the auto-feather system. Not to mention," Eva added, "We would have made some effort to stay clear of them."

"What about the bird remains on one of the engines?"

"I don't know what to make of it." Eva placed her head in her hand. "I suppose," she looked up, "I suppose we were so busy flying the airplane, we just didn't notice. We were close to the ground when the right engine shutdown. Maybe the engine noise startled the geese grazing near the runway and inadvertently flown up into the engine." She shook her head. "It's too farfetched."

"The left engine failed just as you pulled the right engine's T-Handle. This could have been coincidental, right? There may have been another goose. They usually fly in pairs, don't they?"

"Odessa, you need to keep this to yourself. I'm beginning to second guess myself. Until all the facts are collected, this information may unintentionally steer the investigation in the wrong direction. This can be incriminating. Someone will be blamed, but I don't know who."

"You need to take this up with Olivia Cooper."

"I'm not taking this to the president of the company."

"Why not?"

"If Virginia Airlines maintenance is to blame, I can't afford to have her use me to downplay the error."

"Olivia's goal is to protect the best interest of all departments. It will reflect badly on the company."

"Exactly. It will be easier to pin it on a person than a whole department. How long do you think I will last?" Eva asked.

"I'm not a pilot but from what I can see," Odessa said, waving the pages in the air, "Besides the bang, there was nothing else out of the ordinary."

"You're forgetting one thing," Eva said. "I deviated from procedures. I improvised and though it shouldn't have made a difference Olivia could hang her hat on it. If I limited myself to the written procedure, we would not have lost any lives."

"Then speak to Thomas," Odessa suggested.

"Can he be trusted?"

"Absolutely. I can bring your notes to him. He will make certain the investigation stays on course."

"No. They will remain here and you cannot speak a word of this. It's important."

"Okay, but what about the FAA?" Odessa asked.

"I can stall them, but not for long."

Eva wondered how much time she could buy herself. The delay would need to be significant, preferably controlled for as long as possible. She considered omitting information to the FAA inspectors, withholding it temporarily until someone like Thomas could find the cause of the failure.

Why had pulling the right T-Handle shut down the left engine? She needed to know that first, and then disclose the information to the FAA under the pretence that her memory had improved when she was finished the pain medication. That could work. It would be a moot point if geese really had gone into both engines, but she shrugged it off-it was inconceivable.

The drawback of withholding what had occurred in the cockpit may be construed as misleading the investigation. The FAA may see it as the pilots' loss of situational awareness, and smearing Philip's memory was not an option. She is mindful her tactic to delay, be it direct or indirect; Philip's honourable life must remain intact, untarnished and pure, just as he had lived it.

# CHAPTER 13

**MICHAEL HALL HAD** direct and unrestricted access to Cecil Longhorn through their frequent business dealings. A professional relationship developed while he moonlighted at Aircraft Systems and Electronics, a company with which Cecil served as a silent partner with a forty-nine percent stake ownership. Without rhyme or reason, however, communications had stopped following the crash of aircraft 641. Each unanswered phone call fuelled his irritation. Not knowing if Cecil's unavailability was intentional didn't help ease his growing sense of abandonment.

The crash occupied his thoughts every minute of the day. Drinking himself to a stupor had temporarily halted the whirlwind of speculation. The weekend binge drinking had done little to heal his resolve that he had played a role in the crash.

Revisiting each scenario and examining every aspect of his involvement to right a wrong yielded the same result. Michael had exercised all of Cecil's bidding because at the time, he agreed they were suitable measures. Recognizing the risk assessment was conducted in isolation under a veil of secrecy, he wondered if it would pass the test of public opinion. If the facts ever became public, would the families who lost a child, sibling, parent, or a spouse on flight 1001 agree they had done their best? Hindsight suggested he had taken the path of least resistance, and that worried him.

Michael, seated in his usual chair, watched his reflection in the television tube. He wondered if he had been true to himself. It was a sobering thought to consider that he had been willfully manipulated as part of a calculated scheme. It held his fingerprints, and concluded he couldn't prove anything if he wished to go public. Retracing his steps, Michael knew any FBI investigator worth his stripes could easily follow the trail of 641's crash back to him.

*But I'm innocent,* Michael thought.

The cases of beer consumed in the forty-eight hour session of self-pity made him realize he needed a reprieve he could only obtain through Cecil Longhorn. He dialed Cecil's home number as one last attempt. To his surprise, someone answered after three rings. Michael recognized the gruff voice and it can be no other than Cecil's personal bodyguard.

"Sullivan it's me, Michael."

"You're one persistent son of a bitch."

"Don't hang up. I just want to set Cecil's mind at ease. I can be trusted but we need to get our story straight."

"Michael, you're rambling."

"Just put him on the phone. I only need a minute."

Sullivan held the receiver at arm's length. He heard Michael's voice but couldn't make out what was being said. Nor did he care. He allowed Michael to say what was on his mind. In a moment of silence, Sullivan spoke into the receiver. "You can't get the hint so I'll spell it out to you. Stop harassing Mister Longhorn. Whatever you have conjured up in your mind doesn't involve him. If you attempt to step foot at his place of business or his residence, you will be charged with trespassing. Now tell me you understand."

"Whatever."

"You've been warned."

Michael paid no mind to Sullivan's fool-hearted warning. He had changed out of the clothes he had worn for the last two days, washed his face, shaved, and set out for Cecil's office.

Two hours passed when Michael arrived downtown Charlottesville. He parked his car on Main near 4th Street. The keys left in the ignition, a habit from his upbringing in Orange County. Crossing Main Street, he paused in the center of the road to allow an eastbound vehicle to pass before continuing.

He stood on the sidewalk facing the entrance to Longhorn's Investment Brokerage. He tucked in his shirt and pulled up his pants. Then licked his palms and patted down his wavy hair.

"I need to speak to Mister Longhorn," he said to the receptionist. She was sitting behind a semi-circular desk in the large oval lobby at Longhorn Investment Brokerage. Behind her was the company logo in chrome lettering attached to the twelve by six foot sectional wall. Hidden behind it was a full glass door leading into the brokerage offices.

The five-foot eight slender build with shoulder-length brunette hair, the receptionist named Loretta asked, "Is he expecting you?"

"No," Michael said.

"And your name is?"

"Michael Hall," he replied.

"I am sorry, Mister Hall, but Mister Longhorn has a full schedule. May I ask what this is regarding?"

"Isn't he the owner of this establishment, the senior investment adviser? I need to see him," Michael said. He realized the beautiful creature behind the desk was an innocent bystander and lowered his voice. "Just tell him I'm here and there is a matter of an utmost importance."

Startled by his outburst, she offered the typical knee jerk response. "Yes sir. Please take a seat." She contacted her immediate supervisor. She covered her mouth over the receiver. "He's here," Loretta whispered.

"Speak up girl. What did you say?" her supervisor asked.

Michael plucked a magazine from the rack and sat down on the white vinyl sofa. Leafing through the pages, he glimpsed at her direction and returned to the magazine. "Mister Hall is here to see Mister Longhorn," she said.

"Stay calm," said her supervisor. "Did he mention why he wanted to see Mister Longhorn?"

"It is about a matter of utmost importance," Loretta said, raising her voice slightly.

"Okay, hon. Tell him he is in a meeting," Sue said.

She looked up at Michael. "Mister Longhorn is in a meeting and he will be right out once he is done."

Michael returned the magazine to the rack. A siren outside was getting louder. He rushed to the door and confirmed a police squad car was in the distance. Lights danced along Main Street in his direction. "What did you do?" Michael shouted. He took a deep breath and shook his head in disappointment. "Your boss is one son-of-a-bitch."

Loretta recognized his anger was not directed at her but towards Cecil Longhorn. As a precaution, she ran behind the sectional wall where she met Sullivan, Cecil's bodyguard built like an offensive lineman. He charged into the lobby to find the area abandoned.

"Loretta, it's all clear," Sullivan said over his shoulder. He grinned at the spectacle his friend Stan is putting on. "I owe you buddy," he muttered watching Michael Hall chased by the police cruiser with lights flashing and sirens blaring.

"Is he wanted by the law?" Loretta said.

"Nah, I just called them here to send the gentleman a strong message." Sullivan replied. Before he could turn away from the entrance, he watched Michael run across the street. He must have circled back. He watched Michael enter his car and drive off. "He won't be coming back."

"Are you sure?"

"Yeah, I'm sure. I can stay with you for a while if you want."

"No, that won't be necessary," Loretta said. Seated behind her desk, she continued, "I don't want to be too much trouble." She offered a reassuring smile she is fine. "Anyway, the gentleman has an issue with Mister Longhorn not with me."

\* \* \*

David Steadman locked up his desk at the Federal Office Building 10A, headquarters for the FAA in Washington D.C., before setting off to lunch. He yanked his jacket and hat off the coat rack as Shirley approached with a thick vanilla envelope.

"Where are you going?" she asked.

"It's time to eat. Do you want to come along?"

"I don't know." She swung the large envelope side to side like a pendulum.

"Is that what I think it is?"

"Do you want to eat or listen to flight 1001's cockpit recording?"

"I'll get the reel to reel recorder and set it up in the conference room while you get me a roast beef sandwich from the second floor cafeteria," David said.

Shirley rubbed her index finger and thumb together. "It's your turn to buy. Come on, cough up five bucks."

"What happened to the southern belle I used to know?"

"She grew up," Shirley said, walking away. "And don't start without me."

David retrieved the TEAC 7010SL series tape recorder from the audio/visual department. Back on the fifth floor, he laid the recorder on the table and installed the reel. He threaded the tape through the machine and secured it to the other reel. Shirley arrived from the cafeteria when he hit the play button.

"You started without me?" Shirley said.

"No, just getting it ready," David said. "Please close and lock the door behind you."

He placed his finger on the stop button, waiting patiently for sounds to emanate out of the speakers. A rumble sounded and he quickly stopped the recorder. The four-digit index counter was set to all zeros to reference the starting point.

"It's ready to go," David said. "Let's eat before we dive in."

Shirley realized they were eating without saying a word. "Is something on your mind?"

"What?" David said with his mouth full.

"You're a chatter box, particularly when we're working on a case. Why are you so quite?"

"I was just thinking."

"Does it have anything to do with Grace? I thought she was doing fine."

"Oh no, I mean, yes she is doing fine," David said. "But she's not on my mind." He paused. "I was just thinking about the Washington Post article. They claimed their unnamed source is a federal employee."

"The information cited in the paper is wrong," she said. "It's obvious, whoever it is, they are not part of any investigating team. Whoever it is, they're taking liberties to suggest they are a viable source."

David chewed his food while Shirley patiently waited for his reply. There was none. She didn't press the issue and returned to her salad.

"Just suppose," David said, breaking the silence. "The reporter may be on Eastern or TWA's payroll. This is a great opportunity to harm Virginia Airlines. They have been given the major airlines a run for their money and what better way is there to set them back."

"You're over thinking it," she replied. "My guess is that someone is seeking attention. That's it, that's all."

David laughed. "The reel-to-reel is setup with aircraft 641's cockpit voice recovered recording. We should get going."

The FAA investigators are very hopeful the flight crew communications and the related sounds may shed some light on what had occurred on flight 1001.

"Are you done eating?" Shirley asked. Chewing his last bite of morsel, David gestured yes. "Let's clear off the table and get to work." She took his plate away.

David reached for his notepad and placed it in front of him. He glanced at his partner then pressed the play button on the recorder. Background noise exploded over the speakers and he adjusted the volume. "The engines are running. I hoped the recording would have captured the preflight checks and pilot interaction before engine start up."

"Ground, VA1001 taxi with Foxtrot," said a woman's voice over the radio.

"Is that the first officer?" David asked.

"Yes, Eva Muller. The captain's name is Philip Schmitt."

"I've heard his name mentioned several times while I was at the crash site. A great number of people revere him. He's an ace pilot who flew in Colonel Alexander Cooper's squadron during the Korean War."

"Virginia Airlines 1001, Charlottesville Ground, taxi to runway two one, you're on request," said the air traffic controller.

The engine noise rose for several seconds, then lowered as the plane taxied. David suspected it was moving away from the apron area on to alpha taxiway. The aircraft then arrived at runway 21.

"Take-off speeds will be based on a weight of 50,000 pounds?" Philip asked, giving a subtle hint to his co-pilot.

"Yes, let me fix that," Eva replied. There were several faint clicking sounds detected. "There you go."

David pressed the stop button to take notes. "What do you make of this?"

"Sounds like she didn't have the take-off V-chart set to 50,000 pounds."

"I agree. Philip's query matched the weight and balance form they left behind at the station. We can assume they discussed it before engine start. We'll verify with Eva Muller when we interview her," David said.

"Agreed."

David pressed the play button.

"I'll take this leg to Richmond and it's yours on the next leg to Miami." Philip said. "Or do you prefer I take it all the way to Miami and you bring it back?"

"Ah, I prefer to alternate at each stop. It helps break the monotony."

"That's what we'll do."

"Before take-off checklist complete," Eva said.

"Call it in."

"Flight 1001 is ready to go," she said into her microphone.

"Roger 1001. After departure, turn left, proceed direct to Richmond. Cleared for takeoff," the controller replied.

"Power," Philip said. "Turbine inlet temperature is 932 degrees."

David halted the play back and wrote down his comments before asking Shirley for her observations. "What do you think so far?"

Shirley looked up from her notepad. "So far so good. At this point, all procedures are performed flawlessly."

"I agree," David said. "We need to get to the lab to retrieve the FDR data information. This will help confirm the engines were set correctly and achieved 932 degrees for take-off power."

"The lab is swamped. They said we can expect to receive the FDR report by the end of this week."

"Can we expedite it? I hoped to complete a preliminary review before speaking to Eva Muller."

Shirley shrugged. "I will speak to them and see what I can do."

David rewound the tape a bit and pressed the play button. They listened again to Philip commanding power and the accompanying roar of the engines spooling up to take-off power. David visualized Philip, the pilot in command, advancing the power levers. He would set the engine power as close to the intended take-off target as possible and then focus on controlling the aircraft as it rolled down the runway. Eva supported by fine-tuning the power levers to the exact required setting and monitored the instruments.

They listened to the engines rumble over the recorder's built-in speakers for several seconds. "They should be approaching V1 any time now. There's no turning back after that," said Shirley.

David nodded.

"V1," Eva said. Shirley listened intently for the next step. "Rotate." This indicated they had achieved VR and it was safe to lift the nose of the plane.

Both FAA investigators were aware the failure occurred immediately after the aircraft had lifted off and separated from the ground. They put their pens down and leaned in to listen, waiting for the sounds of the hypothesized flock of geese striking the aircraft.

"Positive rate," Eva said.

"The aircraft is off the ground and climbing," David whispered.

"Yup."

"Gear up," Philip said to Eva, signalled her to raise the landing gear.

The FAA investigators heard the click of the gear handle activation followed by a pronounced bang.

"What's that?" Eva asked.

There was a second of silence. The investigators assumed the pilots were referring to their instruments and annunciator panel, assessing the situation.

"It's the number two engine," Philip declared.

David didn't bother to halt the playback to confer with Shirley. The sounds and words showed the first engine failure had occurred. There were no leading indicators to suspect the number two engine was not performing at par. Based on the cockpit audio recording, the engine stoppage was abrupt. Coupled with the blood and feathers he witnessed at the crash site, it supported the story of a bird strike claimed one propulsion source.

"Max power," Philip said.

Eva repeated the command. "Max power." She pushed the number one engine's power lever forward.

"Engine shutdown checklist," Philip directed.

"I'm on it," Eva said. "The T-Handle should be pulled."

"We don't have an engine fire. Is that necessary?" he asked.

"It wouldn't hurt."

A pronounced clunk was heard when Eva pulled the T-Handle. An eerie silence followed. The left engine was no longer operating and they were a mere few hundred feet in the air.

"Philip!" Eva shouted.

The recording reached its end. "Is that it?" David asked.

"I guess so," Shirley said. "The lab mentioned the tape was in poor condition but I thought they meant the audio quality. I had no idea they meant they had only extracted twelve minutes of audio."

"If that," David said.

"At least we have something to work with. One engine shut down automatically and the other was initiated by the pilot."

"It seems that way, and yet it is hard to comprehend."

"Out of all the tasks a pilot performs during a flight, pulling the T-Handle would be the easiest."

"That's what I find to be most troubling as well. What would possess a pilot to pull the left-hand T-Handle when the right engine had failed?" David tapped his pen on the notepad. "It's inconceivable."

"Setting aside that there was no fire indication to prompt her to pull the T-Handle, this aircraft was re-engineered. The systems were modified to reduce weight, increase reliability, as well as reduce operating costs. The engine fire panel is one of those systems."

"I see where you're going with this," David said. "The T-Handles on the VA980 are no longer linked mechanically through a cable circuit. I went over the engineering drawings. All the relays and valves are now controlled electronically."

"So it could have been wired incorrectly," Shirley said.

"If the number one and number two engines are electrically crossed wired, she would have inadvertently shut down the wrong engine while activating the correct T-Handle. To your point, she shouldn't have pulled the T-Handle, but that's a topic we'll discuss on another day."

"I think we have enough information to start our investigation."

David rewound the tape to the supply reel. "No word of this to anyone. We can't afford to have it leaked to the media that the pilot may have erred."

"There was no error," Shirley corrected. "The pilots have the right to deviate from the quick reference handbook as they see fit. Regardless if pulling the T-Handle was justified or not, the number one engine should have continued to operate normally."

"I agree. You're preaching to the choir." He glanced down at his notepad. "But that is how it will play out in the media. They will latch on to the procedural deviation and exaggerate the point to sensationalize the story to sell more newspapers. They may even question if the re-engineered 980 aircraft are airworthy and what other hidden issues may still exist."

"You're absolutely right," Shirley said. "We'll keep a tight lid on this until we can get to the bottom of it."

David approached the recorder to remove the tape reel. "Did the lab make a copy of this?"

"I took it before they had a chance. I'll remind them to do so once I return it."

"For the time being, it will remain locked up in my desk."

"Okay. Let's get our technicians to check the wiring on the fire protection panel to see if our assumptions hold any water."

David stuffed the supply reel back into the envelope. "If we're right, we will need to verify how the OEM, who manufactured the fire protection panel, the airline who installed it, and the associated procedures to validate its serviceability had all missed the flaw."

"Understood." Shirley nodded. "What is our story in the meantime?"

"The truth," David replied. "The CVR tape indicated the pilots executed their duties and there was no indication the engines had experienced irregularities before shutdown." He grinned.

"Good. Let's get to work and interview Eva Muller first before heading off to the hangar. All the technicians will be assembled there minus two individuals. The shift duty manager by the name of Thomas B. Wright, he is away on vacation. The other is Michael Hall, he is off duty for several days and he can't be reached by telephone."

"Advise Virginia Airlines that won't do. We need to speak everyone directly involved with this aircraft. Play it safe and go straight to the top - contact Olivia Cooper."

# CHAPTER 14

**AT THE AIRCRAFT** Systems and Electronics facilities, Michael entered through the employee's side entrance with determination. He needed to gather data to help in his reprieve. It would be his word against Cecil, a prominent member of the community and Charlottesville's elite. No one would believe him without evidence. In the library room, where all the manuals and engineering documents were kept, he rummaged through the large drawers. The engineering drawings for the FA680 to VA980 conversion were missing.

"Michael," Aiden Lynch called. "May I ask what you are doing?"

With his back to the library's door, Michael recognized the voice belonging to the president and CEO of Aircraft Systems and Electronics. He closed the empty drawer and turned around to face Aiden. "I thought I would come in and get caught up on a few things."

"Ah ha, very good," Aiden replied. He grinned to hide his scepticism. "I need to speak to you in my office."

"Yes sir." Michael nodded. "I will be there shortly."

Aiden peered at his watch. "Okay, but make it quick. I have a meeting in twenty minutes."

Michael sighed, relieved, and returned to his task. He scanned the shelving for the binders containing the same engineering drawings printed on smaller paper. Those engineering renditions were more manageable and occupied less space at a workstation. Technicians kept them nearby to reference while wiring and assembling aircraft components. Though they are not the originals, they will serve his purpose none-the-less.

He placed the binder on the table and he turned the pages. To his dismay, the relevant section was missing. All the sections were present except for those he had sought out. He closed the book and went to see his employer.

"Mister Lynch, you wanted to see me," Michael said, walking into the corner office. It mirrored the grandeur and decor of Alexander Cooper's office.

"Please, take a seat. Unfortunately, I only have fifteen minutes but I need to speak to you urgently and it couldn't wait."

"How can I help?" Michael asked.

"I spoke to Cecil Longhorn," Aiden said, leaning in and resting his elbows on his desk with clasped hands. "And I need you to explain a few things for me."

"In regards to my visit to Longhorn Investment Brokerage..."

"No." Aiden interrupted. "I am referring to Cecil's phone call last night urging me to have you dismissed."

"Last night?"

"Yes. Your work here has been exemplary so you can understand why I was taken back by his request. His reason was supposed slanderous and defamatory comments made by you to Virginia Airlines employees."

"That's not true."

Aiden held up a finger. "I know we have had some quality issues lately. All of us, you included, have worked diligently to correct them.

We made great strides to improve our processes and methods identified through exhaustive audits. We addressed every finding immediately. We have introduced a paradigm shift across the board that has brought our checks and balances to a new and unparalleled standard. After having said this, can you understand why I would be disappointed to hear you may have tarnished this organization's reputation?"

Michael tried to piece together Cecil's calculated measures to distance himself, including uncharacteristically denying his phone calls, tarnishing his good name to Aiden Lynch, and this morning's refusal to meet in person. His rebuffing was no coincidence, but a plan to assure Cecil's self-preservation with the public and his close business associates. But why? As far as Michael was concerned, he gave Cecil no reason to doubt his loyalty.

"Michael, do you have anything to say?" Aiden asked.

"If I had said a word about the occurrences and the efforts made at this organization, I can assure you, sir, it wasn't disparaging by any means." Michael swallowed.

"So you admit you spoke about us to Virginia Airline employees?"

"Yes, but only to dispute the technician's derogatory comments," Michael said.

"Derogatory in what way?" Aiden asked.

"Claims of poor quality and workmanship."

"Well, Cecil is saying otherwise."

"He is wrong," Michael said. "Defending your company's reputation made me the center of attention and ridiculed for doing so. I almost lost my job. They transferred me to another crew to give me a second chance."

Aiden rose from his seat and stepped to the window to walk off the discomfort he felt toward Michael's inevitable dismissal. "I thought by discussing this with you I may be able to clear the air. Unfortunately, it has become more convoluted and no closer to understanding the truth."

"The truth is Mister Longhorn is deceitful," Michael said.

"Hold your tongue," Aiden said. "There is no need to vilify his character because you disagree with him."

"That is not my intention. I am stating a fact. Mister Longhorn is a liar, not to mention that he has been deceiving you for some time and you're oblivious to it."

"That's enough!" Aiden said, visibly unsettled. "Cecil may be many things, but he is not deceitful, nor a liar. If it were not for his trust to lend me the money with little to no collateral, I'd still be operating my business out of my garage." He pointed at Michael. "You listen carefully. When my organization was hanging on by its fingernails because of one inexperienced technician, when he purposefully ignored crucial procedural steps, it was Cecil who stepped up and held us together."

"Is that when he became your partner?" Michael asked.

"That's correct," Aiden furrowed his brow, unclear why this has any relevance. "As I was saying, Cecil went to his friend Alexander Cooper to persuade him not cancel the contract." He stopped the finger pointing and returned to his seat behind the desk. "There was nothing wrong with our procedures. I took my lumps as Cecil suggested, added more layers in our quality division, and I'm pleased to say Aircraft Systems and Electronics continues to prosper."

"So you are obliged to follow through with Mister Longhorn's request," Michael said.

"I am indeed." Aiden sighed.

"Okay then. I guess there's nothing more to say."

"Leave your keys and company I.D. card with my secretary."

"Before I go, can I say one last thing?"

Aiden glanced at the timepiece sitting on his desk. "You have thirty seconds."

"My only regret is that I didn't alert you when Mister Longhorn first approached me. I presumed he was acting in the best interest of the company. I can clearly see I have failed you, but more importantly, I had failed myself."

Aiden's secretary poked her head through the doorway. "Your 11am meeting with Olivia Cooper starts right now. She's waiting for you on line two."

"Thanks, Judith," Aiden said. He looked at Michael. "That will be all."

Aiden and Olivia conducting a phone call immediately following his dismissal concerned Michael deeply. He wondered if what had occurred would affect his employment at Virginia Airlines. He couldn't worry about his future employment or career when he lacked the proof to clear his name. He decided to go to the engineering office as a last ditch effort.

"Excuse me," Judith said.

Michael stopped to face Aiden's secretary.

"Are you forgetting you need to leave me your keys and I.D. badge?"

"I'll bring them to you after I clear out my locker."

"You need to leave the premises immediately."

"Can you give me five minutes?" Michael asked.

Judith was no fan of Cecil Longhorn and sympathized with Michael's predicament. She blinked and nodded her approval.

\* \* \*

The engineering area housed four drafting tables and a manager's office. In the center of the room sat a large boardroom table with project plans laid to one side and drawings spread across its center. The far right was clear except for a telephone. Michael rushed to the table, searching for the drawings absent from the library. He found one sheet of the engine fire panel and set it aside. He continued to rummage through the remaining drawings.

"Hey Michael," said Peter Saga, the engineering manager.

"Oh, Peter, you startled me," Michael said. "Where is every one?"

"They are all working on 641," Peter replied. "What are you looking for?"

"The wiring diagrams for the VA980's engine fire panel."

Peter approached the table, "I was not aware we had anything in the queue."

"We don't," Michael said.

"What is this all about?"

"Mister Hall, you need to come with us." A security guard came into the room and walked towards Michael.

Ignoring the guards, Michael said, "I need to get my hands on those drawings. I can really use your help on this."

"I can't," Peter replied.

"And why not?" Michael demanded.

"They were retrieved by Cecil Longhorn."

"When?"

"Mister Hall, do you wish to be carried out?" the guard asked.

"That won't be necessary." He took one step toward the door then faced Peter. "Will you help me get my hands on the fire protection panel drawings."

Peter lowered his eyes and shook his head. "I can't risk losing my job."

\*\*\*

Emma spent her Monday morning retrieving her car from Compton Hollow in Page County. That's where she left it two days prior after she found Thomas to let him know about 641's mishap. She drove him back in his car and it had been a chore to find someone to take her on an hour and a half drive north to recover hers.

She returned to Thomas's home on Middle Mountain at 12:45pm to find a note on the kitchen table. "Gone to check up on the airplane's wreckage, call you tonight."

A young barefoot woman wearing a bohemian dress, string bead necklace, and a thin leather band around her head let herself into the house. "Hello," she called.

"May I help you?" Emma asked.

"Hi, I'm Debbie Bailey. I live next door. Is Thomas at home?"

"No, he went out. Is there something I can help you with?" Emma said.

She held out an empty teacup. "If it's not a bother, can I borrow some sugar?"

"Sure, come on in." Emma walked into the kitchen. "Is that your dog barking?"

"Yes, that's Ginger. She's probably chasing a rabbit."

"It must be some rabbit to make all that racket."

"Ginger!" Debbie shouted through the screen door. The dog paused for a second and continued barking.

Emma grabbed an unopened five-pound bag of sugar from one of the cupboards. "Here you go. You can have the whole bag."

"You're not trying to show me up?" Debbie asked. "I had only asked for a neighbourly cup of sugar."

"Not at all. Use as much as you need and bring back what you don't use." Not waiting for a response, she opened the screen door curious to know why Ginger barked so.

A hundred feet from the house, Emma saw the familiar peregrine falcon busy at work plucking the feathers from its prey. Ginger, the Border collie approached and was chased away by the falcon. Approaching again, the falcon attacked with its talons pointed outwards. She scratched the dog's muzzle, which caused Ginger to yelp and coward to her owner's side.

Stepping off the porch, Emma walked toward the peregrine for a closer look. Debbie followed but cautioned her to keep a safe distance.

Emma ignored the warning and continued to move in closer. When twelve feet away, she crouched to admire the raptor feasting. The tip of the beak was red from the blood. Long leather strands and brass bells tied to each of the bird's legs confirmed it was the same one continually popping into her life.

"Thomas is right, you are a beauty," Emma said. "I've seen you three days in a row. You must live nearby."

Ginger's barking was a distraction and irritated Emma while she studied the bird. She moved away slowly to fetch her camera.

Debbie noticed Emma's walk, her posture, determination, and her muscular physique, not to mention the caduceus tattooed on her forearm.

"Were you in Vietnam?" she asked.

"And if I were?" Emma asked. She remembered the condescending comments she received upon returning from her tour of duty.

"My dad served in Vietnam."

Emma went to her truck and grabbed the camera from the front seat. "A lot of us did. More than two and a half million served in country." She peeled away the cover from the camera and advanced the film. "Sadly though, one out of every ten was a casualty." Circling the peregrine falcon and its prey, she snapped a photograph from the side and then another head on. The camera had enough film to take five shots, "Shit I'm out of film."

"I can take you to where she lives," Debbie said. "When you have more film, that is."

"I would like that," Emma said walking back to her truck. Leaving the camera in the front seat, she picked up the bag of sugar and tossed it to Debbie. "That's a down payment for you guide services. Oh, and tell your dad to drop by any time. It would be good to talk to a fellow vet."

"He can't come here."

"And why not?"

"He left his legs in Vietnam," Debbie replied.

# CHAPTER 15

"**OH, IT'S YOU,**" Cecil Longhorn said, answering the knock at his front door.

"That wasn't the response I expected," Thomas said. "But then again, you never fail to surprise me."

"Your sarcasm suits you. It reflects who you are and why you never have nor will ever amount to anything," Cecil said.

A large burly man in a navy blue suit arrived from within the house and positioned himself between Cecil and Thomas. "Sir, do you wish this gentleman to be removed from the premises?"

"That won't be necessary, he's harmless," Cecil said. He signaled Thomas to come in.

Thomas lowered his sunglasses and stared down at Sullivan. "You can go back to bench pressing. The grownups need to talk."

"Don't patronize the help, Thomas," Cecil said. "I'll pour you a drink and then you can be on your way."

Thomas pushed his sunglasses back on to the bridge of his nose and grinned, taunting Sullivan for a second more before heading to the study.

"I take it you are still partial to single malt scotch on the rocks," Cecil said, passing a glass to Thomas. "I never understood why you would ruin fine whiskey with ice cubes."

"You know," Thomas said, "You are a fucking dick."

Cecil laughed. "And this is a revelation? Don't tell me you came all this way just to tell me that? Hell, I haven't been in anyone's good graces for some time." He paused to reflect on who thought of him favourably. No one came to mind. "I suppose stepping on all those toes on my way to the top didn't help."

"You need to face the facts; you're an asshole."

"Now you're getting personal," Cecil said. He finished his drink and rested his glass on the side table. "Enough with the sweet talk. Tell me what you came here to say and get out."

"Have you seen Michael Hall?"

"Why would I?"

"I was told he came by your office this morning and you ran him off."

"You should get your facts straight," Cecil said. "I didn't see him, so how could I have run him off? Why would you care, and most of all, how does it pertain to me?" He stood and strolled to the bar to refresh his drink. Thomas would love to wipe the smirk off his face with a left hook and an uppercut to the jaw.

Thomas kept his cool and suspended his sarcasm to seek the truth. "How long have you and Michael been working together?"

"You mean how long he has been working at Aircraft Systems and Electronics?" Cecil corrected.

Thomas remembered talking to Nathan while seated in 641's cockpit an hour prior to the crash. Two maintenance crews had abandoned their workstations to listen to Michael talk about why they should unionize. Away from prying ears, they stood in the employee parking lot where Michael argued the benefits for doing so. If they agreed, he assured they would have Longhorn's backing. "He speaks your name with the familiarity suggesting you two are more than acquaintants."

"I can't speak intelligently about a person I only met in passing," Cecil replied. "Why he said what he said or implied to others, I have no explanation. Michael worked for Aiden Lynch, so I'm not sure what you are suggesting."

"Worked? That's past tense. He no longer works for you?"

"You must be hard of hearing. I'm only a silent partner and yes, Aiden did mention he had to let Michael go."

"Why?"

"I am not involved in the daily activities and it would be best to ask Aiden. Regardless, I don't see how that could be any of your business," Cecil said.

Thomas knew being direct would only make Cecil evade the truth. Instead, he cast his first lie. "I have been approached by the FAA. They asked about you."

"I know a great number of people and some are employed with the FAA, so what of it?" His smirk widened.

Thomas prepared to deliver the second lie. "They did not offer salutations. They did, however, have several queries about the fire protection panel."

Cecil's smirk faded. "Of all the systems involved on the aircraft, why that particular component?"

Thomas noticed Cecil's demeanour change and felt he was making progress. The information Nathan and Leonard had brought forth was not much on its own, but combined with what Thomas knew about Michael's unexplained activities performed on the aircraft, it was damning. He would need to continue with the web of lies to see if his theory was valid. Treading lightly to ensure his deception wouldn't backfire and make him out to be the fool, he replied, "Shortly after take-off, both engines shutdown and they flew dead stick into the church. Though the FAA did not say specifically, we can surmise the fire protection panel is common to both engines."

"So what?" Cecil said. "I'm sure the FAA will examine all relevant systems in their investigation. This is rudimentary."

"The only difference is Michael's mysterious tampering with these same panels," Thomas said. He had re-evaluated the line of questioning and decided to put his cards on the table face up. "We're both aware that Aircraft Systems and Electronics had a poor quality record and the board of directors convinced Alexander Cooper not to cancel the contract. Alexander reluctantly gave them another chance because the board had a vested interest in ASE. So, I'll come out and say it."

"Please do," Cecil said.

"Was there a quality issue with the fire protection panel? Was Michael directed by ASE to secretly correct the problem to avoid Alexander knowing there was another quality escape?"

"You'll never change; you always play the conspiracy theorist in matters beyond your grasp." Cecil laughed. "You have nothing but innuendos. I can play the same game, Thomas. Let me see, what have you done to the aircraft while it was under your care? What maintenance action was carried out that brought that airplane down?" Cecil rose from his seat. "Everyone knows a flock of geese shut down those engines. Chasing ghosts is futile, so leave well enough alone."

*Leave well enough alone is a poor choice of words,* Thomas thought. It was not a denial, and based on his dealings with Cecil, this would be as close as he'd come to admitting Michael tampered with the fire protection panels. "I need to get going."

"Wait, you weren't clear," Cecil said. "What questions did the FAA have on the fire protection panels?"

"I didn't say." Thomas grinned. "I'm sure they will seek you out."

\* \* \*

It was Tuesday morning, the third day after the crash. Michael Hall started the day tidying up his house. He moved the cases of beer stacked in the kitchen and living room to the garage, mopped and vacuumed, and made the bed. The open windows did not help to move the warm still air that filled the house. He built up a sweat trying to put the house in order.

Michael went into the refrigerator to retrieve a pitcher of lemonade made the night before. It was the first non-alcoholic beverage he had drank in days. The first glass helped to cool him down a bit, so he poured himself another. He unplugged the toaster sitting on the kitchen counter and carried it to the bathroom.

While undressing to his boxer shorts, water filled the cast iron tub. He held his hand in the water and adjusted the taps for the right temperature. Placing his clothes into the hamper, he remembered the envelope in his shirt pocket. He wedged it into the mirror's wooden frame. Glancing into the mirror, he brushed his hair away from his brow with his fingertips.

As water continued to fill the tub, he returned to the kitchen and telephoned Nathan Aschan.

"Hello?" a woman's voice said.

"Hi, this is Michael Hall. May I speak to Nathan please?"

"I'm sorry, he just stepped out. Would you like to leave him a message?"

"Sure. Let him know I could really use his help to work on my car."

"At what number can you be reached?"

"Nathan has my number."

"Will that be all?"

"Yes Ma'am. Thank you."

\* \* \*

Nathan arrived at Michael's home and entered the garage to find it empty. There were no tools lying around, no jacks suspending the car, and the hood remained closed. Nothing suggested his friend had been working on his vehicle. Perhaps he held off until help arrived.

The front door was ajar and he let himself in. He called Michael's name but went unanswered. The smell of cleansers filled the air. Nathan saw the house had been transformed. Clothes, magazines, newspapers, and beer bottles that once littered the floors and furniture are all gone. The wooden furniture was no longer covered in layers of dust and the recent polish revealed the vibrant wood grains.

"Michael! You have been a busy boy."

Hearing running water, he moved down the hallway and stepped in a puddle. It was coming from the bathroom and he quickened his step to turn off the tap. He pushed the door open and he saw the tub overflowing. Nathan's lifeguard training in his youth caused him to pause and observe. Michael found submerged underwater with a silver object grasped within his hands had halted Nathan's impulse to pull him out.

A black cord attached to the silver object traced to an electrical outlet. "It's a fucking toaster," he muttered.

Uncertain if the fuse supplying alternating current was intact or blown, Nathan rushed to the basement to shut off the main switch. Returning to the bathroom, he lifted Michael's head above the water.

There was no need to check his pulse because his skin was blue, but he did it anyway. He called the police after his attempt to revive Michael had failed. His second call was to Thomas.

The medical examiner pronounced Michael dead at the scene from suicide by electrocution. He recommended a medicolegal autopsy to rule out foul play. The body was carried off in a stretcher draped in a white sheet.

When Thomas arrived, he leaned his motorcycle on its side stand. While removing his helmet he looked on at the residents gathered near Michael's home. Two police officers marshalled the departing ambulance safely through the small crowd. He scoured the area to find Nathan speaking to a police officer.

"You'll need to come to the station to give a formal statement," the officer said.

"Yes sir," Nathan said.

As Michael's dead body was transported away, the crowd dispersed.

Thomas placed his hand on Nathan's shoulder. "How are you holding up?"

Nathan turned, put his hands in his pant pockets, and leaned against his car. He looked away as his eyes welled up with tears. Thomas pulled him into his arms. Nathan resisted at first, and then accepted the comfort from an old family friend.

"I don't get it," Nathan said, wiping the tears away from his cheeks.

"It's hard to tell what goes on in a person's head," Thomas replied.

"What was he thinking?"

"That's hard to say. My only concern now is with you."

"I can't get the image out of my head. Michael's limp body coloured blue." Nathan lit a cigarette.

"Why don't we spend the day at my place?" Thomas said. "We can talk about it - or not. What do you think?"

"If you're thinking this will scar me for life, don't worry yourself. I will be okay." Nathan took a drag from his cigarette. "I'm disappointed in Michael though."

"Alright, but should you change your mind, you know where to find me." He noticed the young man staring off into space. "Are you sure you're okay?"

"Yes, yes, I'm just thinking. I don't believe he killed himself because he had no other choice."

"Why's that?"

"It's the shift log pages."

"I presume you mean the missing log pages."

"Yeah, I found them torn up in Michael's home. I wonder if he was protecting something larger than himself."

"I'm sorry, son, but I'm not following you."

"Michael accepted blame for his decisions, be it good or bad. He was always accountable for his actions. He never had problem falling on the sword for the good of the crew. When the other shift duty managers accused him of possible impropriety, he would go into a tirade. He was a proud man."

"Nathan, you have me at a loss. What does his pride and the shift log have in common?"

"I suspect the shift logs will confirm he had performed undocumented aircraft maintenance. Knowing him as well as I do, I believe he was doing it on behalf of someone else. Protecting what he felt was for the greater good. Whatever part he played on 641, professing his good intentions would be futile."

"I'm not sure about that," Thomas said. "Michael was definitely a complicated individual involved in a number of unexplained issues. It's best not to overreach and make this more than it really is. I suspect suicide is merely another complication in his life we will never understand…"

"Wait a minute." Nathan interrupted. He pulled an envelope out of his back pocket and held it out for Thomas.

Thomas stared at the sealed envelope bearing his name. "Where did you get this?"

"It was wedged into the bathroom's mirror frame," Nathan replied. "I found it while I was waiting for the police to arrive."

"The police don't know?"

"Of course not, it is addressed to you. Michael left a suicide note on the kitchen table, so I'm hoping this envelope may shed some light on the crash."

Thomas grimaced. "You're overreaching again. A flock of geese took 641 down. Remember what Olivia Cooper said?"

"Open it," Nathan said. "Let's find out if I'm overreaching or not."

Thomas took the envelope and ripped it open. He was just as anxious as Nathan. He couldn't give in to conjecture, even though with each passing day, the circumstantial evidence continued to grow and cast doubt on the flock of geese theory.

"What is it?" Nathan asked.

"A key," Thomas said.

"A toolbox key?"

"It looks that way." He looked at Nathan. "Don't say anything about this."

"I don't intend to."

"I mean everything, including your conspiracy theory on the crash. Just stick to what you know, the facts and nothing else."

"I only shared it with you and Leonard."

"Good. Keep it that way. Call me if you need to talk."

# CHAPTER 16

**OLIVIA SAT AT** her desk, leaning back in the high leather chair with her feet up. Preparing for the board meeting, she reviewed the business proposal to expand the airline. She rehearsed the strategy to convey the revenue potential through operations extending to the mid-west. It would require the acquisition of four more aircraft, on top of a fifth to replace 641. She was aware of the board's reluctance to do so in the past because expansion meant taking on more debt in a volatile market.

Her father had faced fierce opposition when he pitched the same proposal nearly four years ago. He underestimated the board's pushback, stemming from Virginia Airlines high load factor and low revenue yields. They resisted the need to return to the days when they had over-leveraged the company to stay in contention with their competitors. Board members included first time airline investors, unaccustomed to the unpredictable revenue flow with high fixed operating costs. The first few years of operation was nail biting. No one wished to repeat that, which might have explained why Alexander did not press as hard as he would have liked.

Olivia knew that this time around, the company was in a better position. It had enjoyed operating in the black and basking in lower debt to equity ratio in recent years, and she felt there was no reason not to enter its next expansion phase. Biting her lower lip, she wondered if the board would cower behind the veil of 641's uncertainty.

If a board member suggested a possible design flaw, she had information to quash the concern. The board was always mindful of the exorbitant costs of the aircraft redesign and Alexander's insistence to do so. She would repeat the FAA's announcement of the cause of the crash to help push her mandate through.

Alexander came into the office minutes before the commencement of the board meeting. He hoped he had more time with his daughter to discuss their approach in detail. They always discussed strategy at a high-level, but this time they had only dealt with the noteworthy bullet points the board needed to know.

Alexander was flushed. "We'll need to open the meeting with 641's review, the maintenance performed the night before, its reliable history, the FAA's observations, engineering design yielded low maintenance and operating costs and..."

"Dad!" Olivia said, raising her voice. "I have it. Relax, everything will be fine. Every aspect we discussed is covered to the hilt and we considered every conceivable question that may come up."

Alexander placed his hands on his hips and sighed. "Okay. I'm sure you have everything well in hand."

Olivia slid her feet off the desk and into her shoes, "If this proposal does not go through, we have bigger problems."

"So it didn't go well when you proposed the plan to Cecil?" Alexander asked.

"It turned out as I thought it would. He was not receptive, but he will think twice before voting against the proposal," Olivia said, putting on her jacket. "How do I look?"

"You look good," he said proudly. "All right then, if Cecil is against it, that could only mean the board will follow."

"He may surprise you today," she said. "I've planted a what-if scenario in his head."

"You didn't?"

"I did. We'll know shortly if it worked to persuade him." She buttoned up her jacket. "I have never understood what you see in him. He is petty, greedy, and self-absorbed."

"Cecil has always been a narcissist, especially when he earned his wings. He was resentful of those who surpassed his rank or flying skills," Alexander said.

"Then why do you keep him close?" Olivia asked.

"He serves a purpose," Alexander said, looking at his watch. "We should get going."

"Is our backup in play?" Olivia asked before stepping through her office door.

"Troy is more than happy to oblige. Should it come to it, I will signal him to offer you his shares."

"As the interim president and CEO, I have the right of first refusal. I hope it doesn't come to that, it's a shit load of money."

"Damn right it is," Alexander said. "But the board will force our hand should they insist on keeping the status quo. Troy's shares will tip the scale in our favour."

"Those shares we help us circumvent the board's rule that no one can own fifty-one percent of the company."

"But together, we will always have majority control," Alexander said, as they walked down the hallway. "We may need to live like paupers for a spell to get back on our feet. It will all be worth it to get this company back on the right path."

"Let's not get ahead of ourselves," she whispered. "Let's hope they come around so we don't need to take drastic measures."

At the end of the hallway, they saw the members mingling through the open double boardroom doors.

"Everyone, please take your seats. We have a lot to cover today," Olivia said. She took her place at the head of the table with her back to the window.

"Alexander," Cecil said, "I was not aware you were going to be here. I would have worn a tie."

Some members were amused. Alexander simply smiled. It was no surprise Cecil would seek attention among the captive audience of his fellow investors. His badge of honour was the influence he had on the board as a presumptive aviation expert.

"How are you doing, Cecil?" Alexander said with his hand extended.

"I'm doing fine." Cecil grinned. "But look at you. I am pleased to see you are up and around. How's the ticker?"

"It's not the ticker," Alexander shot back, still grinning, seeing through Cecil's tactics to undermine him. "It's the plumbing. The condition was caught early and with a good diet my body is working splendidly."

"Excellent news," Cecil said. "We're all glad you can join us again."

Beatrice entered with a stack of leather folders containing the agenda and reference materials. She laid a folder in front of each board member, starting with Anthony Peters. He was an intellectual and a realist that saw an opportunity after the Second World War when he repatriated from England back home to Virginia. A Harvard graduate, with the aid of his father he started the Savings and Loans in Leesburg, Virginia, in 1946 at twenty-eight years old. Thirty years later, he owned several successful Savings and Loan Banking branches in Virginia and surrounding states.

Beatrice placed a folder by Cecil Longhorn and another beside Dean Mathews, a Real Estate Developer, originally from Brooklyn,

New York. He joined his uncle's bridge building company in 1951, Canal Bridge Developers. Established in Ohio then headquartered in Arlington, Virginia, in 1955. Following the death of his uncle, Ned Waters, in 1958 the company diversified its operation in real estate development. In 1965, Dean saw merit to diversify his holdings. He invested in a new airline introduced to him by Cecil, his investment advisor.

Circling around the head of the table, Beatrice laid the folder beside Betty Windsfield, married to an oil tycoon Bran Windsfield. Bran responded to Alexandra Cooper's investment solicitation letter. Mindful of Betty's fascination in aviation, it was only fitting he award the airline shares to his wife as a wedding anniversary. Giving his adoring wife, an experienced pilot in her own right, the opportunity to keep her feet planted on the ground rather than fly her reconditioned Lockheed Electra 10E airplane throughout the Americas, Africa and Europe. The same airplane Amelia Earhart had flown in her 1937 failed attempt to circumnavigate around the world.

"Mister Cooper," Beatrice said passing him the folder. She then turned to Troy Tyler, "And here's your copy."

"Thank you Beatrice," Troy said. He is the only African-American on the board, a veteran airman of the Korean War, and a prospering realtor in Northern Virginia. Alexander holds him in high regard for his continued friendship, patronage and the first person to invest in the airline. His shareholder stake in the company is small compared to the other board members. Troy's mere two percent is now worth 6 million dollars and represents half of his net worth.

Beatrice placed a tray holding the coffee and teapot in the center of the table with the sugar, cream, spoons, and cups. Another tray was positioned beside the first with an assortment of pastries and napkins.

"Gentlemen and ladies, paper and a pen are provided in your folder should you wish to take notes." She focused on Olivia. "Will there be anything else, Miss Cooper?"

"No, I believe you have taken care of everything. Thank you, Beatrice, that will be all." When she left, Olivia addressed the board. "Opening to the first page, you'll notice the agenda has Flight 1001, aircraft 641, listed for our discussion. You'll also find an envelope in the folder containing photos of the crash scene."

The members opened their files. The word 'Confidential' was stamped in red on every item.

"There is a sheet highlighting the casualty stats. As of last night, the number of fatalities is increased by one. The passing of Nellie Stewart brings the death toll to nineteen. She was seventy-five years old and succumbed to her injuries. She had burns to eighty percent of her body and the attending physician was amazed she lasted as long as she did."

"She was one tough cookie," Betty said.

"Have we been contacted by the lawyers acting on behalf of the families?" Troy asked.

"Not yet," Olivia said, "But I'm sure all the families will take part in a lawsuit. It's too soon to tell what legal liability they will be seeking. The cause of the crash is currently considered an act of nature, but our legal team suspects they will claim pilot error."

"That's a sound argument," Dean said. "No doubt they will argue the flight crew were not attentive and did not take satisfactory measures to avoid the collision with the flock of geese."

"That's bullshit," Betty said. "Those of us that pilot airplanes know you can't plow through the sky and swerve around birds flying across your path. Anyway, the near misses I've had with birds always occurred near the ground, either during take-off or landing. It's like a deer jumping in front of a moving vehicle; the best you can do is chug right on through."

"I can only imagine," Troy began, "the Charlottesville Airport management will be cited in the lawsuit as well."

"What for?" Betty asked, shifting in her seat to face him.

"I would guess they will claim the lack of due diligence," Troy replied. "Betty, you would agree there is a responsibility to ensure a safe environment. There is no way to ensure absolute guaranteed prevention against wildlife hazards, however, you can be held liable for making no effort toward minimizing risk."

"Well, I suppose," she said.

"We need to vote on the need to replace our flagship," Olivia said.

"That's an easy yes," Alexander said. "Our revenue yields are at an all-time high. We can't afford to lose our market share to our competitors."

"Here here," Betty agreed.

Troy, Dean, Anthony, and Sean waited on Cecil's reply. "Yes, of course," he said.

The rest of the board agreed and voted unanimously. Alexander felt the victory came too easily, but it was a welcoming resolution nonetheless - and best left unquestioned.

"You'll notice the rest of the enclosed material concerns the fleet expansion by another four airplanes. This will serve as our next phase of growth toward the Midwest, supported through our Chicago, New York, Washington, and Atlanta stations. We have done well meeting the needs of the rural and remote areas along the eastern region. Our marketing analysis is positive to continue our footprint in the west with a mixture of passenger and airfreight services."

"Four more aircraft plus 641's replacement makes five," Sean said, shaking his head. "Didn't we discuss this three or four years ago? I don't mind saying I am enjoying the dividends of late and dislike the thought of reverting back to operating in the red." He turned to Cecil for support.

"Hold on a second. I don't believe we will be operating in the red if the marketing analysis is accurate," Olivia said. "It is true the start-up costs will bite into our profits but I suspect the Midwest can benefit from our services significantly. We will not have the market saturation we experienced on the east coast."

"True," Dean said. "But in the east, can we safely say twenty percent of the population travel by air. Can we expect the same in the Midwest? The average family income is much less there and I'm not sure we can achieve the break-even load factor. However, I suspect there will be an appetite by the commercial sector for airfreight services of perishable foods and premium express shipments."

Olivia smiled briefly. "Dean, you raised a good point but as I mentioned..."

Alexander interrupted. "The aircraft will be configured to a fifty-fifty combo." He turned to Olivia. "Sorry for jumping in. Do you mind?"

"No, please continue, Dad."

"Market analysis indicates business travel to the Midwest is cumbersome. There are a limited number of direct flights and we can improve on them through our four busiest hubs."

"Cecil, you have been quiet," Betty said. "If I'm not mistaken, you spoke out against this plan years ago and freak and frat seated next to you followed suit."

"I believe you voted against it as well," Cecil said.

"Hold on," Betty said, holding out her hand. "Before you grace us with your opinion, I want you to know this time around I'm all in. It is time we branch out, offer the lowest fares legally allowed, and fortify a larger and stronger hold of the market share. The major airlines won't dare challenge us."

"I don't dispute our little airline has done well," Cecil replied. "We had one hell of a bumpy start and the recovery was painfully slow, but I am cautiously optimistic."

"Spit it out, Cecil," Betty said. "We can't wait all day. It's a simple yes or no vote and you bloody well know it is time."

Alexander and Troy exchanged a glance.

"Yes," Cecil said.

"Yes to what?"

"Yes, yes. Yes!" Cecil said. "It's time, but I won't agree to the acquisition of five aircraft. We'll need to move slowly."

Alexander shook his head, signalling to Troy to hold off on the announcement for the time being. With Cecil consenting to the expansion, there was no reason to announce Troy's stock sell to Olivia.

"Troy, what did you wish to say," Dean said, aware Cecil had interrupted him seconds earlier.

"It can wait," Troy replied.

"Okay. I vote yes to the growth plan," Dean said, "and second Cecil's concern to review the number of airplanes we need to buy."

Olivia was pleased with the events unfolding in her favour, in her father's favour, better yet – it would benefit Virginia Airlines. What's more, Betty's barked orders, commanding the fellow members to fall in line and make the rightful decision, touched her funny bone. Resisting the temptation to show her exuberance, she fidgeted in her seat and held her breath.

"Now we're talking," Betty said, banging a fist on the table. "Alexander, we know you're voting yes." She turned to Sean, Anthony, and Dean, "Well boys, the ball is in your court. Show us what your gonads are made of."

Olivia could no longer resist and laughed aloud.

"What has gotten into you, dear?" Betty said.

Olivia covered her mouth and pressed her lips together to collect her composure.

"Was gonads a little too much?" Betty said, smiling.

Olivia exploded into another round of uncontrollable laughter. No longer resisting, she let it all out. The laughter was infectious, causing the members to join in - except for Cecil.

"Yes, of course," Anthony said, chuckling.

"No pain, no gain. I'm in too," said Sean.

"I hate to burst everyone's bubble," Troy said.

Alexander grimaced. What was his ally up to?

"Expansion towards the west is a good thing but I too have apprehensions on the number of aircraft acquisitions," Troy said. Peering over his steel-rimmed glasses at Alexander, he asked, "Are we sure the market analysis is accurate? I need to be persuaded."

"Is your coffee spiked?" Betty asked.

"Cut him a break, Betty," Anthony said. "Troy's not against the growth. He is simply asking if it would be best to ease into it. Rather than buying five aircraft, why not four, three, or even two?"

"I can understand the concern," Olivia said. "There are four airplanes available right now below market prices. All the information is in front of you. I do not think there will be another chance like this. The timing is good, the business plan is sound, and the opportunity to strike is now."

"Well then," Troy said, "I need to hear from your father directly." Facing Alexander he asked, "Can you assure me we need to buy four more aircraft?"

Alexander read between the lines. Troy's wanted to know that their agreement was still in play. Obviously, Olivia buying Troy out was no longer on the table since the board voted for the growth, and yet Troy needed confirmation the alternate agreement would be honoured.

"Absolutely," Alexander said.

Troy smiled, knowing he would receive a four million dollar interest free loan. "That's good for me. I'm in too."

"Finally," Betty said.

"We're not yet done," Cecil said. "I agree with Troy. Let's have a quick vote on the number of aircraft. Based on the four aircraft readily available for a good price, I say we only purchase the four."

"I hate to do this, but I too say four is all we need," Betty said.

The board unanimously agree except for Olivia, who was yet to vote. Everyone looked on patiently, waiting for her response.

"Honey," Betty said, "What do you have to say? We can do a lot with four extra aircraft."

"I guess we can increase our present fleet's utilization to make up for 641's absence," Olivia said.

"Then we're done for the day," Alexander said.

"I suppose we are," Olivia agreed. "We will proceed with the purchase of four airplanes and we're a go for the western expansion."

# CHAPTER 17

**ON THE MORNING** of August 22, Emma finished her first day back at work following 641's crash. Tasked with the duties and responsibilities as the temporary shift duty manager, she was standing in for Thomas while he was on vacation. She had been looking forward to the challenge of leading the crews and overcoming the obstacles to meet her airline's expectations. She would do all that she can to earn Thomas's faith in her.

Her first day at the helm was like herding cats or pushing rope up a hill. She could only attribute it to the accident still fresh in everyone's mind. The staff were sombre throughout the evening and understandably so. Until now, all the aircraft technicians had conducted themselves professionally.

No mention of 641 had come up during the coffee breaks or lunch. No one uttered Michael Hall's name. He maintained 641 and saying his name would steer their discussion into unwelcomed territory. Everyone wanted to leave well enough alone and only concentrate on the work.

Emma undressed in the men's locker room. Being the only wrench turning female in a male dominated work force, there was no women's locker room at Virginia Airlines. It was an issue she was told would be remedied when hired six years ago. The truth was that no one thought a woman could hold their own as an aircraft technician. The presumption that Emma's stay at Virginia Airlines' maintenance department would be short lived had proven everyone wrong except for Thomas.

He had seen Emma's positive attitude, drive, and determination during the interview process. Her mechanical aptitude gained while working on large farming equipment and tractors at her uncle's Massey Ferguson dealership. She then changed her career field to nursing and applied her skills in Vietnam while in the Army Corp. He knew she had all the requirements needed to succeed. Ignoring the advice of human resources and fellow co-workers, Thomas hired her to his crew.

She put her oil soaked clothes into a brown paper bag and entered into the shower area, large enough to accommodate six people. Tilting her head back, the water splashed on to her hair, face, and rushed down over her oil-covered body.

Louis, an experienced technician, had neglected to reinstall the engine's servicing cap, which caused oil to spew during engine rotation. Emma was standing nearby with the fire extinguisher, exercising standard operating procedures. As the engine started, the oil gushed out and covered her.

She wrapped herself in a towel and took a short walk to her locker. Laying the towel on the bench, she pulled up her stretchy nylon low rise briefs. Louis entered and found her half naked.

He marvelled at the tattoo spanning across her shoulder blades. Two prehistoric looking fish arched and faced away from each other. They were connected by a sword that pierced through the belly of the one on the left and in the backside of the other to form the letter H. It was an unusual characterization of the zodiac sign for Pisces.

Emma picked up her bra hanging in her locker when she noticed Louis gawking at her. Facing him with her breasts exposed, she placed her hands on her waist and tilted her head slightly to one side. "Have you not sucked on your mother's tits?" she asked.

"Yeah, I suppose," Louis said.

"Based on your stare, I can only presume you have forgotten how tits looked like. Just as forgetting the importance to reinstall the servicing cap after topping up the engine oil." After holding a stern look a moment longer in sentence, she turned her back to him to put on her bra. "Get out of here. Can't you see I'm getting dressed?"

He reached for the doorknob and paused. "I'm sorry for what happened. I'll try to put 641 out of my head."

Emma sighed, knowing the crash was the reason everyone had dragged their feet last night. She noticed a bunch of keys on the wooden bench belonging to Louis.

"I promise to be more alert and focused when I come back in tonight," he said.

"You better be," Emma said. "Louis!" Turning to face her, he caught his car keys in the air. "By the way, there have been a number of tasks rescheduled due to our lack of productivity. Get 641 out of your head. It is ancient history."

He nodded.

"You and the team will be doing penance on your days off to make up for the poor performance," she said.

\* \* \*

Slide over," Louis said.

"What has gotten into you?" Nathan asked.

"You don't want to know." He looked over the menu.

"What took you so long?" Diego asked. "I thought you were right behind us."

"I couldn't find my car keys."

Diego leaned to one side to look out the window of Jimmy's Diner. "Looks like you found them after all."

"Has everybody ordered?" Louis said, changing the subject.

"Nah, we waited for you," Diego said. "Get your face out of the menu." He took the menu from Louis. "You're not fooling anyone. You have ordered the same breakfast as long as I can remember."

Louis slouched in the bench seat. "It doesn't matter. I'm not hungry anyway."

"Get over it," Diego said. "We all screw up one time or another. Just don't make it a practice."

"Did you see Emma covered all over in oil?" Zac laughed. "When she learned why it happened, I thought she was going to kick your ass."

"What happened?" Nathan said, joining in on the laughter.

"It's nothing," Diego said. "I'm starving." Looking around for Jenny, a long time waitress, he noticed her coming out of the kitchen with a pot of coffee.

"Everyone having coffee?" she asked with a smile.

"You bet," Diego said. "I'll have orange juice too."

"I already have it written down," Jenny said, flashing the order pad at him.

Diego smiled. "We'll all have the usual."

"That was easy," Jenny said. "I'll be right back with the orange juice."

"Have you guys heard Nicolas is back in town?" Leonard said.

"Nicolas Diaz?" Diego questioned.

"Who's he?" Nathan asked.

"One of Virginia Airlines best aircraft mechanics," Leonard said. "He left us to oversee ASE's operations in Miami."

"To set the record straight," Diego said. "He didn't leave, Thomas fired him. Supposedly, he had been smuggling drugs on our flights."

"That's just a rumour," Louis said. "If that were true, Thomas would have notified the police. Anyway, we all know Thomas, Nicolas and that pilot killed on 641..."

"Philip," Leonard interrupted.

"That's right, Philip," Louis continued. "They all served together in Korea. They're all close friends."

"Whatever," Diego said. "I know what I know. Just do yourselves a favour and stay away from him. Nicolas and his circle of new friends are bad news."

"He's in town because of Michael," Leonard said.

"Who's going to Michael's wake tonight?" Nathan asked.

"We're working tonight," Louis said, scowling.

"You really need to chill. Nathan's just asking, that's all," Leonard said.

"Okay, look. It's best you hear it from me rather than from Emma tonight," Louis said.

"Don't bother, I already know," Diego said.

"There's no way you could have known. I just received word before I had left the hangar. She must have discussed it with you previously."

"She didn't say a word," Diego said. "I can tell by the expression on your face."

"Let us in on the secret," Nathan said.

"Seeing how our compadre is behaving, all mournful and all, it looks like we'll be doing penance," Diego said.

"Penance, what's that?" Zac blurted, folding his arms on the table.

"Really? What are they teaching you kids in school nowadays?" Diego scoffed.

"I know the meaning of penance. I meant how does it affect us and what does it involve?"

Jenny returned to the table with the food. She looked at Zac and Leonard. "I'll be right back with your dishes."

"Emma is applying the old motivational tool Thomas introduced long ago," Diego said. "We will be working through our days off."

"Is that it? I don't mind," Nathan said. "I can use the extra money."

"Oh no, that's not how it works," Louis said. "It wouldn't be penance if you're rewarded. Isn't that right, Diego?"

"There's no pay. We will work hard, but it will be for a good cause," Diego conveyed, biting into a bacon strip. "We'll be helping veterans. Eat up boys, you'll need your strength."

\* \* \*

"Right this way, sir," said the maitre d', leading Cecil Longhorn to his table at the Gray Fox Country Golf Club.

"Cecil," said Aiden, raising his martini glass to toast his partner's arrival. "You have great taste in restaurants."

Cecil smiled and sat down. "I have been a club member for a long time," he said, laying a napkin over his lap. "I have been coming here nearly twenty years after moving back to Virginia. I first lived in a farmhouse not too far down the road," he pointed toward the window. "I babysat the house and managed the 750 acres farmed by neighbouring residents. Best two years of my life."

Aiden waved to the waiter and pointed to his glass for another. "Would you like one too?" Cecil nodded and Aiden gestured for a second. He drank what was left in his glass. "I never took you for a farmer. You have all the wants and mannerisms of an aristocrat, but playing in dirt, I can't picture it."

"You are correct." Cecil chuckled. He placed an elbow on the armrest. "I must confess, I didn't like the physical act of farming. My intrigue was in the ability to create revenue through a well-managed and cultivated soil."

"I grew up on a farm," Aiden said. "And detested every minute of it. I knew it was time to leave when I grew accustomed to the smell of manure." He snickered. "So you toiled in manure as well."

"Yes, there's no escaping it," Cecil said. "The land depended on its nutrients." He held his tongue when the waiter approached to place the drinks on the table.

The waiter noticed the menus remained untouched, lying in the same place he had left them on the edge of the table. "Are you ready to place you order or do you need more time?"

"We will call you when we're ready," Aiden said.

"Would you like to hear today's lunch specials?" The waiter asked. Without waiting for a response, he started into his rehearsed line up of dishes the chef has planned for the day.

Cecil held up his hand. "That won't be necessary." The waiter ignored the gesture and continued rambling. "I said, that will not be necessary!"

The waiter stopped in midsentence, "Yes sir, my apologies."

"Very well," Cecil said with a glare sharp as a dagger. It caught the waiter's attention like a car wreck. "Now go!" The waiter cowered away. The onlookers returned to their food after realizing there was no commotion, just Cecil's known habit of toying with the help.

"What a strange individual," Aiden noted.

"He's young, with low self-esteem," Cecil said, reaching for his martini. "He is just like your son, but at least this individual will eventually improve." Removing the olives from the glass, he said, "Your son after all will never have the intelligence beyond that of a nine-year-old child." He consumed the olives.

Aiden felt a chill run down his spine. An ill word spoken against his son did not sit well with him. As the nurturer, mentor, and most of all a protector, he shielded his son from the harsh and ignorant misconceptions people had towards his condition. "And your point is?"

"You know all too well," Cecil said. "To no fault of his own, Peter's mental capacity will cast a shadow on the success we have worked so hard to achieve."

"That's absurd," Aiden said, glaring at his partner. "What I said last time holds true today. I will not send my boy away."

Cecil scowled. "You don't have much time to do what is best. You're not just doing this for your well-being; it is for Peter's benefit as well." He took a drink and without lowering his glass, gulped another mouth full of martini. "You need to do what is right to alleviate any glimmer of impropriety."

Aiden snapped his fingers and waved to the waiter for another round. The waiter was taking an order at another table and had nodded his acknowledgement. "Frankly, you are overestimating our exposure," Aiden said. "It's a pity you weren't as diligent as you thought when dealing with our predicament a year ago. Perhaps ignoring my suggestion to self-disclose has pushed you to continue the lie." Cecil smirked while Aiden continued. "I'm sure you are aware that should the authorities know the truth, you alone will be incarcerated."

"I'm not here to hold your hand," Cecil replied. "But I will if I need to, for as long as it takes to make you see the light."

The waiter arrived with the drinks. "Are you ready to order now?" Cecil simply stared back at him. "Okay, I'll give you two more time to decide." He scurried away with empty glasses.

"I don't need hand holding," Aiden snapped. "I can manage my son and deal with the situation you have created. It is best we carry on as we always have. There's no need to overreact." He raised his glass. "A toast to business as usual. Cooler heads will prevail, and I assure you we will be better for it."

Cecil rapped his knuckles against the table's hard oak surface. It wiped away Aiden's smirk. "Our financier in New York will not want to be exposed nor have his interests jeopardized. If you do not send your son away, they will use more permanent methods. Do you understand me?"

Aiden slowly nodded.

"We need to remove all perceived risk and show that we have matters well in hand," Cecil added.

"Peter did not ask to be born with Down Syndrome. Most of all, no one would consider his condition has cast a shadow over the work he did at Aircraft Systems and Electronics. He is an exemplary employee who has never complained, argued, or tired. With an I.Q. of less than seventy, who figured out an error in the engineering drawings when no one else could?" His eyes welled up. "The elite intellectuals who are prejudiced to my son's condition are the same people that ignored his repeated warnings. He was proven right after all. Wasn't he?"

"If I'm not mistaken," Cecil said softly. "His warnings fell on your deaf ears as well. You of all people are without prejudice, and yet Peter failed to persuade his own father. What does that make you?" He gently twirled his glass. "Peter's inability to convey the issue rationally caused all of us to discount him. We're only guilty of not taking him seriously. It had nothing to do with his condition."

"We cannot excuse our absentmindedness," Aiden said, rising from the table. "But one thing is for certain: He will not pay for our mistake. I will not send him away."

"I see. You have made your point. Remember this, we are vulnerable should the FAA or the NTSB question Peter. I just want you to know that this is not my cross to bear. Whatever happens, it is all on you."

# CHAPTER 18

**AUGUST 26 WAS** the day of reckoning for the crews on Emma's shift rotation. It was the day for paying penance for their lackluster performance. Their performance yielded the lowest productivity she could remember. Returning to work shortly after losing one of their airplanes, crew, and some of the passengers weighed heavily on the minds and hearts of the aircraft technicians.

The workweek started on the wrong foot. Emma conceded that after much deliberation and guidance, the team had picked themselves up by their bootstraps. Her persistence had succeeded in turning around the sombre mood. "Stop dwelling on the past. We can't undo what has been done," she had said. "Look forward and do your best. The memory of those who passed is better served by carrying on. To do otherwise would be disrespectful." The team's productivity had returned to some normalcy on the fourth and final day of their workweek rotation.

Emma packed her pickup truck with tools borrowed from Thomas's barn and drove down the road to Debbie Bailey's house on Middle Mountain. Her team would be helping Debbie's father, a disabled Vietnam vet. It was a practice started by Thomas to round up volunteers to help veterans. Two or three times a year, he would find fault with his staff and commandeer their time off.

No one minded Thomas's antics when seeking their help. Deployed to a veteran's home, they would do meager tasks like mending fences, painting, roof repairs, to elaborate renovations such as building wheelchair ramps. The local merchants donated the materials for the free advertisement it brought them.

Emma turned into the dirt driveway, pleased to see her team had arrived ahead of time. However, she thought it odd they were all crouched behind their vehicles. Then she noticed Leonard, who has no military experience, lying on the ground and cowering. "What the fuck is going on here?" she mumbled.

Three gunshots rang out, aimed at Leonard's 1966 Pontiac GTO side mirror. A fourth shot separated the mirror from the car and two more finished the job. Todd Bailey sat in his wheel chair perched on his porch with rifle in hand. He showed off his shooting ability while poor Leonard continued to hug the ground, quivering.

"Get off my property," Todd said.

Emma slammed the gear into neutral fifty feet from the house, applied the emergency brake, and jumped out of her pickup truck. Diego inched around his 1965 Chevrolet Impala holding a Colt M1911 handgun. Keeping his head down, he waited for Todd to reload before making his move to disarm the wheel-chaired heretic. She made eye contact and signalled him to stand down. There was no need for anyone to get hurt, especially when it involved an isolated vet who meant no harm.

"What's wrong with you people?" Todd yelled. "Get off my property!" He set his sights on Emma and shot a round eighteen inches to her right. It did not faze her. She didn't miss a step as she continued toward the porch.

"Boys," Todd yelled, "This pretty lady can teach you a lesson or two." He took aim. "She has bigger balls than you will ever have." He squeezed the trigger and fired the last cartridge, causing the rifle to eject the clip. The bullet hit a large rock protruding slightly above the ground between her feet. It ricocheted and grazed her left calf. She stopped for a moment to inspect the wound and quicken her pace up the porch steps. Her boys watched as she grabbed the unloaded rifle, spun it around in one smooth transitional motion, and rapped the butt end against Todd's forehead.

His head jerked back from the impact. "Are you fucking crazy?"

"You're damn right I am," Emma yelled back. She rested her hands on the wheelchair's armrest. "We are here to help a comrade in arms, you fat fuck." Then pushed the chair away, "If you're going to shoot, shoot to kill or fuck off." Pain rushed up her leg and she leaned against the post supporting the porch roof. "Be useful and get me something to bandage up my leg."

Diego holstered his gun and rushed to Emma's side. Louis, Nathan, Zac, and the rest of the team followed suit.

Leonard joined the group a little shaken up and kept his distance, watching those he had worked with sprung into action around Emma. This morning's event unveiled itself in a split-second. It lasted minutes and yet felt like hours. There was too much to absorb, his senses and thought progresses overwhelmed him. He needed time to digest what had just occurred. It was the first time he had experienced a gun pointed at him. He saw Diego tend to the injured leg while the others positioned themselves in a circle to form a protective perimeter. This what it must have felt like in combat, he thought.

"Eh Leonard, do you need a change of underwear?" Zac said, unable to refrain himself, "I've never seen anyone hug the ground like that. And, I fought in 'Nam for Christ's sake."

The group joined in on the laughter. Brian Kelley, a lead mechanic with light brown hair, blue eyes, and a muscular build, stepped away from Emma and pointed to the GTO. "He did a number on your car, boy." His dry humour gave rise to more laughter.

"Enough," Emma said.

Todd returned with antiseptic, antibiotic ointment and bandages he carried on his lap. He passed them to Diego. "Are you a doctor?"

"Me? Nah," Diego replied. "I was an Army medic." Focusing on the leg, his hand applied pressure on the flesh wound to stop the bleeding. "The wound needs to be cleaned up. Zac, go fetch a container of water."

Zac rushed into the house and returned with a pitcher of cold water.

Todd watched the group working as a unit, their movements coordinated with little to no verbal instruction. The four men attending to Emma all had a tattoo of a skull wearing a green beret. A banner below the skull read Vietnam 1966–68. Another two strangers stood nearby, and he noticed tattoos of an inverted triangle, black with a yellow border, and a stripe running diagonally from the top left to bottom right. The upper right quadrant of the inverted triangle had a silhouette of a horse's head. U.S. 1st Air Cavalry, he thought. The other three were just young enough to have escaped the draft.

Suddenly, an overpowering sense of belonging rushed through him. He could not recall the last time he had been in the company of his peers. The spectacle made him remember that above all, he could rely on his brothers in arms.

He sobbed softly, but Diego and the others paid no attention. Leonard walked away, dumbfounded at the whole situation. He went to his car to examine the damage.

Emma grimaced and bit her bottom lip as Diego poured water over the wound. She stared at Todd slowly regain his composure as he wiped his tears with his shirtsleeve. He stared off into the horizon as if nothing had occurred. She can see he was not doing well and broke the awkward silence to draw him into a discussion. "Looks as if you left a part of yourself in 'Nam."

Todd smirked. "My legs were tired of walking so I got rid of them. I got myself this chair instead."

Emma noticed his electric wheel chair had no battery and one of the tires was nearly flat. "That fancy chair can take you far if you took care of it," she said.

"You're one cold fish," Todd said. It wasn't meant to be derogatory; he preferred it over the sympathy most people held towards him.

"I wasn't always this way. I was in 'Nam too. The things I saw and did... I've had enough pity parties to last ten lifetimes. I cried myself to sleep many a night and then I grew up. Once I embraced the nightmare I was living, I could finally become an active participant."

Todd slouched in his chair and covered his mouth with his hand. The familiarity in her voice had brought him back to Vietnam, to the nurse handing him his leg. "This belongs to you," she had said. "Don't drop it."

"You're all bandaged up," Diego said. "You should be fine but it is best someone takes you to the hospital to check it out."

"I'll be fine," Emma replied. "It's just a scratch and you will not use this as an excuse to get out of work today."

Leonard stormed up to the porch. "You fucking ruined my car and you are going to pay for the repairs." He looked at the team and saw they were all scowling at him. He realized he would have better odds drawing blood from a stone. "Ah, forget about it. I've got insurance."

"Let's get to work," Emma said. "Leonard, take Nathan and Ed - you have lawn duty. The grass is three feet tall, no easy task. Brian, you and your crew have the house exterior."

"Paint duty," Brian said. "We're on it."

"Scrape off the loose paint first," Emma said. "I have brushes and rollers in my truck and eight gallons of paint. Let me know if you need more."

"And for me and Fred?" Diego asked.

"Fence duty," Emma replied. She pulled a piece of paper out of her bra and passed it to him. "Bill Sanders owns a lumber yard outside Waynesboro. He offered pine boards to our cause. Not sure it will be enough so we'll focus on the fencing along the road first."

"Got it," Diego said. He paused. "How are you holding up?"

"I'm good," Emma replied. "Get going."

Todd noticed the caduceus tattooed on her forearm. Everything was coming together and he had a gnawing feeling he knew Emma. Her hair was shorter and purposefully uncombed. Then there was the tone of her voice. It was almost identical to the one he recalled first hearing it in 'Nam. Without a doubt, he was certain the woman sitting on his porch was responsible for putting him in the wheelchair for the rest of his life. He pointed to Emma. "You're the fucking bitch."

Diego reached behind his back, pulled out his M1911, and pointed it to Todd. "What the fuck is your problem? Jesus fucking Christ!"

Todd grabbed the handgun and pressed the muzzle against his forehead. "Go ahead, tough guy, pull the fucking trigger."

Emma folded her arms. "Diego! Put your gun away. Put it back in your pants where it belongs."

Diego pulled his gun from Todd's grip, "This idiot called you a fucking bitch." Then pointed the muzzle at Emma. "I don't have a clue why you're grinning." Puzzled with Emma's demeanor, he rubbed the muzzle of his gun on his back while waiting for an explanation.

"Diego, put the gun away," Emma said. "And stop using it as a backscratcher, especially when it's loaded." She smiled. "That was my call name in 'Nam, you idiot. Actually, I had several - the Bitch or the fuckin' Bitch, and my all time favorite, the dragon lady. You boys may not be aware that I served in the Army Nurse Corps, stationed at the 7th Surgical Hospital in Cu Chi." She reached for Todd's hand. "I was the one who put the saw to this man's legs." She gave his hand a little squeeze and looked into his eyes. "We almost lost you. I'm glad to see you made it."

# CHAPTER 19

"**THERE YOU ARE,**" Shirley said. The conference room table was covered with books, folders, and engineering drawings.

David Steadman lifted his head from the table. He had been sleeping. "What day is this?"

"Have you been here all night?" Shirley said, closing the door behind her without taking her eyes off David.

"I guess today is Monday," he replied. He rubbed his eyes and rotated his head to work out the kink in his neck.

"You haven't been here all weekend?"

"I have been going over everything," he said. "I could really use a glass of water and some food."

Shirley brought him a glass of water and covered her nose when his body odour hit her like a brick wall. "Oh, you desperately need to get cleaned up." She stepped away. "Get your ass up and I'll drive you home."

"We don't have that much time," David replied. "I'll wash up and fill you in on the way."

She scanned the table and noticed David's notes in his leather-bound notebook. She pulled up a chair and began studying his hypothesis. David laid out the evidence like a forensic scientist. Page after page connected the information from the cockpit voice and flight data recorder, eyewitness accounts, interviews conducted with the passengers and Virginia Airlines technicians. Shirley could find no fault in his analysis.

The notes only lacked Eva Muller's testimony. As the only surviving flight crewmember, she would be the key. Should her testimony collaborate with David's hypothesis, it would show the failure was preventable. His analysis focused on the fire protection panel. Missed wired or otherwise, when activated by Eva, it shut down the only serviceable engine keeping the airplane in the air. Several pages listed questions for Eva and remaining maintenance personnel. It contained a set of specific questions based on the evidence collected from the on-board recorders.

David washed up as best as he could in the men's bathroom and admitted he was better for it. He felt refreshed after a gruelling weekend marathon in which he had stopped only to eat food delivered to him. He had catnap now and then when exhaustion got the best of him. He reappeared at the door, buttoning up a clean shirt he had tucked away in his desk. "We should be heading out," he said. "I have lined up several interviews with Virginia Airlines staff today." He put on his jacket. "First we will need to stop at Eva Muller's home. She is not well enough to travel so we'll go to her."

The drive from D.C. to Charlottesville was pleasant. There was traffic but it was moving well. Shirley held the map and navigated them to the apartment's driveway. They parked in the visitors' area and David grabbed his briefcase and the portable reel-to-reel recorder from the back seat. "I think it's best you take the lead and question Eva. She may prefer to open up to another woman."

"It shouldn't matter, but I get your point," Shirley said. "I would suggest we chat with her first to get a sense how she is doing."

They got in the elevator and took it to the sixth floor. "The more I think of it, you have to pose the questions. If you recall," he looked at Shirley, "it didn't go as well at the hospital."

"Eva was drugged up and in pain," she said. "We pressed her too hard so soon after the accident. I was glad the doctor kicked us out since she was in no condition to speak to us." She watched the numbers above the elevator door lit up one by one as they passed each floor. "As I said before, let's feel her out. You know the material like the back of your hand and it is only fitting you depose her directly."

\*\*\*

Brandon Smithers, one of four attorneys employed at Virginia Airlines, was seated in a chair next to the sofa where Eva laid. Her left leg, still in the cast, was propped up on two pillows and her left arm was supported in the sling.

Brandon was tasked with prepping the airline's employees for their interviews with the FAA and NTSB. He would ensure the information they provided was concise and straight to the point. He instilled confidence in the employees through Q&A dry run sessions, reciting the list of do's and don'ts, and ending with the same encouraging words: "Everything is going to be alright. Answer each question directly without imposing your thoughts and theories. Be yourself and you should do just fine."

Eva rehearsed her testimony several times, coping with the pain through preparation.

Eva's mother approached and sat on the edge of the coffee table. "I'm sorry, honey," Eleanor said, offering her daughter a dose of pain medication laced with codeine. "I should have given them to you more than an hour ago. I can tell you're in pain."

She took the pills and swallowed them. "That's alright, Mom. The pain just started a few minutes ago."

"You're a brave little girl," Eleanor said proudly.

A knock on the door got everyone's attention. "They're early," Brandon said. "I'll let them in." He looked at Eva while buttoning his suit jacket, concerned her pain and the medication would make her unfit to answer questions. "Are you sure you don't want me to delay this meeting?"

"If it were up to me, I wouldn't do this at all," Eva said. She sat upright and repositioned the pillows propping up her leg. "Let's not prolong the unavoidable. I'll survive."

"Okay, but if at any time you wish to stop, just let me know."

Brandon opened the door and after the introductions, the FAA inspectors provided their business cards.

"Eva, this is David Steadman," Brandon said. "He is the inspector in charge of the operation. With him is Shirley Attwood, who is assisting in the investigation into 641's incident."

Eleanor arrived from the kitchen with two chairs. "Please, have a seat."

"Thank you," David said as he placed the portable reel-to-reel on the coffee table.

"This is my mom, Eleanor," Eva said.

"Hello, I'm Shirley." They smiled and shook hands.

David unlocked the latches and pulled off the cover. "We will be recording our meeting. This is standard procedure." He held the plug in his left hand. Eleanor pointed to the electrical outlet by the sofa.

Eva felt unsettled by having her responses recorded. It would capture her answers as well as her stumbling reflections and tone. She turned to her attorney for advice.

"That will be fine," Brandon replied. "Do you know how long this interview will take?"

"Oh, I don't know," Shirley said. "Dispositions held last week with the maintenance staff averaged slightly more than an hour. So…"

"Let's play it by ear," David said. He unravelled the cord attached to the microphone and placed it on the coffee table. "We have a lot of material to cover and we can stop any time Miss Muller needs a break."

"Eva is in a lot of pain and is taking prescribed medication for it. I would strongly recommend we run through the questions in a timely fashion to ensure the session is conducted quickly," Brandon said. "It is important we minimize questions to those relevant to her experience on flight 1001."

*There it is,* David thought, *a shot across the FAA's bow.* He smiled. "Of course." However, he did not intend to comply unless he got what he needed. He connected the microphone's cord to the receptacle on the recorder. "Shall we begin?"

"Yes, please," Eva said softly.

The lawyer pressed David's buttons and he was determined more than ever to conduct the questioning himself. He held out his hand and Shirley got the hint. She passed him the folder containing the prepared questions. He pressed the play and record buttons simultaneously.

David began by stating the date and time. He then announced their location, purpose of the meeting, reason to depose Eva, identified each individual present, and stated their respective professions.

Eleanor arrived with a wooden coffee tray she had bought for Eva as a house warming gift. She placed it on the side table closest to Eva and Brandon and poured coffee into one of the cups. David reached to stop the recording but Shirley beat him to it.

"My apologies," Shirley said. "This is an active investigation. She cannot be here."

"It's my mistake," said David. "Mister Smithers, I need to remind you of the conditions and requirements for deposing Miss Muller at her home."

"Not to worry," Eleanor said. "I will get out of your hair."

"You're very kind," Shirley said, seeing no harm in allowing the hospitality. "I'll take my coffee black."

"Mister Brandon, you are dreadfully quiet for an attorney," Eleanor said. "How do you take your coffee?"

"Milk and sugar, ma'am."

In short order, the meeting recommenced. David referred to his notes in the green folder and Eva answered question upon question in perfect calmness. She stated her qualifications as a pilot and described her arrival to the aircraft, referencing the logbook, her walk around the airplane before departure, how she and Philip decided who would be pilot-in-command, and the first engine failure.

"The unexpected engine shutdown occurred following the gear-up selection," Eva said.

"How long after the gear-up selection did the engine shut down?" David asked.

Remembering Brandon's guidance to respond to questions with facts and absolutes, she said, "The right engine shut down shortly after gear-up selection."

"So it is safe to say the engine did not shut down simultaneously on selecting the gear up."

"That is an accurate statement," Eva said, waiting for the next question.

They looked at each other for another second before David continued. "Why did you see fit to pull the T-Handle?" He purposely didn't say which one, the left or the right, she had activated.

Eva was not certain what motivated this question. She had purposefully left it out in her written statement to Virginia Airlines and to the FAA. She had rehearsed the ordeal repeatedly in her mind until coming to the revelation with the help of her friend Odessa. She's almost positive that it was a mechanical failure and not her actions that caused the crash.

They know, she thought. Somehow, they know. They must have found something in the cockpit voice recorder or the data recorder. "The T-Handle was pulled for added measure."

"Added measure for what purpose?"

"Do not answer that," Brandon said. "I need a minute with Eva to review this new information."

"Is that necessary?" David asked. He understood Brandon's concern, but if the omission to her statement was done consciously, it would be a problem. "There is nothing irregular here, or is there?"

"I wrote my statement shortly after the accident while heavily medicated. It's not an excuse, but the information holds true besides this one oversight," Eva said.

Shirley stopped the recording. "It might be best we step outside and give these two a minute alone."

David wanted to press ahead but did not argue the point. "We'll be right outside," he said.

Brandon watched the FAA inspectors exit through the front door and turned to Eva. "How are you holding up?"

"I'm fine but when he brought up the T-Handle, it hit me like a tidal wave. I knew I had neglected to mention it in my statement."

"Is that all?" Brandon asked.

"What do you mean?"

"There is anything else you may have left out in the written statement? If there is, now is the time to let me know."

"There's nothing more," Eva said.

"One last thing I need answered. Did you cause the left engine to shut down when you pulled the T-Handle?"

"I pulled the right engine's T-Handle," Eva replied.

There was a moment of silence. "Did the left engine shut down after you had activated the right T-Handle?"

"There was so much activity," Eva replied. "Everything happened so fast. If you're asking if there is a chance the right T-Handle shut down the opposite engine, I would say yes." She leaned her head up against the sofa's backrest. "I've replayed that day over and over again in my mind." She sat up again to face him. "I am not positively sure, but there's nothing else to explain it."

"This is not good at all," Brandon said. "As morbid as this may sound, I'd rather it was the geese. If those wires were crossed, it could have huge implications for the whole company. The situation has become messy."

"I know." Eva nodded towards the door. "You should let them back in."

# CHAPTER 20

**THE TAPPING IN** Emma's head caused her to wince and take an abrupt deep breath. Awoken from a deep sleep, she shielded her eyes from the sunlight entering through the window facing her.

Disorientated, she sat up quickly, looked at the surroundings, and removed the light blanket wrapped around her. The pain in her leg reminded her the day's events and she realized she had fallen asleep at Todd Bailey's home. Putting her head back down on the couch cushion, she stared at the ceiling as the hammering of nails erupted again.

"Good, you're up," Todd said, rolling into the living room with a food tray on his lap. "I made you some lunch."

"What time is it?"

He placed the tray on the coffee table, careful not to spill the glass of ice tea filled to the rim. "It's nearly half past one," Todd replied. "You went out like a light while I put on a pot of coffee." He pointed to her leg. "How do you feel?"

"The bullet went in and out," Emma said. "No bones shattered and the artery is intact. It will heal in no time."

"I'm sorry," Todd said.

"Don't worry about it. Anyway, the rap on the head gave you one hell of a welt. That makes us even." Reaching for a sandwich, she grinned. "Tuna is Thomas's favourite."

"Who do you think brought it over?" Todd said.

"Thomas? When?"

"At least once a month," Todd replied. "He brings a box of canned food. He always has a lame excuse about leaving town and not wanting the food to go bad. How the hell does canned food go bad?" He snickered. "It's a thoughtful gesture. His departed wife started it."

"I'll be damned," Emma murmured, taking a bite of her sandwich. She nodded and smiled. "You've added just the right amount of onions, celery, and mayonnaise."

"The vegetables are from the garden." Todd pointed to the window. "I'm glad you like the sandwich. Do you want another?"

"That won't be necessary. I need to get outside and check on the guys."

"You don't have to," Todd said. "They have been checking up on you every fifteen minutes." He turned to the screen door. "Speaking of the devils, here they come."

The three lead mechanics stepped through the doorway and surrounded Emma. Diego and Brian immediately took a seat on either side of her on the couch and Leonard crunched in front of them. She elbowed the boys sitting next to her. "Guys, for Christ's sake, give me some space."

"The bitch is back," Diego said awkwardly to hide his concern. He rubbed her back in a circular motion.

"Fuck off," Emma said. "You three better have your work complete before I'm done eating or there will be hell to pay."

"We're not nearly done," Brian said. "The siding had a lot of wood rot. We cut the lumber meant for the fence and had just enough to replace all the affected boards."

"That explains the racket," Emma said.

"The front yard is all cleaned up and manicured," Leonard said. "Nathan and Ed went to town to pick up more gasoline to take care of the yard behind the house. We were thinking of clearing two acres out back. That should be enough."

Emma shook her head. "Put yourself and Ed on Brian's detail. If we expect to paint the house by day's end, we need all hands on deck."

"Actually, Emma, the crew on fence duty were helping Brian with the repairs," Diego said. He chuckled. "He took all our fucking lumber. The fencing will have to wait for another day."

"You lazy fuck! When we carried the wood off to the house, I didn't see you put up a fight," Brian said.

Emma held up a finger. "You two banter like women. I'm pleased we focused on the house, since it was the priority. Anyway, we can tackle the fence tomorrow."

"What?" Leonard said. "I have plans tomorrow."

Diego gently shook his head gently signalling that was inappropriate.

"Sorry. I'll be here tomorrow, bright and early."

"No," Emma said, "Ann will kill you if you don't keep your promise and go ring shopping with her tomorrow."

"And she'll kill us too for holding you back," Brian said.

"If that's the case, we will be fine without you," Diego said. "I'm too young to die."

Emma smiled. "It's settled. We'll make do without your black ass. Now everyone get back to work." She waved them off.

Diego stayed behind. "We're good?"

"Get out of here," Emma said. "I'm perfectly fine and will join you shortly."

Todd took the food tray and she watched him wheel away into the kitchen. She realized he was a good man after all, though you would never know it by looking at him. Who could blame anyone for fearing an armed recluse on wheels?

While taking in the view of the immediate surroundings, Emma noticed the damaged and outdated furniture, worn area rugs, cracked plaster on the ceiling and walls, and plywood nailed over a broken window. It wasn't just neglect, but a lack of funds that had put the estate into this condition. She guessed that his only income was his disability pension.

Having her team fix up a few things was great, but it wouldn't make him self-sufficient. Todd needed a helping hand, not a hand out. *He needs to get his land back to a viable farm it once was*, she thought. *How the hell am I going to manage that? He needs a job to get him back on his feet.* She laughed at the poor choice of words. *That's fucking sick.*

A loud thud from the kitchen startled her. She heard grunting and moaning. "Todd, are you alright?" She rose from the couch and favoured her right leg to limp toward the kitchen. "Todd, have you fallen?"

"No!" Todd said. "I'm fine. I'll be out in a second."

"Are you sure you don't need a hand?"

"I can," Todd paused while he lifted the battery on to his wheelchair. "Take care of it myself." After he positioned the battery correctly, he attached the wires to the positive and negative lugs. He spun the wheelchair around to grab both armrests to pull him off the floor and back into the seat. He dragged a dishtowel across his brow and tossed it into the sink.

"What have you been up to?" Emma asked supporting herself against the door jam. "With all the grunting and groaning, I wasn't sure if you were bench pressing or pleasuring yourself."

"You are so much like Thomas," Todd said. "You're both lousy liars." Pushing the joystick forward, he rushed through the doorway and Emma quickly hopped out of his way. Stopping abruptly, he said, "It's best you sit on my lap."

"Excuse me?"

"Come on," Todd encouraged. "I don't bite."

"What for?"

"Debbie mentioned your interest with falconry."

"True. But what does that have to do with me sitting on your lap?"

"I want to show you something and in your condition, it would be a long haul."

"Speaking of Debbie," Emma said, stepping in front of him, "Where is she?"

"At her boyfriend's place in town." He scowled.

She sat on a pillow he laid on his lap.

Emma's crew was busy painting the house siding. They stopped long enough to witness the spectacle. They watched a wheeling madman and their team leader wiz away towards a large shed fifty yards from the house.

"Diego," Brian called from the ladder twenty feet above the ground. "Pull out your gun and shoot at his tires. He's kidnapping our boss."

Grinning, Diego replied, "I'll shoot you if you don't hurry up."

"Yeah right." Brian smiled.

Placing the last two gallons of paint by the house, near where Brian and his team were working, Diego looked at Emma. With her arm around Todd's shoulder, she smiled and waved. "It's amazing how she tamed the beast. She isn't afraid of anything."

"He wasn't kidding," Brian said. "She has a big set of balls on her. You're wrong about one thing."

"Oh yeah, and what would that be?"

"She's terrified of Thomas," Brian said. "She jumps when he calls on her. She carries out his instructions quickly and to the tee without deviation."

"That's not fear," Diego said. "She respects him."

Arriving at the shed painted dark green, Emma noticed it was in impeccable condition - far better than the rest of the property. "This horse stable is in great shape," she said. "Is this new?"

"No and no," Todd replied. He slowed his wheelchair as they approached the double doors secured with a padlock.

"I didn't realize I had asked two questions," she said, swinging her feet to the ground. "I should have put on my shoes."

"It's not a horse stable and it's not new." He inserted the key into the padlock.

She heard distinctive bells coming from a barred window and realized what was happening. "You're a falconer?"

"That's right," Todd said with pride. He swung open the door and waved her to enter the mews. "Ladies first. I think you will be pleased."

She entered the mews and noticed the structure divided into two equal parts by chicken wire. Behind the wire mesh screen stood three perches measuring two, three, and four feet tall with their tops covered in Astroturf. Two-hawser rope perches, each measuring two and half inches in diameter, were strung across the partitioned room to form a v-shape. Scanning the room, she failed to see the bird of prey.

"Where is she?" Emma asked.

"It's a he," Todd said, putting on his leather glove. "And he's by your feet. Do me a favour and close the door. I don't want him to get away before I can attach the leash."

In all the excitement, Emma had forgotten the pain in her leg and limped, not hopped, to shut the door.

"Up, up," Todd instructed. The peregrine falcon obeyed and flew away from the rubber-matted flooring. The falcon exited through the opened partition's screen door and on to his hand. The leather glove protected his hand from the bird's talons.

"He is smaller than the falcon living in these parts," Emma said.

"Males are roughly a third smaller," Todd said. "That's why they're called tercel, stemmed from the Latin word meaning a third."

"I read the one book available at Charlottesville Library," Emma said. "I suppose there isn't much interest in these parts to learn the art of falconry. From what I can gather, it's a lot of work to train a raptor."

"Falconry is not a hobby, it is a way of life," Todd said while lightly stroking his bird's chest. "It requires your time every single day, throughout the year, to care for it and keep up with its training."

"He is a handsome bird," Emma said, inching closer.

"This little fellow is the reason I get out of bed every morning." He gazed at the bird like a proud dad. "Isn't that right, Thunder?" Todd motioned with his free hand and Thunder spread his wings. "That's a good boy." He slowly opened his fist to expose a defrosted mouse. Thunder snatched it away and feasted on it.

"He must be hungry," Emma said, watching the raptor devour the mouse in seconds.

"Mice are only part of his diet," Todd said. "Thunder's preference is to feed on birds." Pushing the joystick forward, the electric wheelchair moved to the entrance. "Would you like to see him in action?"

Emma pushed the mews' double doors wide open and at that moment, two turtle ring neck doves flew by.

"Watch this," Todd said. He tossed Thunder into the air and the raptor gave chase. The doves split apart, flying in different directions to increase their chance of survival. Thunder followed the slower of the two. They turned so quickly, Emma had difficulty following the flight path.

The dove gave Thunder a run for his money but within a short straight away, the raptor's talons reached out and grabbed hold. Snatched out of the sky, Thunder took his prize to the ground. The light breeze carried the plucked feathers he tossed into the air. The dove was still alive while the raptor began to feast. Its efforts to wiggle loose were useless. Unable to break free, Thunder plunged his beak in to tear another strip of flesh. It took ten minutes for the dove to succumb to its wounds.

Todd placed a mouse in the palm of his gloved hand and blew the whistle. Thunder looked up, beak dripping with blood, and responded to his master's second call.

# CHAPTER 21

**EVERYONE REASSEMBLED IN** Eva Muller's living room. The FAA inspectors casually switched places without drawing attention. Shirley was now tasked with operating the reel-to-reel recorder while the other chair allowed David to sit closer to Eva and her attorney. David had received new information that required putting the set of questions aside for the moment. "Before we begin," David said, "I used the phone in the lobby to call the office."

Brandon noticed David's behaviour was different, more subdued and serious.

"I've been told the Federal Bureau of Investigation will be involved," David said.

"What brought this on?" Brandon asked. "Involving the FBI can only mean a crime has been committed."

"You are correct," David replied. "The evidence provided by one of your employees implied airplane tampering, which is a federal crime."

Brandon failed to restrain his skepticism. "A Virginia Airlines employee, you say?"

"Indeed he was," David said.

"Was?" Brandon paused to formulate his next question. "So this ex-employee voluntarily provided an unsolicited written statement?" He leaned forward in his seat.

"I have been told the statement is detailed and comprehensive. It alleges inappropriate actions exercised on your company's fleet," David said. He noticed Brandon's apprehension. He placed his hand on Brandon's knee and smiled. "Unofficially, I will tell you it absolves your company. You can breathe easier now, counsellor, at least for the time being."

Brandon sat back in the seat. "Does this person have a name?" He laughed. "So I may thank them."

"It was Michael Hall," Shirley said softly. "He did not come forward. His statement was prepared before he died."

They sat in silence for a moment before David suggested they continue with the interview. Without being told, Shirley pressed the play and record buttons on the recorder. The recommencement of the question period started with a personal reference.

Though Eva had been quiet while the others spoke of the new evidence in the FAA's possession, she had grimaced occasionally and readjusted the pillows holding up her leg. She asked Brandon to get her another drink and painkillers. Taking them provided no immediate relief, but she insisted they continue nonetheless.

David referred to his notes. "We left off after you confirmed the T-Handle had been activated."

"The number two T-Handle," Eva said.

"Excuse me?"

"I mentioned I pulled the right engine's T-Handle."

"Okay, I don't believe that was stated previously," David said, leafing through his notes. He pulled the pen from his shirt pocket. "To ensure I understood correctly, you and the captain agreed to pull the T-Handle and for the record, you said..."

"As I mentioned," Eva swallowed, "I pulled the T-Handle on the affected engine."

"I'm not trying to be difficult but I need to be clear with the chain of events. For the record, can you specifically state which side was selected?" David purposely repeated the question for an absolute and undeniable response.

"The T-Handle pulled belonged to the right-hand engine," Eva said. A quiver in her voice exposed her nervousness for the first time.

"Understanding the QRH did not specify the need to pull the T-Handle, before the break you mentioned the decision to do so was for an added measure? What constituted that need?"

"Shortly after take-off, it was unclear what caused the right engine to shut down abruptly. Therefore, halting the fuel and hydraulic fluid to the engine was considered a valid precaution." Sticking to the facts helped ease her racing heart.

"Was there a fire indication?"

Eva reminded herself to take it slow. Before responding, she took a deep breath. "No."

"Did the turbine inlet temperature rise prior to the number two engine shutting down?"

"Not that I can recall."

"Did the turbine inlet temperature rise after the engine had shut down?"

"Definitely."

"Was that a factor in deciding the added measure was needed?"

"Not at all." The voice in the back of her head provided encouragement, reminding her to be herself and to take it slow. "But as I stated, the decision was solely based on the uncertainty about what had caused the engine to stop."

"Have you ever had a similar experience using the T-Handle as a precautionary measure?"

"No, this was the first time." Eva fidgeted with the sling supporting her left arm. She thought the FAA's fixation on the T-Handle bordered on obsession. She believed her responses were clear, accurate, and forthcoming. Yet the FAA's repetitious and redundant questions focused on one aspect of a short-lived flight. It can only represent they are on a fishing expedition. Perhaps the responses revealed the measures she considered self-evident were not as obvious to the two inspectors. The short answers, though correct, were not filling the void to explain a double engine failure. There was nothing more that could be said on the matter. No further actions had been taken by the flight crew or observed beyond what had already been said. "I hope I have been of some assistance?"

"You have been very helpful," Shirley said. "We have a few more questions and we'll be on our way."

"Another T-Handle question?" Eva said, smirking.

Sensing the sarcasm, David said, "It just so happens I have one more question pertaining to the T-Handle. Did you pull the left engine's T-Handle?"

Eva recomposed herself. "I have been very clear on this." Tears welled up in her eyes. "I must sound like a broken record when stating this repeatedly, I pulled the right engine's T-Handle."

Wiping the tears rolling down her cheeks with her hand, she then provided a step-by-step first-hand account to halt the misconception, perceived or otherwise, there was any wrong doing by the flight crew. Starting with the take-off roll she explicitly recalled the engine parameters, airspeed leading up to and including aircraft rotation. She expressed the characteristics of the aircraft handling during positive climb to the point they had experienced the startling and surprising uncommanded right-hand engine shutting down.

Recounting the vivid details left nothing to the imagination. It was emotional, explicit, compelling and her ability to communicate unequivocally provided enough stimulation to make you feel you were there. Eva's composure and account of the incident made her a credible witness. She took a sip of water and the captivated audience muttered no words, they clung to her every word spoken and anxiously awaited for the climatic part where the airplane crashed into Aviator's Baptist Church.

"On activating the right engine's T-Handle," Eva said, "Philip noticed and called out that the left engine had shut down." She took Brandon's handkerchief and held it in her hands. Her tears had dried up. "I cannot confirm or deny that the left engine shutdown and T-Handle activation were concurrent, or one action induced the other." This was a white lie but she did not want to confuse the situation.

"When the left engine shut down, the silence was deafening, as you can imagine. It felt like the rug had been pulled from under our feet. Without the engines pulling us through the air and with the nose pointed upwards, the airplane struggled to stay aloft. While the plane started to flounder a few hundred feet above the ground, Philip expected it and slammed the column away from him to push the nose over." She placed her finger over her lips to hold back the surfacing emotions.

"Eva..." Brandon began.

She held up her hand.

"Philip did not waver," she continued. "I remember the look on his face. He was so calm. He never gave up." Her eyes began to well up again. "If not for the electrical wires strung along the road, the plane would have missed the church and we would have crashed into the open field." She used the handkerchief to dab away the tears at the corner of her eyes. "Philip's courage saved lives, including my own. I will never forget that as long as I live."

Shirley reached for the recorder to turn it off. There was nothing left to discuss. All the information needed for the investigation had been collected.

"I appreciate your candour," David said. "And I apologise for making you relive that awful day." He lifted himself slightly off the seat and sat back down. "Eva, you don't need to answer if you don't want to, but I'm compelled to ask about Philip."

"What do you wish to know?"

"You exited the airplane through the captain's direct vision window..."

"And you're wondering why Philip didn't climb out first?"

"Well yes," David said. "For you to exit out of his window and Philip to remain in the cockpit, I can only presume you needed assistance."

"That's right," Eva said. She took a deep breath and closed her eyes. "I couldn't believe we had made it, that we had survived what was surely our last seconds on earth. I can't explain it, but an uncontrollable sense of giddiness swept over me. I didn't care that I was suspending in mid-air like a marionette from my seatbelt harness." She smiled sadly. "My giddiness turned to laughter and I covered my mouth to muffle the embarrassing outburst."

Eva sighed and exposed a grin saying, "It was such a liberating feeling to stare death in the face and escape it. To break free from the grim reaper's hold on you by the skin of my teeth. That feeling was short-lived when I turned to check up on Philip. His hand pressed against the left side of his head covered in blood. My impulsive laughter had stopped as fast as it had begun."

Eva's Journalism major obtained from Boston University gave her the uncanny ability to articulate her experience brilliantly. David, Shirley and Brandon were all on the edge of their seat listening attentively to her words spoken softly. At certain times, her voice was just above a whisper and it was not for effect.

David saw his daughter in Eva. Both are principled, determined, and strong without question. *Perhaps,* he thought, *these are the attributes career oriented women need to push through the noise to succeed in a man's world.* By all indication, Eva's sound constitution had served her well to be the first woman pilot at Virginia Airlines. Good on her he conceded.

From the onset, Brandon had been leaning forward when Eva recited the events. His arms crossed over his knees, a stance somewhat similar to everyone else present in the room. A posture favoured by all to provide the ability to inch forward as much as possible from a seated position, for no other purpose than to capture every word spoken. He nodded occasionally, a reflection of his pleasure in Eva's representation of the facts. Surprised she has held up well when considering her circumstances. No less, he was pleased in himself for a job well done. Thinking, "I am really good." Proud in the fact he had prepped her so well because she has been right on queue. She has the FAA inspectors eating out of her hand.

Eva's eyes remained shut and those present remained silent. "Philip was dangling as well and yet found a way to free himself. He placed his feet on the dashboard, which helped him take his weight off the harness to unbuckle it."

"I could not do the same. I insisted that he leave and get help. There was no convincing him. He stubbornly made his way to me. Grunting and moaning, climbing over the center console. There were moments he stood still and the cockpit shifted. I heard awful creaking and screeching sounds." She wiped her runny nose with the handkerchief.

"We didn't know how much time we had before the plane ripped apart, or worse. I managed with Philip's help to get myself to his window. I squeezed through the opening and with great difficulty started down the escape rope. Then came the explosion."

She opened her eyes. David, Shirley, and Brandon waited to hear the ending of her extraordinary tale. "It's okay," Brandon said. "We can figure out the rest on our own."

"I'm sorry," Eva said. "I cannot remember anything else. I do not recall falling or dislocating my shoulder and breaking my leg in three places. I'm not sure how long I was unconscious but when I came to, I recall lying in a stretcher. While looking up at the cockpit barely hanging on, flames shot out of the window."

"I understand," David said. "You have answered my question."

"We should be on our way," Shirley said.

# CHAPTER 22

**LOOKING OUT THE** window Thomas watched the apron activity at Washington National Airport. The marshaller guiding the airplane toward the terminal gate had crossed the batons and caused the plane to ease to a full stop. A ramp attendant waited nearby for the lead marshaller's signal to position the passenger stepladder at the plane's entrance door. The two propellers slowed to a stop after the engines were shut down.

Seated in the last row, Thomas pulled his gaze away from the window when a chime sounded, triggered by the pilot selecting the fasten seatbelt lights off. The passengers immediately sprung to their feet to gather their belongings from the overhead shelving. Unlike the other passengers, he preferred to remain seated, as he knew it would take several minutes for the door to open and deplane. Arriving a little over two hours before his scheduled meeting with the FBI, he contemplated how he would pass the time.

The ladder positioned against the airplane, the ramp attendant ascended the stairs two steps at a time. Standing on the top platform, he peered through the small circular window on the door. No red flag was visible confirmed the emergency escape slide was deactivated. It's safe to open the door.

Thomas felt the humid air fill the cabin and decided to leave his top shirt button undone and neck tie slack. He laid his jacket over his forearm and flung the strap of his English leather messenger satchel over his shoulder.

"Where are you off to?" Camila Ross asked. She fanned her face with the emergency card plucked from a seat pocket. She's one of the two flight attendants that worked the flight from Charlottesville to Washington DC. Six feet tall, she is Virginia Airline's tallest flight attendant, and so slender she had earned the nickname Olive Oyl, a cartoon character playing Popeye's girlfriend. She is reputedly Virginia Airlines best flight attendant, a full-time employee during the summer months and worked part-time during the school year.

"I'm meeting up with the FBI," Thomas said. "They wish to ask me a few questions about aircraft 641." He held out his hand. "Let's not talk about the crash. That's all anyone wants to talk about. I understand the need to do so but I can use a break."

"Yeah, I can appreciate that," she whispered. After a short pause she offered, "It's scorching hot out there." With cheeks sucked in and twisted lips she added, "I'm melting."

"Thanks for understanding." Thomas smiled.

"Too bad this was a short flight leg," Camila frowned. "I would have liked if we had a minute to chat and get caught up."

"That would have been nice," he said, nodding in agreement. "So how are you doing?"

"Not bad, not bad at all. I will be starting my doctorate program in a few weeks. So I am excited about that."

"Are you still pursuing a Criminal Psychologist career?" He asked. Recalling their last discussion held weeks prior.

"You don't forget a thing do you?" Camila said, moving her head side to side. "I was on the fence for a short time." She held her hand up with thumb and forefinger slightly apart. "I wasn't sure if criminal psychology would be rewarding as clinical psychology. I like the idea to help people work through their problems."

"Two totally different spectrums," he commented, intrigued with the dilemma. "What made you stick with Criminal Psychology?"

"I read the FBI is starting up a Behavioral Analysis Unit to assist in criminal investigations," she said. "Considering the number of unsolved serial murders, I came to a realization getting the bad guys off the streets would be more rewarding."

"Good for you. By all indications, you are pursuing your dream. Thomas leaned in and gave her a quick hug. "If there's anything you need, just let me know."

"Actually," she slurred, slightly embarrassed to be imposing so quickly.

"Yes?"

"I have two weeks left before heading back to school and they have based me out of Charlottesville," she winced. "I can't afford to stay at a hotel..."

"You need a crash pad," Thomas interpreted.

"Starting tonight if you don't mind."

Thomas rubbed his head.

"I will do the dishes," she offered. "I would do the cooking but should you wish to see your next birthday, it's best I stay out of the kitchen."

Thomas grinned while he dug into his pant pocket and pulled out his house key. "I have a huge home. You're welcome to it."

Camila kisses him on the cheek, "You are a life saver." She pointed to the cockpit and whispered, "The new First Officer offered to help me out, but I don't trust him. Ten Finger Louie can't keep his hands to himself."

"I'll speak to him," Thomas said authoritatively.

She put her hand on his chest. "You're sweet but that won't be necessary. I will deal with him in my own way."

He bit his bottom lip, held his thoughts to himself, and gave a reluctant nod. "I'll see you tonight." He started down the aisle and noticed a pilot exit the cockpit. He did not recognize the pilot and presumed it was the infamous Ten Finger Louie. He turned to Camila. "Hey honey! Do not forget we are having dinner with the Coopers' this evening. Don't be late."

"What?" Camila replied. She stopped picking up the empty cups and newspapers stuffed in the seat pockets to look up at Thomas.

"The Coopers', they are expecting us for dinner tonight," Thomas reiterated for Ten Finger Louie's benefit.

Acknowledging his antics to shield her she played along. "What about the Rockefellers? Will they be joining us as well?"

Thomas gave a look at the first office when he said, "Fuck the Rockefellers. They will talk our ears off." He blew Camila a kiss and headed for the airplane's door.

Dan Evans, a long time Captain employed at Virginia Airlines had witnessed the spectacle and joined in. "Thomas, don't you worry. We will help Camila tidy up the aircraft so she can be on her way quickly. Isn't that right, Lou?"

"Absolutely, Sir," Lou said.

"That's much appreciated Dan," Thomas said, then exited the airplane.

Lou eyed Camila, admiring her long legs and curves. He tilted his head slightly as he watched her bend over to cross the passenger seat belts in a neat and orderly fashion. "So he really knows the Coopers'?" He asked.

"As a matter of fact, they know each other very well. They served together in the Korean War," Dan said. He noticed the co-pilot gawking over Camila. "I don't think you got the hint that she's off limits."

"I do get it," Lou responded. "Look but don't touch."

"Grow up." Dan said, as he removed his hat and jacket. "There's no use in standing around, let us help out the girls."

\* \* \*

The taxi stopped at the side of the road at 950 Pennsylvania Avenue, in front of the Department of Justice Building. It had houses the FBI headquarters since 1936 and, like the FAA, Congress had approved a measure to build them a new facility to amalgamate all the FBI divisions under one roof. The construction of the new building was nearing completion but had experienced delays and costly overruns amounting to well over one hundred million dollars.

Thomas stepped out of the cab. He yanked a twenty-dollar bill from his wallet and gave it to the cab driver. "Keep the change."

"Thank you, sir!" the driver said. He did not bother asking if Thomas had meant to give him an extravagant tip. He thought it would be best to accept the offering and make his way back to Washington National Airport to pick up his next ride. "You have a good day, sir." He smiled and drove off.

Stepping into the Department of Justice Building, he approached the security desk. The guard wore the same uniform as the District of Columbia police. "How may I help you?" he asked.

I am here to see Special Agent..." Thomas paused. The name had slipped his mind. He fumbled through his suit jacket, digging for a folded piece of paper. He found it and said, "Special Agent Reese."

The security guard ran his finger down a page in the visitor's log with the day's date to confirm Thomas's name and his appointment were registered. He glanced to his left, then his right, to ensure no one was listening. "You're early. It's best you wait outdoors on the south side."

"Excuse me?" Thomas said, returning the folded paper back into his jacket pocket.

The guard rose from his seat. "A good friend of mine by the name of Ed Stone once said, 'Why waste time when you can enjoy a good ole fashion dog'." He extended an arm, pointing down the hall leading to the building's south entrance.

"That is the same way I came in," Thomas said.

"Get going. Your appointment won't be for another twenty-three minutes."

Thomas picked up his satchel off the floor and followed the instruction. Mentioning an old hometown friend gave the guard's peculiar instructions some credence. In 1949, after graduating high school, they went to the recruiting office together and joined the air force. Neither of them gave their families prior notice. Thomas's military interests involved turning wrenches on airplanes while Ed pursued law enforcement. With slightly less than ten years of service, Ed was promoted to technical sergeant, the second highest enlisted rank. He was a perfect fit for the FBI thanks to his years spent with the Air Force Office of Special Investigations.

At twenty to three, Thomas stood on the south side of the building at the corner of Constitution Avenue and 10th Street. Feeling the heat and humidity, he loosened his tie and undid the top button of his shirt. "What in the hell am I doing?" he whispered.

To his surprise, on the right was a food truck parked by the curb. Based on the security guard's comments, it must be the vendor specializing in hot dogs. If there was any doubt, the sign mounted above the chalkboard menu reaffirmed it: "DC's Good Old Fashioned Dogs."

"Hi, I'm Thomas," he said.

"Good to meet you," the vendor replied. He had an Eastern European accent. "Would you like a hot dog or a Polish Sausage? They are both very good."

"You don't understand. My name is Thomas."

"Mister, I'm Pawl, but I heard you the first time."

Thomas was puzzled. He looked around and glanced at his watch. This is a waste of time, he thought.

"I'll have a hot dog," said a man, approaching the truck.

"Mister Stone," Pawl said. "I thought I was not going to see you today."

"Don't be silly." Ed Stone smiled. "A man has to eat, doesn't he?"

Pawl looked at Thomas. "This is a very very smart man. He is the best FBI agent in all the America."

"Pawl, if you continue to tell people I'm from the FBI, I will have no choice but to shoot you."

"First eat, kill me later." Pawl chuckled. "It is unhealthy to shoot someone on an empty stomach."

"What's going on Ed?" Thomas asked. "I'm here to answer a few questions and then be on my way. I am not so sure about the cloak-and-dagger routine you're putting me through."

"Turn away. Make like you don't know me," Ed said without looking at his old friend. "It's nothing major but I thought it would be prudent to give you a heads up."

"I'll have a hot dog as well," Thomas said.

"Now you're talking," Pawl said.

"They know about your past," Ed whispered.

"What about it?" Thomas said. As quick as the words came out, he knew there was only one thing about his past no one else had known. Well, almost no one - except for Sarah, Alexander, and Ed.

"Do I need to say it?"

"No. That won't be necessary," Thomas said.

"It's nothing serious," Ed said. "They can't prove anything however they will bring it up during the interview process none-the-less. It's just to throw you off kilter, a tactic to prime you up for the questioning session."

"Here you go, Mister Stone," Pawl said, passing the hot dog.

"I wasn't sure how you would react," Ed said. "I just wanted to put your mind at ease, that's all. So there's no need to flip out if they ask."

"Is that it?" Thomas asked as he reached for his hot dog.

"I have to go," Ed said. While he walked away he said, "Pawl, my new friend is paying for the dogs."

Recalling how much money he had on hand, Thomas shook his head. He didn't have enough for his taxi ride back to the airport.

# CHAPTER 23

**SPECIAL AGENT SAM** Johnson was an elderly man with a receding hairline, slightly overweight, wearing a light blue plaid sports jacket and navy blue slacks. With a little more than a month remaining until retirement, he was tasked with mentoring the new recruits. He escorted Thomas to Special Agent Reese.

"I guess junior is not in his office," Sam said. "It's best you take a seat here." He pointed to a chair up against the wall facing the office door.

"It's five minutes to the hour," Thomas said, looking at his watch. "I'm early."

"You know what they say," Sam said, standing with his hands on his hips. "To be early is to be on time, to be on time is to be late, to be late is to be forgotten."

"Bull," Thomas said.

Sam laughed. "I suppose you don't care much for punctuality."

"If that were the case, I wouldn't be here waiting for someone else. I believe it was Admiral Bull Halsey who coined that phrase?"

Sam looked at the floor. "Well, I wouldn't know anything about that. I heard it from my father growing up in Alabama." He smiled. "He was one tough son-of-a-bitch, yes he was."

"Do you know why I'm here? Special Agent Reese only mentioned it was about aircraft maintenance. I found this odd and presume it really pertained to the crash. I'm not sure I can be of any help."

"Why don't we wait for junior? I'm sure he will let us both in on the secret." Sam looked down the hallway in both directions. "Ah, there he is."

Special Agent Reese rounded the corner and gave a quick nod acknowledging their presence. "Mister Wright?"

"Yes, you can call me Thomas."

"And you can call me Stephen." They shook hands. "Please come into my office. Will you be joining us as well?"

Sam unbuttoned his suit jacket. "I believe I will."

"Very well. Special Agent Johnson will be observing us while we go over a few questions," Stephen said with a forced grin. "It shouldn't take long, just..."

"I'm not sure how I can help," Thomas said. "But I will answer any of your questions as best I can."

"I appreciate your cooperation. As I mentioned, it is just a few questions to help us understand Virginia Airlines accident. Let's start with..." Stephen looked at his notes. "What do you think happened on that flight?"

"It crashed," Thomas said.

"What I mean to say is, do you have any idea why it fell out of the sky the way it did?"

"I wasn't present to witness the incident but if the information in the newspapers is accurate, both engines stopped turning."

Sam covered his mouth with his hand to hide his amusement. He waited to see if the new FBI recruit would find his legs and seize control.

Stephen removed a silver case from his jacket pocket, opened it, and held it up to Thomas. "Cigarette?"

"No thanks."

The agent leaned back in his chair and lit his cigarette with a matching silver Zippo lighter. In his limited experience, he had expected Thomas to spew everything he knew, but he was not intimated by the surroundings.

Opening the blue folder, Stephen asked, "It shows here you have ten percent ownership of Virginia Airlines."

"That's correct."

The agent waited for a second for additional information. There was none.

Thomas crossed his leg and waited for the next question.

"And you're not a board member?"

"That is accurate."

"So let me get this straight, you have ten percent of the organization and you're not a board member for the company?"

"Alexander Cooper serves as my proxy. He has full control to act on my behalf," Thomas replied calmly. "It is all specified in the board's guidelines and by-laws. I can send you a copy if you feel it will be useful for your investigation."

"That won't be necessary," Sam said. "We trust the word of a millionaire. Isn't that right, junior?"

Stephen glared at Sam.

"I am at a lost," Thomas said. "Did you call me here to talk about my investment portfolio? I have better things to do." He pivoted in his seat to confront Sam, the older and presumably wiser of the two. "I am concerned that the FBI is investigating my airline's crash because it can only mean you suspect a criminal act has been committed." He returned his gaze to Stephen. "Why not start by stating the crime you believe was committed. Based on the questions raised so far, I am perplexed. Can we start over and have a frank and open discussion?"

"There's no reason to get your back up," Sam said. "You'll need to excuse junior's line of questioning, he is new at this." He ran his tongue along his bottom lip. "I can assure you, he means no ill will."

"The NTSB asked us to get involved," Stephen said to regain control as the lead investigator. "Information obtained through interviews held with Virginia Airline employees suggested there had been unlawful aircraft tampering by one of your technicians."

"What's the individual's name?" Thomas asked. "Have you brought the individual in for questioning?"

Sam rubbed the palm of his hands over his pant leg and chuckled. "We would have, if he were still alive. He took his own life."

"Michael Hall," Thomas said. He reached for and felt the impression of the key Michael left him through the cotton fibers of his shirt. Relieved it was still in his possession.

"That's right," Sam said. "We have received testimony that one of your shift duty managers tried to dismiss him for performing undocumented work on more than one aircraft. Yet, your organization kept him on and moved him to your shift rotation."

"There wasn't enough information to support the claim," Thomas said. "Human resources moved Michael to my shift to address the personality conflict that ensued after the allegations were brought to light. He became my responsibility."

Stephen took a long drag from his cigarette and exhaled the smoke to one side. "You asked us to be frank and I will oblige." He took another drag. "You and an inexperienced aircraft technician were the last individuals to perform operational checks on the aircraft in question."

"Yes. Both engines needed to be run as part of the leak check requirement following the fuel and oil filter change."

"On an airplane worked by an individual known to have conducted undocumented aircraft maintenance."

"Allegedly," Thomas said.

"Then shortly after, the plane crashed."

They stared at each other for a moment.

"Have you reviewed the list of tasks performed that evening?"

"Yes, we have," Stephen replied.

"And you are aware I personally performed the operational runs?"

Stephen nodded.

"If any unlawful measures or tampering of the engines had taken place, it would have been noticed during the run. I am confident the accident was not related to any maintenance performed that evening. Anyway, there have been reports the plane flew into a flock of geese."

"That does not seem to be the case," said Sam.

"The engine manufacturer," Stephen began, searching for the organization's name in his stack of papers.

"Allison Engine Company," Thomas offered.

"Yes, a division of General Motors had dismantled both engines. They confirmed only the right engine swallowed a Canadian goose. It triggered the auto-feather circuits to shut down the engine."

"And what about the left engine?" Thomas asked.

"Nothing definite as of yet."

Thomas shook his head in dismay. Bringing him from Charlottesville to Washington was nothing but a witch hunt. "So what am I doing here?"

"Well son, there's another problem. You see, you don't exist." Sam chuckled.

"Excuse me?" Thomas furrowed his brow. "Are you kidding me?"

"I wish I were, son," Sam said.

"There is no record of Thomas Benjamin Wright until 1948, a year before you joined the Air Force," Stephen said. "Can you explain how that could be?"

Thomas silently thanked Ed Stone for warning him about this. Though he knew it was coming, it did not stop his heart from racing. He reminded himself it was just to push him off kilter. "So what you're saying is, the FBI doesn't really know everything."

"Oh, that's a good one," Sam said, amused. "But son, this is not funny. No it is not." He wet his lips. "You may not have anything to do with the aircraft going up in flames, but you are an anomaly in our investigation. The FBI does not like loose ends."

Stephen smiled smugly at Thomas.

Thomas knew it was a mistake to meet with the FBI. What they had unearthed about his identify could not be avoided. "Am I under arrest?" he asked.

"No, not right now," Stephen said.

"What does that mean, not right now?"

"Charges are pending," Sam said. "If you cooperate, we may be able to help minimize your use of an alias and the associated felony charges."

"This is not a fishing expedition," Stephen said. "We have you dead to rights."

"Bullshit," Thomas said. Years before, Ed Stone and he had orchestrated the alias, masterfully executing Benjamin Williams's disappearance and resurrecting Thomas Benjamin Wright. Running off to join the military was the icing on the cake. It was the only vehicle, Ed and Thomas had to escape Mariana, Florida.

"You two are talking out of your ass," Thomas said with his chest out and head held high. The FBI may have had an inkling of impropriety but they couldn't prove it. They were insinuating evidence in the hope Thomas would reveal his guilt. Sitting up straight in his seat, he said, "Contact Colonel Cooper. He has access to my safety deposit box and will personally deliver my birth certificate."

Sam and Stephen shared a glance. Closing the file, Stephen said, "That won't be necessary. We had to be certain. We admit small-town records, especially in the south, can be questionable." He sighed and looked at his watch.

"You might as well let him in on the secret," Sam said. "For crying out loud, he is part owner of the company. Once he hears it, he may be willing to help us out."

"There have been a lot of loose ends in this investigation," Stephen said.

"Just spill the beans, junior."

Stephen set the blue folder aside and removed another from his top drawer. This one had the word confidential in large bold lettering stamped in red. "The fire protection panel was inspected and functionally tested serviceable. The hypothesis the FAA shared with us could not be proven."

"They suspected the T-Handles may have been cross-wired," Sam said.

"This is just circumstantial evidence, but two of my technicians pieced together the same hypothesis. But their theory was flawed."

"How so?" Sam asked.

"There was only one replacement of the fire protection panel," Thomas said. "Considering the remaining aircraft had these panels installed for nearly a decade, at the very least, the cross wiring would have been detected during an engine change. Pulling the onside T-Handle, the technician would have noticed fuel and hydraulics leaking out when disconnecting the lines from the engine."

"There's no other tasks that may have identified the issue?" Stephen asked.

"Yes, there are," Thomas said. "During line checks, which occur every fifty hours. The technicians physically check that all relevant shutoff valves function properly. However, the T-Handles are both pulled, so there would be no way of knowing."

"Replacing oil and fuel filters on both engines on a given night shift would also cause both T-Handles to be pulled together," Sam said.

"I was afraid you may go down that path," Thomas said. "Yes, during the work we carried out before 641's flight, we would have pulled both T-Handles."

"That is a moot point," Stephen said. "Even though we were certain 641's fire protection panel wiring was routed correctly, Olivia Cooper humoured us and had all the aircraft checked for good measure." He glanced at the first sheet of paper in the confidential folder. "It's final; cross wiring is a non-issue." He turned the folder to his desk drawer. "Aircraft Systems and Electronics do most of your component overhauls as well as manufacturing the redesigned parts for your fleet."

"That's correct," Thomas said. "We kept our maintenance costs down by contracting this work out. This was preferable to setting up our own in-house shops that would require equipment and larger facilities, additional staff, and so on."

"ASE also built your wheel assemblies," Stephen said, "replacing the worn tires with new back on the same rims."

"Yup, at their Miami location," Thomas said. "And then they are sent to our maintenance stations throughout our system." He recalled there were two wheel assemblies in 641's cargo compartment. "641 departed Miami for Newark but diverted to Charlottesville for sluggish flight controls."

"So you were aware that these wheel assemblies was on-board the aircraft?" Stephen asked.

"Of course I knew," Thomas said. "They were left alone. The tire's sidewall had the airport code - EWR – written in white chalk. It meant they were intended for our Newark station. We notified Miami to remove the tires when 641 arrived that morning so they can reroute them back to Newark."

"EWR is the designator for Newark Airport?" Sam asked.

"Yes."

"What does the asterisk beside EWR mean?" Stephen pointed to an eight by ten photo.

"It doesn't mean a thing," Thomas replied.

"Son," Sam said, leading forward, "take another look. We need you to be certain."

Holding up the photograph, Thomas noticed one tire had an asterisk and the other did not. "It has no meaning whatsoever to my knowledge. It is merely someone being creative. If you notice," he gave the photo back to Stephen, "only one out of the two tires has it." He shrugged. "It's obvious you two think there's more to this than I know."

"Show him, junior."

Stephen reached to the lower right-hand drawer of his desk and pulled a brick sized package wrapped with duct tape. "We found thirty-two of these stored in the tire marked with the asterisk."

Thomas glared at Sam and Stephen. "Are you going to tell me what's in it?"

"It's a kilogram of cocaine," Stephen replied. "This is the purest form the agency has ever seized. We measured the purity at ninety-five percent or better. It has a street value of forty thousand dollars."

"The agents reviewing the wreckage noticed there was something wrong when one tire weighed seventy pounds more than the other," Sam said. "We followed the breadcrumbs to ASE, and posted agents around the clock there and at Miami Airport." He rose and sat on the edge of the desk. "In three days, we estimate thirty wheel assemblies marked with an asterisk were shipped to Virginia Airlines. We estimate half a billion dollars in cocaine were trafficked in just three days. We tracked the shipments to Chicago, Newark, Saint Louis, and Denver." He slammed his hands together. "Can you imagine that?"

"This is huge," Stephen said, "and we haven't even scratched the surface."

Thomas leaned back and closed his eyes. The fire protection panels deemed serviceable and Michael tampering with them; his airline involved in cocaine trafficking; and an employee committing suicide - all at the same time. This can't be a coincidence.

# CHAPTER 24

**RETURNING TO VIRGINIA,** Thomas drove to Middle Mountain, his refuge in the Appalachians. The picturesque vistas, as old as the earth, have the power to overwhelm the senses and make any concern into an inconsequential and benign issue. Nature's wondrous powers however could not trivialize two events in his life. The first being Sarah's untimely passing because of 1969's medical advancements could not cure her cancer. The second is his company-intertwined in a drug smuggling ring; fortunately, the cancer plaguing his organization is not biological.

He decided there is no choice but to treat everyone working at Virginia Airlines as a suspect. Including front-line employees loading and offloading tires marked with an "X" would need management's support and inherent protection. There would be no other way for the staff to deviate from procedures without detection. If it were up to him to devise and carry out a successful smuggling operation, he considered, it would need to recruit every personnel from overseeing aircraft movement, Loadmaster to the individuals handling the freight.

Once the goods are in transit, protecting its passage would be the priority. Assuring it did not fall into the wrong hands. Its detection would sabotage the cost effective air distribution channels across the nation; and worst yet, start an FBI investigation that would lead to the apprehension and arrest of all those involved. Protecting the goods equates to and is directly proportional to the ringleader's self-preservation.

His disappointment that these activities had occurred under his watch turned to anger. He hit the steering wheel three times with the palm of his hand. *I should have known,* he told himself.

He is reminded of Nicolas Diaz's last day worked at Virginia Airlines. It ended shortly after loading a cardboard box on an airplane. He lost his grip and caused the box to fall to the ground hard, ripped it apart and exposed its contents. Thomas watched Nicolas frantically stuff the unexplained packets into a duffel bag.

"Don't say a word," Nicolas said, as he walked by Thomas and stood by a garbage container.

"What have you gotten yourself into?" Thomas asked. "Whatever is going on here, we can work it out."

Nicolas threw the torn box into the garbage. "Do us both a favour and forget what you have seen."

"We've known each other for twenty-two years and in all that time, I have never known you to be a drug smuggler."

He eyed his old friend. "This is all on me. I fucked up."

"How is Diana doing?" Thomas asked.

"The ALS is taking her away from me." Nicolas began to tear up. "Look who I'm talking to, you had gone through a similar experience with Sarah."

Thomas glanced at the duffel bag. "And the medical bills?"

"Well Thomas." Nicolas straightened his back and sniffed. "They keep piling up."

The aircraft technicians returned from their lunch break, entering into the hangar single file. Thomas placed his hand on Nicolas's shoulder. "Let's go to my office. I'll call Philip and the three of us will work it out."

At a distance, the maintenance crews watched Nicolas wave Thomas's hand away.

"I'll need to get this locked up in my car," Nicolas said.

He never returned and that was the last time Thomas laid eyes on him. He remembered looking into the garbage and saw ASE's logo on the cardboard box. He realized now, Nicolas wasn't the first and obviously not the last to smuggle drugs on his airline. He regrets foolishly thinking Nicolas had acted alone. If he had known the drug cartel was involved, Thomas would have handled the situation differently and forced an old friend to seek help.

Thomas welcomed the opportunity to assist the FBI. To serve his penance, sort of speak, by assisting bureau's sting operation, eager to provide their agents with the access and cover to infiltrate Virginia Airlines workforce.

Thomas steered his Morgan roadster into the driveway. While approaching the house, he noticed all the lights were on. He remembered the tall and beautiful blonde flight attendant was staying at the house. With everything that is going on, he would have preferred to be alone. It's only for two weeks until Camila Ross returned to Catholic university full-time to complete her masters in psychology.

The front door swung open and Camila leaned on the doorknob, wearing nothing but one of Thomas's pajama top. "I wondered what time you would be arriving," she said. "I just got out of the shower when I heard you drive up."

"It's late," he said. "I hope you didn't stay up for me."

"I couldn't sleep. I thought I heard someone in the house."

"It may have been Debbie Bailey, a neighbour of mine. She has a key and from time to time she checks up on the house when I'm not at home."

"How did it go today in DC?"

"It went as well as it could be expected," he said, laying his satchel on the kitchen table. He reached into the refrigerator and grabbed a beer. Thomas noticed her eyeing it. "I'm sorry, I should have asked if you were flying in the morning."

"I was, but crew scheduling called and said I will be starting late," Camila said, reaching for Thomas's beer. She took a sip and returned the bottle. "It's your last beer, I checked the fridge earlier, but we can share it if you don't mind."

"There's more in the pantry," he said. "I'll stock the fridge later." He reached into the cupboard to pour her a glass.

"We can drink out of the same bottle," she said in a warm and seductive tone.

"You don't mind swapping spit with a coworker?" Thomas jested.

She hunched her back, distorted her face and dragged her leg across the kitchen floor like Igor, Frankenstein's assistant. "Would that be so bad?" Camila noticed her antics were not amusing him. "A little too much?"

"No, it was funny," Thomas replied, and then grinned. "It's hard to focus with you in my pajama top." He paused to look away and started toward the porch. "Let's just say when you raise your arms, you keep showing me your natural hair colour."

"I am a natural blonde," Camila replied. At that moment she realized she had unintentionally revealed more of herself.

"Let's finish our drinks on the porch," Thomas suggested.

Camila joined him after putting on a robe she gathered from the bathroom door. "Is this better? I didn't mean to flaunt my privates," she said.

"Not to worry, I only peeked once." He smiled.

She covered her face. "I'm so embarrassed. I wasn't thinking."

"Don't give it another thought." A Ford truck approached had caught their attention. Thomas squinted to make out the vehicle. "It's Emma." He drank the last bit of beer. "I suppose she will be spending the night as well."

"A girlfriend?" Camila asked.

"No. But an old flame to be rekindled," he replied, leaving his seat to greet Emma.

The driver's door opened and Emma swung her legs to favour her right foot to support her body weight. She tucked the crutch into her left armpit and slammed the door closed. "Who's that," she asked, nodding to the porch.

"I will introduce you," Thomas said. "What happened?"

"I'll live. It's not as bad as it looks. I'll fill you in when we're alone."

Emma navigated on her crutches down the pathway. She climbed the two steps on to the porch with little effort and took a seat beside the woman wearing Thomas's bathrobe. "I recognize you," she said, leaning her crutches against the house. "You're one of our flight attendants."

"Yes, I am," Camila replied. "I recognize you too. You're the one everyone calls the Dragon Lady."

Emma shook her head, "That's one of my better nicknames bestowed by the opposite sex."

"I apologise," Camila said. "I didn't mean to be rude."

Emma extended her hand. "And you're Olive Oyl."

"Touché." Camila smiled. "I deserved that."

Thomas arrived with three tall glasses and a pitcher of ice tea.

"Did you forget to stock the fridge with beer?" Emma guessed.

"You read me like an open book," Thomas replied. He pulled a chair close to sit between the two women. "So, what did I miss?"

"Olive Oyl couldn't follow through on her psychoanalysis of me," Emma said.

"I was not psychoanalyzing!" Camila said. "Mind you, I am a psych major." She giggled to hide her embarrassment.

"Look at you," Emma said, squeezing Camila's forearms. "You're beautiful and proportional. I have no idea how these guys came up with the name Olive Oyl. You're perfect."

Thomas watched the friendly banter and poured the drinks, following the conversation like a spectator at a women's tennis match. "Camila was reassigned and will be based out of Charlottesville for her last two weeks with Virginia Airlines. She will be staying with us before heading back to school full-time in D.C."

"There's nothing you can do for her?" Emma asked. She wanted to keep the lovely temptress out of Thomas's sight and mind. "You can't pull some strings to prevent the transfer to Charlottesville? It seems silly to move her with only two weeks remaining."

"I agreed to it," Camila said. "Reluctantly, mind you, but once crew scheduling told me they were hurting for flight attendants, I agreed. It's the closest station to my home in Georgetown. I can drive home on my days off."

Thomas raised his glass. "This would have been better with beer."

Emma reached across the small circular table and held his hand. They looked at each other with mutual affection.

"I'll leave you two lovebirds alone," Camila said.

"Get your ass back down," Emma said. "We'll have one more glass of non-alcoholic beverage before we hit the hay."

Thomas refilled the glasses.

"You're growing on me," Emma said winking.

"That's something you don't often hear her say," he said. "It's a big compliment. Should you ever get to know Emma, you'll understand why."

"Well, thank you," said Camila.

"Let us in on the secret," Emma said. "How did you get the nickname Olive Oyl? You're beautiful, but before you go half-cocked, I'm no lesbian." She took the half-filled glass of ice tea from Thomas. "You are definitely eye candy and it does explain why the men go gaga over you."

"It's exhausting to hear about my good looks." Camila frowned. "The attention I receive based purely on genetics is ridiculous."

"Boo hoo," Emma said, laughing. "The dice rolled in your favour at birth."

"If you're guessing the nickname is an endearing reference," Camila hesitated, "You would be wrong. Newark's station manager, Ramirez, started it after I put a stop to his repeated advances."

"You don't have to worry about him," Thomas said. "We terminated his employment for inappropriate behaviour with a ticket agent."

"Rumour has it that he sexually assaulted a passenger as well, a frequent flyer if I'm not mistaken," Emma commented.

"I don't want to get into that," Thomas said. As a Virginia Airlines shareholder, he received briefings on all employee investigations pending termination. It was not proper to disclose confidential matters with present company.

"Ramirez may no longer be employed with us, but I can assure you he is still around," Camila said. "He drives a truck for ASE, loading and offloading aircraft tires."

"And how long has he been doing that?" Thomas asked.

"You know he had been moonlighting with them while employed with Virginia Airlines," Camila replied.

"He performed functions for ASE while he worked on shift at Virginia Airlines?"

"Well, yeah," Camila said. "It's no secret, Ramirez bragged about it to everyone. How he was earning two pay cheques on an eight hour shift. But he didn't do much for ASE. He simply offloaded aircraft tires from our Miami inbound flights." She paused, "Now solely employed with ASE, he offloads tires throughout the New England area."

"You don't mean he handles tires in all six states?" Thomas said.

"Not at all," Camila responded. "We don't fly to Rhode Island or New Hamshire. Otherwise, you'll find him in Bangor one day, another day in Burlington, Boston the next and so on. He makes the same rounds every week but most of the time is spent at the La Guardia and Newark airports." She sipped her tea. "I'm getting the impression this is all new to you."

Thomas felt his blood pressure rise and face flush. "I wasn't however I'm pleased to see he is working after we had let him go." Her innocent and inconsequential observation was unfolding into the workings of a multimillion-dollar smuggling ring. He was beside himself.

Emma noticed him tense up and sensed there was more to the story.

"I'm sure there's a logical explanation that a menial task would need his services at various stations," Camila said.

"Oh, I'm sure this is ASE's way of ensuring their products are handled correctly," Thomas said. "They have had quality issues in the past and this may be an effort to rule out handling and shipping damage."

"If that were the case," Emma said, "why would they focus solely on the tires? All other parts shipped on our flights are directly handled by our stores personnel and ramp attendants."

Thomas shot a look at Emma. Her perceptiveness was not helping his efforts to down play Camila's observation.

"Tires are not packaged in boxes lined with foam like the other aircraft parts," Thomas said. "And their weight is more susceptible to mishandling. It's reasonable for ASE to pay particular attention to tires."

"That makes sense," Camila agreed. "Ramirez always has two people helping him when lifting tires into the boxed truck or into the aircraft's cargo compartment."

*I'm sure he does,* Thomas thought. The tire's concealed contents would obviously be too much weight for one person to lift safely.

# CHAPTER 25

**AUGUST 27, 1974.** Ten days after the crash, the FAA investigators gathered in the boardroom at their Washington headquarters. David Steadman and Shirley Attwood waited on the arrival of Allen Horowitz, the FAA's best aeronautical engineering and lab technician. In a telephone conversation, Allen confirmed they had concluded what caused 641's failure. He did not wish to review the facts over the phone and requested a face-to-face, recorded meeting.

"Mister Steadman," Allen said, hanging his hat and jacket on a coat stand positioned by the door. At the age of forty-five, he kept himself in good shape. He stood five feet eleven, with a medium build. His most distinctive feature was the receding hairline at the temples that exaggerated the size of his forehead. That and his high intelligence caused his closest friends to refer to him as The Brain.

"Mister Horowitz," David said. He reached across the boardroom table to shake Allen's hand. "Joining us is Miss Shirley Attwood."

"Allen and I met once before," Shirley said.

"Yes, I remember," Allen said. "But this guy," he pointed to David, "I know all too well. He is nothing but trouble." He opened his briefcase and removed the small reel. "When he says let's go for one drink, don't believe him. It never stops at one," he said, laughing.

"Is that the same CVR recording?" Shirley asked. Waving her reel, "I have the original copy."

"I bought only a segment of the recording," Allen said. "Our sound engineers managed to remove as much noise as possible." He removed four folders from his briefcase and passed them around.

David returned the extra folder to Allen. "You have forgotten there will only be three of us present."

"That, my friend," Allen said raising an eyebrow, "Is for the NTSB. I heard through the grapevine they are not happy with you for not providing them with regular updates."

David's held his jaw firmly closed, fighting the impulse to say something rash. "That's fine, they have my number." He looked at his watch. "Shall we proceed?"

"Very well," Allen said, opening the folder. "We discussed the maintenance portion yesterday; however, it's worth discussing it for the record and for Shirley's benefit." He turned to her. "May I please have some water."

Shirley and David exchange glances and he knew all too well what was running through her mind. David pushed the tray containing a pitcher of water and six glasses toward Allen. "Here you go."

Allen poured himself a drink and pulled a pack of cigarettes out of his shirt pocket. He lit it with a wooden match and blew out the flame. Shirley slid the ashtray with the precision of a curler tossing the granite stone along the ice; it stopped inches away from his stack of papers.

Allen winked at her and turned to his report summary. "We completed an exhaustive review of aircraft registration N1960V, manufacturing serial number 80089, for the twelve months preceding the accident and found no anomalies. Virginia Airlines maintained the aircraft to all regulatory and approved procedures." He took a long deep drag from his cigarette and flicked it into the ashtray. "Based on our analysis, the aircraft was in an airworthy state. The weight and balance..."

"Allen," Shirley said. "I just looked over your report summary and I don't see anything stating why the left-hand engine performed an uncommanded shutdown."

"Shirley is correct," David said. "We know all this information." He picked up the report and tossed it to Allen. "Hell, we're the ones that collected the data for you. The only piece of this puzzle we need to find is why the left engine failed."

"Okay guys," Allen said. "My intent was to build up to the failure, gradually bringing you along to the final conclusion."

"Really!" Shirley said. "Allen, quit the foreplay. You're not good at it. Just jump right in and give us what we need."

"Shit," Allen said, shaking his head. "I like your style." Shirley scowled at him and wiped the grin off his face. He threw his report in his briefcase. "Before you hit the play button, you'll need to know we will be listening to a small portion of the CVR. It will play four times, and each play back will have various frequencies removed for noise reduction."

The soundtrack played four times as Allen said. It focused on a few seconds before the serviceable engine shut down.

"I heard the T-Handle pulled four separate times." David shrugged. "When we first heard the recording, both Shirley and I decided there can be only two scenarios. The first is the activation of the wrong T-Handle."

"However," Shirley said. "The first officer emphatically says that did not occur."

"That's correct, and in our interview with her, she came across very credible. Then again, there are no data to prove otherwise. The second scenario is irrelevant now since we know the wiring wasn't crossed."

"I think it is best you replay the recording," Allen said. "The answer is there."

David and Shirley shared another glance.

"I didn't hear anything on the first run," Shirley said.

"Me neither," David said.

David rewound the twenty-second recording. Before pressing the play button for the second time, he said, "Here goes nothing."

"Please raise the volume, it may help identify the issue," said Allen.

After listening to the recording again, Shirley said, "I think I heard a click of a pen immediately before the clunking sound from the T-Handle."

David did not need to be told, he automatically rewound the tape to play it again and set the volume to full. After depressing the play button there was a beep, static and a clunk sounding over the speakers. A second beep emanated, then what resembled a fingernail tapping twice on a hard surface and a clunk after that. The third beep rang out and David recognized Shirley's description of the two clinking sounds of a ballpoint pen then followed by the same old clunk. The fourth and last segment with the least amount of noise, he heard the familiar sound of switches activating and deactivating that followed by the clunk. He stopped the recorder and sunk into his seat.

David must have listened to the recording countless of times, but he had not detected any other sound before pulling the T-Handle. "Good work, Allen."

"Do we know what caused the clinking noises?" Shirley asked. "There's no switch in the cockpit that specifically shuts off fuel to the engine." She looked at the two men waiting for her to catch up. "The throttle lever for the left engine was found at max power. Therefore, the fuel cut-off micro-switch wasn't activated by the throttle lever." She paused. "A second micro-switch is at the T-Handle. Guys, I'm not connecting the dots."

"I'll show you," Allen said. He removed the fire detection panel from the box and placed in the center of the table. "Applying roughly four inch pounds on the right engine's T-Handle causes it to extend nearly a quarter of an inch."

Shirley approached and stood beside David as he tried to repeat Allen's demonstration. "A four-inch pound to extend it a quarter of an inch is not that much."

"We measured several fire protection panels at Aircraft Systems and Electronics where they are manufactured," Allen said. "They all fell within the four to six inch pounds range, which meets the specifications."

David pulled the T-Handle to its full extension of three-quarters of an inch. "More force is needed to extend it completely."

"Correct," Allen said. "It takes roughly twelve inch pounds to engage the leaf spring lock mechanism."

"I'm only hearing the clunk," Shirley said. "What is making the clicking noise?"

"It's the left engine's T-Handle," David said.

"Pulling the left engine's T-Handle slightly, you'll hear the switch activate, then releasing it you'll hear it deactivate," Allen said. "So let's see if I can reproduce the sounds to match the recording."

Allen applied slight pressure to the left engine T-Handle, released it, and pulled the right engine T-Handle. He repeated it several times until his timing matched identically to the recording. "The micro-switch installed one hundred and eighty degrees out caused a premature activation."

"Therefore, the first officer probably reached up," David said. "She noticed her hand resting on the left engine's T-Handle and quickly repositioned to pull the right T-Handle instead."

"In essence," Shirley said, "Eva's statement is accurate."

"Accurate but incomplete," David said.

"But the left engine's T-Handle was never engaged and she cannot be faulted," Allen said. "She caught herself in time and activated the correct T-Handle. As I have shown, the weight of the co-pilot's hand is enough to cause the switch to open. It was incorrectly installed; however, it triggered a domino effect within its circuits to turn off the fuel, hydraulics, and pneumatic shut-off valves."

"I don't get it," Shirley said.

"What don't you get, sweetheart?" Allen asked.

"First, keep it in your pants, cowboy," Shirley said. "Second, how can a split-second activation of a switch remove electrical power to all those components? At best, the engine would have hiccupped and continued to perform."

"It was more than a split second, but I get your meaning. The small amount was enough to starve the engine of fuel," David said.

"That's correct," Allen said.

"I'm in total agreement, Eva's actions had mistakenly caused the shutdown," said David.

"There it is," she said. "It's an interesting conclusion to a peculiar event."

David held the fire protection panel in his hands. He scrutinized the micro-switch on the left hand T-Handle. "The allegation of aircraft tampering is making sense. The reason why the FBI couldn't prove Michael Hall had tampered with the aircraft because mister Hall was correcting the problem. For whatever reason, no one wanted to disclose this quality issue to Virginia Airlines or to the FAA."

"I don't know," Allen said. "Your theory has too many variables."

"Hold on," Shirley interjected. "I think David's on to something."

"Before we head down this path," Allen began, "we only know of one micro-switch installed incorrectly on one panel. You're suggesting this is a systemic issue, but there is no evidence to support it."

"Fair enough," Shirley conceded. "So using David's theory, Virginia Airlines employees revealed that one of their own people performed undocumented maintenance on more than one aircraft." She referred to her notebook. "Based on our interviews, they alleged there had been at least four aircraft Michael conducted undocumented maintenance."

"The same individual who had moonlighted at ASE," David added.

"Yup. He also took his own life days after the crash." She looked at the mass of papers. "There's enough information here to conclude our investigation on the crash. The quality escape on the fire protection panel is a secondary issue."

"I have one question," Allen said. "If this Michael guy had corrected all of micro-switches on Virginia's fleet months ago, why did he ignore aircraft 641?"

David searched through a stack of papers and pulled one out. "Here it is. This maintenance log page dated July 4, 1974."

"This unit was replaced one month before the crash," Allen said. "So what?"

Shirley shook her head. "For a smart person, you don't pick up on the easy clues. Michael Hall corrected all the units installed on the aircraft. This fire protection panel was sitting on a shelf in Stores."

"You're saying he didn't know there was a fire protection unit in Virginia Airlines inventory."

"Until it was replaced, he thought he had addressed all the questionable units." She turned to David. "You're quiet."

David placed the fire protection unit on the table. "If he had known there was one outstanding unit that needed to be corrected, we'll never now. But if I had to guess, he damn well knew."

"He killed himself three days following the accident," Shirley said. "Wouldn't that suggest he had known?"

Allen shut his briefcase. "This is very fascinating guys. Before heading off I will only add one comment, our evidence can only verify one panel and one switch. No matter how compelling this theory may be, it doesn't account to a hill of beans if you can't prove it."

\* \* \*

"What time is it?" Emma asked.

Thomas rolled over to reach for his watch. "Ten past nine."

"Shit! I'm late."

"Late for what?" He snuggled against her. He kissed her shoulder, neck, and nibbled her ear lobe.

Emma felt his arousal pressing against her backside. "It seems you're ready for some action this morning."

"I've been ready for more than a week." He gave her a peck on the cheek. "Discovering you in your birthday suit was a pleasant surprise. It's been a week and I can't believe we still haven't consummated our reunion."

His willingness to get back together pleased her immensely. She pressed against him, thrilled by the thought of him inside her. She arched her back to position herself to ride along his manhood. Her vagina began to self-lubricate. Thomas felt the wetness upon him and pressed harder. Their slow and synchronised movements, the expectation they would join as one aroused her further. She felt Thomas run his hand along her hip and thigh, and then she bit her bottom lip.

"I can't wait any longer. Put it in," Emma moaned.

Thomas pulled away from her and reached into the nightstand for a prophylactic. He tore the package open and pulled the rubber out.

"Tom!" someone called. "Are you up?"

"It's my cousin," Thomas said.

"For fuck sakes," Emma said.

"Quiet, she can hear you."

"Tom, are you still in bed?" Odessa said while opening the bedroom door.

With determination, Emma walked with a slight limp toward the bathroom. "Good morning, Odessa," she said in an unwelcoming tone, her sights kept straight ahead.

"Good morning, honey." She turned to Thomas. "Did I come at a bad time?"

He picked up the wrapper off the bed and discreetly dropped it into the nightstand drawer. "Not at all, we simply slept in. We had a long night."

"What's with Emma's leg?"

"Give me a minute to get dressed and we'll chat." Thomas slowly slid out of the bed. Standing in the kitchen, he witnessed his cousin brewing coffee and cooking grilled cheese sandwiches. He gave her a hug and a peck on the cheek.

Odessa ran her hands up and down his arms. "You're looking good, cuz." Returning to the stove to flip the cheddar cheese sandwiched between two pieces of white bread. "I hope you don't mind me barging in."

"The door is always open for you. How's your mother doing?"

"She's doing mighty fine. If it wasn't for your support, life would have been different." She removed the sandwiches from the pan and placed them on a plate. "Sit down and eat. I get you some coffee."

"It's been a while," Thomas said. "I should drop by and visit."

"Mom would love that."

"You're working today?" he asked, noticing her uniform.

"Yes." She placed a cup of coffee beside Thomas. "I went in first thing this morning and came here after the morning departures."

"Is something wrong?"

"With mom and I, no." Odessa turned off the gas stove and placed the pan into the sink. "The reason I'm here concerns you. I called you Friday and yesterday." She poured herself a cup of coffee. "I wanted to let you know that the FBI came to the house and asked several questions about you."

"They asked about my past," he said, squirting ketchup on to the edge of his plate. "They questioned me yesterday at their DC office." He took a bite into his grilled cheese sandwich dipped in ketchup. "Mm, that's good."

"I can assure you that your secret is still safe. That's the main reason I came."

He put down his sandwich and looked out the kitchen window. His eyes welled up as he thought of his mother, who passed away while giving birth to him. His father, a falsely accused rapist, placed on trial, sentenced, and executed within an hour. The mob hung him from a tree in Florida's Mariana Courthouse Square on New Year's Day in 1930. The lynch mob agreed there was no way the mayor's daughter willfully had sex with a black man.

Odessa placed her hand on his. "Are you alright?"

Thomas sniffed. "Yeah, I suppose I am."

"Then what is it?"

"I'm not sure what our family back home thinks of me." He turned to her. "I am not ashamed to be black."

"Well, part black," Odessa said, chuckling. "Otherwise you would be the whitest black person I've ever known." They both laughed. "I know you had it rough growing up in Mariana. You were beaten up in the black community for being white, and then beaten up by the whites for being black. No matter which side of the tracks you stood on, it was a lose-lose situation."

"I wish I were black," he said.

"Sure you do," she said skeptically. "It's easy to say that when you can pass for a white person."

Emma stepped into the kitchen, embraced Odessa, and kissed her on the cheek. "Sorry for being a bitch earlier."

"That's all right." Odessa grinned. "You were just being yourself." She and Thomas laughed.

"You made breakfast. You're a gem."

"Dig in. It's probably cold by now."

Emma took a bite. "It's delicious."

The telephone rang and Thomas rose to answer it.

"Sweetie, what happened to your leg?" Odessa asked.

"I was shot at."

"If you don't want to say, I'll understand."

"No, that's what really..."

"You won't believe who was on the phone," Thomas interrupted. "Todd Bailey. He said the gang is all at his house."

"Good. I'll need to hurry and get there as well," Emma said. "I have the boys fixing up his place. It's coming along better than expected."

"Good for you," he said proudly. "I'm glad to see you have resurrected the day of reckoning tradition."

"Before I forget," Odessa said. "I need to tell you that Eva submitted her resignation."

# CHAPTER 26

**EATING CROW IS** the most difficult facet of life, Stephen Reese thought while he walked to Special Agent Sam Johnson's office. It would not be easy to tell the old man, his supposed mentor, that he was correct once again. As a matter of principle, Stephen would follow through and convey the obvious, taking his lumps like a good little soldier, and move on.

"Stephen! Come in," Sam said, seated at his desk. "Just finished reading your report and the information Thomas Wright provided is very good, very good indeed." He traced the edge of his desk pad. "He has given us a lead that will put a big dent in the case. Hell, he has saved us months."

"Okay, okay!" Stephen said. "I have to admit you were correct." He unbuttoned his jacket and pushed it aside to put his hands in his pant pockets. "I grant you the alias issue was a red herring and bringing Thomas on-board was the right thing to do."

"Yes, it was a good idea, wasn't it?" Sam said with glee. He put his hands together interlocking his fingers. "Not to worry, junior, admitting defeat will become easier with time."

"You think so?" Stephen said, expecting a belittling punchline.

"It's only easier when you have to do less of it." Sam chuckled. "I, on the other hand, don't put myself in the position to be wrong." His fledgling protégé gave him a blank look. He was pleased to see his boy in training toughening up. He had developed the needed poker face all FBI agents used while working in the field. Satisfied his trainee was slowly coming along he sprang to his feet. "Are you ready to catch these drug smuggling bastards?"

"Your presence will not be needed," Stephen said.

Sam smiled. "I don't think I heard you correctly."

Stephen, standing toe-to-toe with his mentor, replied, "I am the lead investigator and have determined you're not needed. There is nothing much to this lead. Questioning Carlos Ramirez is a menial task not worthy of your expertise."

"I like you, son." Sam returned to his desk. "You have balls. They're tiny, mind you, but you have balls nonetheless." He took a seat and put his feet on the desk. "I believe you're right. You don't need me." He grabbed his pipe and Zippo lighter off the desk. "It's best you go upstairs and advise our superiors you are ready to be on your own."

Stephen buttoned his jacket. "I think I'll do that. You don't have much time remaining with the bureau. I'm sure they can put you to better use." He knew the cocky old fuck was setting him up for a fall. He realized the safest path was to suck up his pride and wait out his mentor's remaining time. Then he would be free of this disparaging, derogatory, and judgmental asshole once and for all. "On the other hand, the two of us would cover more ground if you came along."

"Junior, that is the most intelligent thing you've said all week. Delighted to see you have come to your senses. Sit down, we'll need to strategize."

Stephen suppressed his pride and reluctantly inched toward the chair facing Sam. "Before questioning our lead, we might as well head over to ASE and get a sense of their operation and how Ramirez fits in."

"We can do that," Sam said. "But we can't let on that he is a person of interest. Ramirez is the key that will lead us to other contacts and show us the routing of the drugs from the airports to the streets."

"I see your point. Any mention of Ramirez may trigger them to hunker down and halt operations," Stephen agreed.

"We'll use the bait and switch technique to get our foot through the door and retrieve the needed evidence."

"That will be a little tricky. We don't know who we are dealing with and there's too much at stake to openly sniff around. It's too risky. I suggest cloak and dagger."

"At this stage of the game the cloak and dagger method needs too much prep work. Sending undercover FBI agents to infiltrate ASE would take too much time. We will use the Virginia Airlines crash to set the bait, and once inside, we'll switch our focus to the smuggling ring."

"That may work. I'm sure they will be just as eager to discover the cause of the crash, and in turn, help us in our investigation."

Sam leaned back in his chair. "If I were running an organization that manufactures, overhauls, and repairs aircraft components to serve as a front to a multibillion dollar drug supply chain, would I give a damn about Virginia Airlines crash?"

"You suspect their cooperation would be half assed at best."

Sam puffed on his pipe. He felt something gnawing at him. "They have no reason to cooperate unless they have a vested interest. Obtaining a search warrant will be counterproductive. It will cause them to clam up and shred all relevant documents."

"So what do you suggest?" Stephen asked.

"In collaboration with the FAA, we'll get an injunction to halt ASE's operations altogether. Stopping their aviation activities will impact their drug smuggling business. Their inability to move their merchandise will force their hand. They will have no choice but to cooperate."

Stephen was taken aback. "Don't you think that is a bit extreme? They will question our justification."

"You're giving them too much credit," Sam replied. "They will have no reason to suspect our investigation into the Virginia Airlines crash, and Michael Hall and their aircraft components are all related to their smuggling ring."

"Under those pretences," Stephen said, "ASE will trip over themselves to assist us."

\* \* \*

The work was progressing well on Todd Bailey's home. Emma's boys completed the house exterior in record time. They applied two coats of white paint and painted the trim around the windows and doors in evergreen. Rusting farming equipment once scattered throughout the property was stored in the barn. The four acres surrounding the house manicured to perfection. Emma thought it gave the property a picturesque look.

Approaching the driveway, she noticed there were more Virginia Airlines employees. This explained why so much work been accomplished ahead of schedule. The day of reckoning had surpassed all expectations. Able-bodied people volunteering their time to help veterans were an extraordinary sight to see. She parked her pickup truck alongside the dozen other vehicles lined up in front of the farmhouse.

"I called you hours ago," Todd said from the front porch. "What took you so long?"

"Good afternoon, Todd," Emma said exiting her truck. She left the crutches behind.

"I have been waiting all morning for you to arrive." His agitation reduced as he watched her limp toward the steps. "I have something to show you."

Emma leaned over and gave him a kiss on the forehead. "The swelling went down I see."

"A bag of ice helped." He gazed at her wrapped leg. "How's your leg?"

"It's a little sore but not that bad. I'll live. Sorry for being late. I should have mentioned I needed to drop by my office. I am taking part in the bird strike committee Olivia Cooper..."

"Virginia Airlines' president?" Todd said.

"Yes, that's right. She is sponsoring a program on how best to mitigate wildlife hazards at our airports. The FAA was present and told us of their efforts over the past decade."

"And what have they done?" Todd asked. "The only way to avoid birds at an airport is to make it less attractive."

"You should be part of the committee," she said. "That was one of the items talked about at great lengths."

"Emma," Diego called. "Going for a late lunch, see you when I return."

She gestured her acknowledgement with a thumbs up. Turning to Todd, she said, "So what do you have to show me?"

Todd's face lit up. "It's waiting at the falcon's mew." He patted his leg. "Sit on my lap, I'll take you there."

"That won't be necessary. I'm able to walk the distance." Todd's enthusiasm puzzled her. "Can it wait until I chat with the my crew?"

"Once you see it, you'll understand." He pushed the joystick forward, propelling his wheel chair down the ramp and onto to a path.

When they arrived, he unlocked the mew, "Ladies first."

"What are you up to?" Emma asked. He grinned.

She heard bells ringing and looked up to see two peregrine falcons. A female, obvious by its larger size, stood next to Thunder, Todd's male falcon.

He watched her expression. "Are you pleased?"

"I'm ecstatic. How did you manage to buy another?"

"She wasn't bought; this is the same peregrine living on Turk mountain. The bird you've seen flying around these parts."

"How on earth were you able to catch her?"

"She is a frequent visitor," Todd said. "When she first appeared she was on the brink of dying of starvation. I suppose she was attracted to my mews because of Thunder. I fed and took care of her for several weeks and released her back to the wild." Todd put on his leather glove and entered the cage.

"Why haven't you mentioned this before?"

"She hasn't been around for weeks. I didn't want to mention it in case she didn't come back," Todd said, approaching the peregrine. "I weighed her last night, she's slightly under nourished."

The peregrine hopped from the four-foot tall perch on to Todd's gloved hand. Her wings spread and flapped slightly to balance herself and she immediately reached for and tore at the meat held in his hand.

"She is magnificent," Emma said.

"If you're serious about falconry, she can be yours. You will need a license and I can be your sponsor. We can keep her here and I will provide you with the necessary training. All you need to decide is if you are willing to put in the time every day for as long as you have her."

"I am interested." She limped into the cage and shut the enclosure door behind her. "I am definitely committed to do what it takes, but are you sure you're up to it?"

"It's the least I can do," Todd replied, placing the peregrine back on the perch. "It's not just about what you and your team have done around the house." He glanced at her bandaged leg. "Well, I appreciate y'all entering my life and all."

"Our bond does not end at the battlefield."

"Before we start with the training." He changed the topic. "You need to do something. It's important."

"And what would that be?"

"You'll need to decide on a name for this lovely bird."

"Once I become skillful in falconry, I intend to bring her to the airport," she said. "To ensure a bird strike will never take another aircraft down. She will serve as a scarecrow." She moved closer, keeping a safe distance from her newly acquired falcon. "I suppose Scarecrow is as a good name as any."

"She will serve your purposes well and will do more than scare birds away. Some she will kill and feed on."

"A killer scarecrow." Emma winced.

"What's the matter?" Todd asked.

"I hadn't thought about that."

"Utilizing an apex predator will solve your problem. Scarecrow will keep birds away from the flight paths."

"But imagine kids watching her fly, then seeing her feasting on live prey. What message will that convey to the public?"

"And how would that be worse than witnessing airplanes fall out of the sky?" He laughed. "Watching a falcon eat will not instill a fear of flying in your paying passengers. It's life."

# CHAPTER 27

"**IS THAT YOU,** Aiden?" Jackie, his childhood sweetheart and wife of twenty-six years said. "Dinner will be ready in just a minute."

He joined her in the dining room, towering over his 5'2" spouse. In typical fashion, she was wearing a formal evening gown with an apron draped around her neck and tied off at her waist. Aiden leaned over to give her the customary peck on the lips. "What's for dinner?"

"Meat loaf, it's been such a long time so I thought I would try a new recipe. You know how much Peter loves his meat loaf."

"Our son is a sick puppy."

"Aiden! Don't say that." She tapped him on the arm. "I thought I would prepare his favorite dish to pick him up. He hasn't been himself since you told him he can't work with you at ASE."

"It's just temporary until the FAA completes their investigation." He watched her place a bowl of mashed potatoes and a plate of string beans on the table. "We already discussed this. I prefer not to rehash why I'm keeping Peter at home for the next several months."

While removing her apron she inventoried the table and realized she had forgotten the napkins. "Honestly, I don't know what has gotten into Cecil." She brought the napkins from the kitchen. "How on earth Peter can be seen as detrimental to the regulatory authorities, I'll never know."

Aiden was not in the mood to argue. He had raised the same point to Cecil, to no avail. "I'll get Peter," he said and vanished up the staircase.

Jackie checked her hair in the gold framed mirror, a French nineteenth century country style piece she and Aiden purchased at an antique shop in Pennsylvania.

"He's not in his room," Aiden said. "Is he out back?"

"Sorry honey, I forgot to mention he went next door to show Blake his new comic book." She pulled his chair away from the head of the table. "You get started while I go get him. I'll only be a minute."

"Don't be silly. I can wait. Anyway, it's Peter's turn to say grace." He embraced his wife, pressing his cheek next to hers. "And I can't wait to hear what he has to be thankful for today."

She tightened her embrace. "Welcome back."

"Back? Oh, have I been that transparent?"

She pulled away from him to look into his eyes. "You haven't been yourself since your meeting with Cecil at the country club. You are yourself again, so can I presume all is well between you two?"

"As a matter of fact, I haven't spoken to him all week." He put his hands on her shoulders. "His preoccupation with a missing package has kept him away from my office. It doesn't get any better than that."

"Do I need to worry why you've been spending every night in your den alone?"

He kissed her on the forehead. "Cecil was just being Cecil. He likes to hear himself speak."

"In other words, it was an idle threat? Peter's safety is not in jeopardy?"

"My only regret is that I brought it up to you."

"Of course you should have brought this to me."

"Hush," he said, holding his forefinger lightly against her lips. "I'm not saying we should keep secrets. I'm just saying I should have remembered Cecil's inability to deal with high-pressure situations."

"Over complicate and overcompensate."

"Something like that."

"So in the words of Franklin D. Roosevelt, there is nothing to fear but fear itself," Jackie said.

Aiden felt her change as she started toward the front door. "Jackie!"

"I need to get Peter before the food gets cold," she said.

"Is everything okay?"

"I didn't think you would lie to me," she said, putting on her white shoes.

"I have no idea what has brought this on." He was perplexed, struggling to grasp what caused her to question his integrity. His efforts to instill confidence and assure everything would be fine had backfired in a split second.

"Whatever your reasons are for doing so, I will trust you. I'm not happy about it but I'm sure you will fill me in when you're ready."

The front entrance door flew open and Peter frantically rushed into the house. "Mommy, Mommy! Come quick!"

"Calm down, Peter. What's the matter?" Jackie asked.

"Blake needs you. He's hurt bad."

"Tell me where he is."

He pointed at Bank Street. "Over there."

Jackie bolted out the door and noticed Blake, the neighbor's son, lying on the road. She rushed to his side.

"What happened, son?" Aiden asked, putting his arm around Peter's shoulder to comfort him.

"A car hit him. Blake pushed me and a car hit him and rode over him."

"Aiden, call an ambulance," Jackie yelled. She knelt on the road next to the body. She rolled him on his back to administer CPR, her hands positioned one on top of the other to begin the chest compressions. The palm of her hand felt the contour of a crushed rib cage.

Bones creaked and crackled as she pushed down hard and fast on his chest. Tears roll down her face, knowing it was futile. Completing the first round of chest compressions, Jackie moved in to fill his lungs with air.

Reaching for his nose, she realized the true severity of the head trauma. Blake's nose was completely flattened, his lower jaw was detached, and a cracked skull exposed his brain.

As the neighbors and on lookers gathered around, Nellie Smith knelt down with her. She put her head on her son's chest and sobbed quietly.

Aiden told his son to go to his room and stay there. Standing on the veranda, he watched the paramedics' failed attempt to break through the crowd with their stretcher in tow. The neighbors formed a tight circle huddled around the boy, joined hand in hand, crying. He realized it could only mean one thing. The accident was fatal.

He dabbed the sweat from his brow and upper lip with a handkerchief. Tucking the handkerchief back into his shirt pocket, he replayed Peter's words: Blake pushed me and a car hit him. He knew the neighbor's boy had saved his son's life.

The first police cruiser to arrive radioed at once for backup to help with crowd control. He helped the paramedics reach the body.

Jackie noticed their presence and step aside. Nellie was not so accommodating and put the paramedics in a precarious situation. The police officer intervened with gentle persistence and broke Nellie's grip on her boy. Rachael, a neighbor living across the road, whisked the sobbing mother to her home. It was clear the injuries were fatal. Nothing could be done to save the boy. The trauma had killed him instantly.

Peter peeked out the open door. His father blocked his line of sight and he couldn't see his friend. "How's Blake, Dad?"

"Get back inside," Aiden said, escorting him away from the doorway. "Son, be a good boy and go back to your room please."

"Why won't you tell me how Blake is doing? Everything is a secret with you. I want to know," he said, stomping his feet.

Jackie returned to the house and barged past her husband and son. She ran up the staircase and locked herself in the bedroom.

"Blake is hurt," Peter guessed, shaking his head. "He must be hurt bad."

"You may be right."

"Mommy's crying."

Leading his son back to his room, he said, "Stay in your bedroom." Then he whispered the words he hoped he would never have to follow through on. "I will let you know how Blake is doing very soon."

"Okay, Dad."

Jackie was on the bed with her back to the door.

He gave Jackie her space but sat on the other side of the bed. He patiently waited for her to come to terms. He wanted to be near when she was ready to talk.

Twenty minutes had passed when she muttered, "He's dead."

"I guessed it." He sighed. "He was a good boy."

"There was nothing that could have been done." She wiped the tears with her fingertips. "Nellie said it was a black Cadillac. It looked like the same vehicle Cecil drives around in."

"Did she get a glimpse of the person driving the car?"

"No. It happened all too fast she also didn't get a chance to notice the license plate."

This was no accident, he realized. Aiden knew that his sole priority was to protect his family. He went into the walk-in closet to retrieve several suitcases. He opened it on the bed and started filling it with clothes. He was giving in to Cecil's demands, but not by choice. He would only hope it was not too late to take his son as far away as possible.

"What are you doing?" Jackie asked. She watched her husband grab outfits off the rack she hadn't worn in years.

"You need to take Peter away from here and we're not going to argue about it."

"This wasn't an accident, was it?"

Aiden paused. "I'm not sure." His eyes well up and the strength drained from his arms, causing Jackie's clothes to fall to the floor. Speechless, he covered his face and cried inconsolably.

Jackie rushed to him. "We'll go to the police," she whispered.

He shook his head.

"Better yet, we'll go to the FBI and tell them everything. We tell them what Cecil and his Columbian friends have been up to."

Aiden nudged her away and sat on the edge of the bed.

"They will protect us for our testimony and we can finally be rid of them and get our lives back."

"We would be signing our death warrants," Aiden said. "These people play for keeps. They will never let up and the price they will put on our heads will guarantee it."

She sat next to him on the bed. "It won't have to be that way," she said. "The FBI will give us new identities, a home, and a life far from here. It wouldn't be perfect but we can make the best of it."

He wrapped his hands around hers. "I'm not going to let us fall on our sword because of Cecil. We can't leave behind a life we have worked so hard to build for each other. There will be a way to deal with Cecil, but to do so, I can't be worrying about you two."

Jackie did not ask for specifics nor did she wish to press for clarification. Recognizing he had always been a good provider amid all the difficulties they had endured through the years, she trusted his good judgment. Their lips joined into a long and heartfelt kiss, and then slowly changed into heavy petting. She pulled back, "That can wait. We have too much to do if we plan to send Peter away."

"You're right," he said. "I'll help you finish your packing and get to work on Peter's belongings."

"Oh no. I'm not going anywhere."

"You need to go. Who else will watch over Peter?"

"I'm sure my sister would love to have him. She can show him around Paris."

"I would prefer he stays with your aunt in Dublin."

"And what's wrong with my sister?" she asked.

"You must admit, she is a little batty," he said. "But that's not the reason."

"I'm waiting." She folded her arms and smiled.

"Too many people are familiar with your sister's whereabouts in France. However, it's not common knowledge your aunt had just moved back home to Dublin. He'd be safe there with her."

"Okay. I'll call and talk to her about it."

# CHAPTER 28

**AUGUST 29, TWELVE** days following Virginia Airline's crash. The activity at the Charlottesville Airport was as normal as could be, Cecil Longhorn thought while strolling through the terminal. He watched passengers forming the first of a series of lineups they would endure before they reached their destination.

As he approached the Virginia Airlines counter, an announcement sounded over the speakers that the flight to Miami was ready to board. Cecil walked past the sixty-three passengers waiting to be served and heading to the front of the line. He startled the new ticket agent. "May I please have my ticket?"

"Excuse me," she said, puzzled with his boldness. "Sir, you will need to go to the back of the line."

He waved the passengers away from the counter and turned to the agent. He leaned slightly forward to look at her nametag. "Joy, is it?" He flashed his credentials. "Joy, my name is Cecil Longhorn. You should have a ticket waiting for me."

She noticed the Virginia Airlines company ID card reading Board of Directors in large letters. "I'm sorry, sir," she said. Opening the bottom drawer, she leafed through an accordion folder. "There is no ticket here for you. Are you sure your flight leaves today?"

"Of course. What kind of question is that? Where is your supervisor?"

"My supervisor is not on shift however, my manager Odessa had just stepped away and should be returning soon," she said without lifting her head to face him. For good measure, Joy checked every drawer and found an envelope with the words 'Dick Head' written in red ink. Her instinct to look inside was correct. "I found your ticket, sir."

She kept the envelope close to her chest to conceal the inappropriate words. Before she had an opportunity to extract the ticket and dispose of the envelope, Cecil snatched it from her.

With a raised eyebrow, he read the words then slowly folded the envelope and placed it in his jacket pocket. "Little lady, you are fortunate I have an important engagement in Miami."

"Are we boarding?" a passenger asked.

"What's the holdup?" another said.

Joy put on a brave face as she glanced at the passengers. "Your ticket please," she asked Cecil, holding out her hand.

"I will deal with you later," he said.

She removed the coupon for the flight from Charlottesville to Miami. The remaining portion of the ticket she returned it to him.

Odessa arrived at the counter at gate three. "Why haven't we started boarding the passengers?" she asked. Joy gestured with her eyes to the person standing next to her. Recognizing him, no explanation was needed since she was aware of his character and disruptive tendencies. "Hello, Mister Longhorn. How may I help you?"

"He is boarding the flight now," Joy said.

He knew tangling with Odessa was pointless. She was in Olivia's good graces and her past insolence had gone unchecked. With a disappointed shake of his head, he said, "I don't know what kind of operation you are running here. It's a wonder our airline makes any money." He walked through the open door leading to his airplane.

"Don't worry about him," Odessa said. "Put on your happy face and let's get these passengers boarded quickly."

* * *

Virginia Airline's Fairlane aircraft, model VA980, landed on runway nine and taxied on to the apron at Miami International Airport. The pilots followed the yellow guidelines as it maneuvered toward concourse three, passing parked aircraft belonging to Eastern, Air Florida, National, and Pan Am Airlines.

Cecil stepped out of the aircraft and noticed a man dressed in a black suit and sunglasses leaning against a limousine. He held a sign with Cecil's name on it. "Who sent you here?"

"Cecil Longhorn?"

"Yes," Cecil replied. "This must be a mistake. I have my own driver waiting on the arrival level."

"It's no mistake," he said, opening the rear limo door. He unbuttoned his jacket and revealed a holstered handgun. "Mister Berra insisted that I drive you to the helipad."

"Take off your damn glasses when you're speaking to me," Cecil said. "And since when do limo drivers carry guns?" He held up his hand. "Don't bother to explain. As I mentioned, I have my own means of transportation and I won't be needing you."

"Before you walk away, Mister Longhorn, you'll need to see this," the driver said. He pulled a small navy blue velvet pouch from his pocket.

Cecil loosened the golden drawstring and emptied the content on to his palm. It was Juan Pablo Berra's most treasured possession, an eighteen-carat ring, an heirloom with his family's coat of arms. He returned it into the pouch.

"Mister Berra said you would understand and cooperate." He held the door open and waited for his reluctant passenger.

The driver seated behind the steering wheel placed an amber beacon on the roof above his head and plugged its cord into the cigarette lighter. They remained airside, following the vehicle guidelines on the apron that lead to a service road. It ran parallel along alpha taxiway to the north end of the airport.

"This is convenient," Cecil said, as they approached the helipad.

"Aircraft owners' has its privileges." The limo driver was also the helicopter pilot. They boarded the Bell 47. "Please put on your seat belt."

Cecil reached for both ends of the seat belt and then pulled on the strap. "Before you start up this contraption, what is your name?"

"Paulo," he replied. "Put this on."

Cecil placed the Davidson Clark headset on as he watched the kid, who was half his age, run through the checklist. "I don't understand why we need to fly to Key Biscayne. We would be halfway there by now if we had gone by car."

Paulo pressed the start button and the Lycoming engine came to life. The main rotor blades started to spin as the engine's RPM passed through 1,600 RPM. He held the throttle at 2,400 RPM to allow engine oil and cylinder temperature to rise.

Cecil grabbed Paulo's right arm. "I asked you a question."

With his free hand, Paulo tapped his headset and reached to the center console to turn on the intercom system. Cecil heard static and Paulo's voice. "Can you hear me now? Sit back and relax. It won't be long."

Cecil released his grip to allow the pilot to continue with his pre-flight checks. He looked through the bubble dome surrounding the cockpit and wondered what was in store for him. Juan Pablo was deeply concerned about the shipment of cocaine hidden in one of the aircraft tires placed in 641's cargo compartment. Its discovery by the FBI, FAA, or the NTSB while investigating the crash would be problematic. Fortunately, he thought, no one was the wiser. No one noticed the weight difference between tires. With great persistence, he persuaded the FBI to release them to ASE for economic reasons. The cocaine returned kept the smuggling secret intact and Juan Pablo's anxiety in check.

The helicopter lifted and in minutes cruised a thousand feet above the ground. They flew by Key Biscayne on an eastward heading into the Atlantic Ocean. Sixty-four nautical miles off the coast of Florida, the helicopter descended to a helipad on board a Canadian built 265-foot customized yacht. Paulo hovered two feet above the moving ship before planting the helicopter firmly on the pad.

"Welcome, Cecil," Juan Pablo said when he climbed out. He signalled him to join the group on the upper deck.

Cecil gave the velvet pouch to its rightful owner. "It worked as you knew it would."

"Of course it did." Juan Pablo smiled and embraced Cecil. "Those FBI pricks have been watching me like a hawk. The only way I can get all of us together is to fly everyone on board."

"Who are these people?" Cecil asked.

"We will not refer to anyone by name," Juan Pablo replied. "Put this on."

Cecil received a small white badge with the number six written on it. Juan Pablo pinned a similar badge on his jacket's lapel with the number nine.

"You've got to be kidding. There's no one around for miles," Cecil said, pointing to the ocean. "What's the point?"

"Everyone, gather around in a tight circle." Juan Pablo motioned everyone into a huddle with himself crouched in the center. "The walls have ears," he began. "I made certain we had at least one safe haven onboard this ship, and we're standing in it. Though the aft upper deck is clean, always, and I mean always, exercise extreme care."

A stout Cuban man in his forties with black curly hair sported a badge with the number two. He whispered, "If you know the ship is bugged, why not take care of it? We are miles away from shore and it would be a shame we have come all this way for nothing."

"I share the same concern," Cecil said. "The issue before us is how we will conduct a productive meeting with everyone listening in."

"Number two and six," a tall Englishman said. Dressed all in white from his shoes to his cap, and wore a four-striped epaulet on either shoulder. "As the new inductees to the Banda de Víboras, you should be speaking less and listening more." He turned to the group. "We all know the feds love to be a fly on the wall and as long as they can listen in on us, they will keep their distance."

"As you have figured out," Juan Pablo said, "this is our capitán. As the commanding officer of this ship, he will be referred to as Number One."

"Everyone, please follow me," the captain said. He led the group to the ladder leading down a flight of steps to the top deck. "Gentleman, you can speak freely on the main deck. The listening devices Mister Berra mentioned, excuse me, I meant mentioned by Number Nine, are in the staterooms and salons throughout the ship."

"Capitán, please tell everyone where we are standing," Juan Pablo said.

The captain realized he was standing near the emergency designated area. "Very good. This rectangle area on the deck highlighted in white hash lines is where we gather during an emergency. You'll notice we have eight life rafts that are more than enough for the twenty-six crew members on board and yourselves to safely evacuate." He leaned against the bulwark.

"For the sake of safety," Juan Pablo said, "Let's sound the alarm so our guests may be familiar and know what to expect."

The captain noticed Juan Pablo was being condescending. He pushed it out of his mind while removing the portable two-way radio clipped to his waist. "Captain to bridge," he called, turning to face the ocean.

"First mate here, Captain."

"Sound the general alarm," he said. "This is a drill. I repeat, this is only a drill"

"Understood, sir."

Returning his sights to the group, he stared down a two and a half inch barrel of a Smith & Wesson Model 19 revolver. Juan Pablo pointed it directly at the captain's face with the hammer cocked.

"What's the meaning of this?" the captain demanded.

"You English, always thinking you're better than everyone else. Believing people with more skin pigmentation or speaking another language does not match the superior British intellect."

"I have no idea what you are referring to. And I resent you holding a gun to my head."

The alarm began and he yelled to be heard. "I must admit, of all the people, I never would have thought you would betray me."

The captain signaled no with his head.

The extended blast sounded. "I know you are working with the feds you fuck," said Juan. He fired his 357 magnum. The bullet entered the captain's left cheek and forced the skull and brain fragments rearward as it exited. He extended his arm to stop the body leaning toward him while the other hand grabbed the captain's waist belt. In one sweeping motion, he lifted the body and tossed it into the water.

Paulo stepped forward. "I'll advise the first mate we have taken care of the rat."

"Wait!" Juan Pablo said. He reached into his pocket and extracted two epaulets of a captain's four-bar designator. "Congratulate the first mate on his promotion."

"He has been waiting a long time for this," Paulo smiled.

"Tell your brother he deserves it and if he fucks up, he too will be swimming with the fishes."

"Yes uncle, I will let him know," Paulo replied.

"Gentlemen, I'm sorry you had to witness this," Juan Pablo said. Noticing the blood on his left hand, he wiped it on his white shirt. The group watched respectively and without uttering a word. "We have been watching him for several months. If he spent more time managing the affairs of the ship, he would have known we swept for bugs every time the vessel is boarded." The bloodstained shirt annoyed him, a reminder of a trusted friend gone rogue. He removed it and threw it on the deck.

"After all this, there are no bugs?" asked Number Two.

Cecil elbowed him in the ribs and Juan Pablo ignored him.

"Dinner will be served in five hours," Juan Pablo said. "Unfortunately, there is an urgent matter to which I need to attend and I suggest you take this opportunity to rest up. We will reconvene in the salon for the best European cuisine and wines money can buy." He tucked his revolver into his pants. "There is a great deal to discuss.

Given that our time together is limited, we will work through the night if need be."

# CHAPTER 29

**GAZING OUT OF** his stateroom window, Cecil Longhorn noticed an island barely visible on the horizon. He figured it was Andros Island, Bahamas largest and closest island off the coast of United States. He would do almost anything to switch places, to stand on the island looking out at the ship rather than being confined. Pacing back and forth along the window, the captain's murder weighed heavily on his mind.

Regardless of the captain's long-standing association with the Band of Vipers, he had done wrong against an unwritten set of rules. It prompted Juan Pablo Berra to fire his gun at the captain's face and no one flinched when the bullet decimated the back of his head. Nausea swept over Cecil. His eyes fixated on the deck flooring to fight the inclination to vomit.

Looking out of his cabin window, he muttered, "How did I get myself into this mess?" Cecil banged his head repeatedly against the glass.

He took a deep breath and recalled how his association with the drug cartel began. It started when a stranger walked into his office at Longhorn Investment Brokerage one late evening. The stranger introduced himself as Juan Pablo Berra, a financial lawyer practicing in the state of New York, serving as a representative to investors situated in Latin American countries. Carrying a large brown paper bag, he placed the contents on to the desk.

"I have the first deposit," Juan Pablo said. Ten piles of US bills were stacked neatly side by side. He picked up one stack. "You're reputation is well-known among those in prominent positions. They say you are a smart investor, a man who can be trusted, and who does not ask questions." He placed his elbows on the desk and twirled the one-hundred thousand dollar bundle. "Am I wrong?"

"Discretion is the foundation my organization was built on," Cecil replied. "Trust instills confidence and to that, I can assure you our services provide the highest standards and impenetrable levels of secrecy. That means..."

"Yes, yes, it comes at a great cost. Here's one million dollars, our first installment. Show us what you can do."

That was the day. A fifteen percent money-laundering fee was all it took to entice Cecil. No documents or contracts were signed, just a handshake to seal the deal. There was no morality dilemma to overcome because Cecil is simply the money guy, a distinction that has become part of his ideology to justify his participation with organized crime.

It was purely business. Legitimizing dirty money was worth the low risk for a quick and high profit gain. He had done the same for large legitimate businesses that continually sought new and innovative ways to evade paying taxes. The goal was to setup the offshore banking accounts and shell companies while assuring no paper trail existed to alert the Internal Revenue Service and other government agencies.

He achieved the objective in ninety days and incrementally tested the money-laundering infrastructure with each expansion phase. As confidence increased, Juan Pablo, through his surrogates, doubled and tripled both the frequency and quantity of dirty money pushed through the system. The tens of thousands of dollars arriving at Cecil's office each day raised some eyebrows, so he developed a system he called the Longhorn Charitable Drop Boxes.

Cecil provided Charlottesville's residents with a year-round opportunity to donate their clothing at one convenient location, and it would then be dispersed to various charities. It had proven advantageous as a money drop off box. Funds inconspicuously hidden in the clothing, garbage bags, and duct-taped boxes masquerading as donations were dropped off. For added security, the money laundering crew replaced the metal box with another on a regular basis rather than empty it on site. The contents were then removed off-site within the confines of a secure facility.

Seduced by large quantities of funds and the resultant commissions, walking away became difficult for Cecil. The enabling factor was the ridiculous ease of earning an outrageous amount of money. He became addicted to money.

Entering 1964, slightly more than a year after it began, the cash flow bottlenecked the system's efficiency. Preserving irregular transaction amounts to simulate actual business activities resulted in millions of dollars stockpiled in various warehouses.

To take money laundering to the next level, he needed a paradigm shift. Besides using shell companies, it would require the purchase of legitimate companies in the service sector. A small company in a specialized industry would have the added benefit of channeling more funds disguised as start-up, organizational growth, and research and development costs.

Cecil knew one investor, Aiden Lynch, for whom he had managed a financial portfolio for years. Aiden owned and operated a company out of his converted barn. His business focused on overhauling and repairing electrical components for transport and private airplanes. It also provided some aeronautical engineering services. Cecil decided it was an excellent prospect to charge ridiculously high prices to expedite the transfer of a large amount of funds by undetectable methods.

Glancing at the palm trees barely visible on the distant island, the blue hue reminded him of the pine trees at his bed and breakfast property. It was situated south of Front Royal, Virginia, on a historic property he once owned along the Shenandoah River. Finding himself in his current predicament, he remembered the day he spent with Aiden in April of 1964.

Stepping away from his car, Aiden had marveled at the landscape surrounding the bed and breakfast. "This is a beautiful stretch of land you have here."

"Don't I know it," Cecil replied with a smirk. "This place sells itself. It draws people in from all over the nation." He put his hands on his hips and looked toward the river, "I don't get out here often enough. The hustle and bustle of tourists gets old."

"Are Monday's typically slow?" Aiden asked, noticing they were the only ones present.

"Don't be fooled," Cecil replied, "During the summer months, Monday's are just as busy. I just made sure we had the place all to ourselves." The wind picked up as the sky darkened and he noticed the clouds had moved in fast. "A storm is moving in, we should head inside."

Stepping into the foyer, the silk Persian rug captured Aiden's attention. He suspected it was one of the original pieces belonging to the old house. The brick house was painted all in white with red shutters and a tin roof. Construction began in 1777, but it was halted that same year when the tradesman departed to enlist in the Virginia County Militia. Completed in 1784, a year after the American Revolutionary War ended, it was appropriately named The Freedom House. The modest home had undergone several renovations and expansions through the decades to its present grandeur.

A stout handsome woman draped in an apron pushed her way through the kitchen door. "I wondered when you would be arriving," Abigail Winnfield said. "Lunch will be ready shortly."

"Abigail, this is Mister Lynch," Cecil said. "He will be joining me today."

"I will lay a second place setting," she replied, returning to the kitchen.

Cecil led Aiden into the conservatory, the largest room in the house. They took a seat at one of the ten tables Abigail had prepared.

"I must confess," Aiden said, breaking the silence, "I was surprised when you asked me to meet you here. I know how much this place means to you."

Abigail arrived with the second place setting. "It won't be long, just another ten minutes."

"That's fine," Cecil replied. He waited for her to leave then glanced at Aiden, "I have a business proposition for you."

"It must be serious for you to wine and dine me."

"How would you like to see your business grow tenfold? You could move the business out of your barn into a facility near the airport with your competitors."

"I started off in my garage and growing the business has been a challenge," Aiden said. "Mind you, when TWA threw some business my way, I quickly converted the barn. A five-thousand square foot overhaul facility to meet the initial contract with the expectation to handle future growth." He shrugged and grinned. "You can probably guess there was no extra work sent our way. It is a competitive market and I am only using a fraction of my facility. What do you know that I don't?"

"I have a new associate eager to have his clients invest in the U.S. and your business perfectly meets their criteria," Cecil said.

"If their intent is to lose money, they have come to the right industry," Aiden said, laughing. "However, if your associate is serious, and I mean really serious, they have to corner the market."

Cecil could not convey the true intent was to launder money and not to literally grow the business. Working with Aiden closely on his financial portfolio had shown him to be a prudent and scrupulous investor. Yet, he would not shy away from questionable or possibly illegal investments if packaged correctly. Those types of investments had been rare. Nonetheless, Aiden focused on self-preservation, not concerned if the business activity is legal or not. He would never rig a horse race, but had no difficulty profiting from it. "What do you recommend?"

"Your investor should buy into an airline," Aiden said.

"And what will that do?"

Aiden leaned forward. "Owning part of an airline will guarantee Aircraft Systems and Electronics receives the needed contracts to grow. This would break the airline's unfounded patronage to maintenance, repair, and overhaul companies doing no one any favors but themselves. If the volume of parts passing through my facility remains high and consistent, we can easily keep our operating costs low and reflected in our pricing with excellent profit margins to boot."

"I believe your suggestion is worth pursuing," Cecil said. "Money is not an issue."

"I hope you're hungry, gentlemen," Abigail said, wheeling the food cart into the conservatory. "Mister Longhorn, you haven't asked but I brought a bottle of red wine for your meal."

"You read my mind." Cecil smiled.

"If there's nothing else," Abigail said, as she removed her apron, "I will be on my way." She put the folded apron on the cart. "Place the dishes on the food cart. I will take care of them in the morning."

"Abigail, as always, everything is perfect. Thank you," Cecil said.

With a slight bow, she left.

"Steak, lobster tail, mashed potato, asparagus, and salad, wow!" Aiden said. "This is very elaborate. Is there something more to this? I'm not complaining but we could have done this at your office. What are you not telling me?"

Cecil moved away from the cabin window and stepped to the stateroom's desk. Remembering that was not the day Aiden learned of the drug cartel's money-laundering scheme. That would happen later. However, Aiden's recommendation to buy into an airline worked fabulously. Juan Pablo's financiers made Cecil's ability to buy into Virginia Airlines possible and the required contracts awarded to ASE. Everything worked to plan, and yet Cecil found himself on this dreadful ship nine years later while Aiden, his sidekick, was safe on the mainland. He would have preferred to be anonymous, inconspicuously working behind the scene as the money guy.

He took a stroll on the main deck. The sea air and light breeze helped him regain his wits and suppress the paranoia. The stout Cuban standing by the bow of the ship caught his eye. He looked forward to human interaction.

The Cuban man extended his hand and introduced himself, "My name is Hugo Lopez." He removed the numbered badge. "I guess I won't be needing this anymore." He tossed it into the ocean.

"I am Cecil Longhorn."

"Longhorn?" He cupped his crotch and chuckled. "Are you bragging?"

Cecil ignored the gesture. "I come from a long line of Texan cattleman. My great great grand pappy changed our family name to the commodity that made us rich."

"Very good," Hugo said, smiling. "So that means you are hung like the rest of us." Cecil did not share in his humor. "You are a serious man, a man that does not say much." He puffed on his cigar. "You're the money guy, am I right?"

Cecil lowered his head to look him in the eye. "A hit man, I'm not."

"I noticed your reaction during the captain's sudden end," Hugo said. "Your face must have turned three shades of green. Watching someone murdered in cold blood and up close is nothing for us working in the trenches. You, on the other hand, I can only assume work in the ivory tower cooking the books all day."

"Not exactly," Cecil said. "But in a roundabout way, yes, I am the money guy."

"I knew it!" Hugo replied enthusiastically. He sucked on his cigar.

A Hughes helicopter, blue in color with a sleek aeronautic design and modern look, approached the ship and entered a circular flight path. As it flew by the bow where Cecil and Hugo stood, they noticed the pilot was alone. The bottom-side of the whirling aircraft's fuselage had three yellow letters in bold: FBI.

"What the hell?" Cecil said.

"Not to worry," Hugo said. "That's Juan Pablo's ace in the hole and the last guest joining us today."

A guard carrying a machine gun with its strap slung over his shoulder approached the two standing by the bow of the ship. He stopped to wave at the pilot and to Cecil's amazement, the pilot waved back.

"I'll be damned," Cecil muttered.

"Everyone is asked to assemble in the salon in fifteen minutes," the guard said.

"What is this about?" Hugo asked.

"Mister Berra is distraught over President Ford's unconditional pardon of Richard Nixon."

Hugo faced Cecil. "Do you find this fucker funny?" He turned to face the guard. "Do you think you're fucking funny? Do you want me to shove that pussy gun of yours up your fucking ass? Now that would be something to laugh at."

"Easy does it," Cecil said. "No use yelling at the help. It's only sarcasm."

"Is that what you call it? Step aside, Cecil, and watch how easy I will bend this fucking guy into a pretzel."

The guard held his M16 assault rifle pointed at Hugo's chest, his eyes hidden behind mirrored teardrop glasses. A bead of sweat trickled down his face.

"Hugo, it's not worth it," Cecil said, pulling on his new acquaintance's arm.

"Hugo Lopez?" the guard asked.

"That's right," Cecil replied.

"Psycho-pez?"

"Only good friends of mind call me that," Hugh barked with his arms folded. "You are no friend of mind, asshole."

Lowering his gun, the guard apologized profusely. "I had no idea, sir. I meant no disrespect."

Hugo grabbed the guard's glasses, crushed them in his hand, and threw them overboard. "You're a dead man."

"Kill him later," Cecil said. "We have a meeting to go to."

# CHAPTER 30

**THE HUGHES HELICOPTER** approached the stern of the ship, trailing behind the yacht at a safe distance. The prevailing winds shifted in strength and direction made it difficult to sustain straight and level flight. While the helicopter bobbed in the sky, the ship's crew scrambled to clear the helipad. The erratic hover ended when the marshaller signaled him to land.

"Welcome back, Mister Stone!" the yacht's marshaler said when the helicopter landed.

"Where's Paulo?" Ed Stone asked. "I'm not shutting down the engine. I need to go quickly."

The marshaler nodded and backed away, bent over to stay clear of the rotating blades. Always staying in the pilot's line of sight, he exited the helipad from the side and rushed into the cabin to page Paulo.

In the salon lined with teak wood lacquered in high gloss, the Band of Vipers gathered. "Gentleman, dinner will not be served for another hour," Juan Pablo said. "However, troubling news has been brought to my attention that affects us all."

"Is that the reason the FBI has boarded your ship?" Cecil asked.

"No!" Juan Pablo snapped. "He is on the payroll. I called him here to fill us in directly." He made eye contact with each of the vipers.

"The FBI has a warrant for our arrest. On our return to the mainland, it will only be a matter of time before we are behind bars."

Hugo rose. "I know I am a new inductee to the Viper membership and if you don't mind me asking, what the fuck did I get myself mixed up in?"

"Hugo, sit down," Juan Pablo said.

"Sit down my fucking ass," Hugo said. "I was happy managing operations out of Albuquerque."

"Ah, Mister Stone, you have arrived," Juan Pablo said, waving him over.

"What would you like to drink?"

Special Agent Edward Stone rushed into the salon carrying a large metal suitcase. He placed it on the table with a heavy thud. The Band of Vipers watched the FBI agent dressed in a navy blue flight jumpsuit with yellow FBI lettering, embroidered gold wings and his name in white thread. He removed his green aviator glasses and stowed them in his chest pocket.

"I don't have much time," Ed Stone said. He pointed to the case. "There sits one hundred million dollars in bonds and cash to be divided among you as you see fit. There is only one condition: Do not return to the United States."

The reaction was as expected. Not to return to United States meant abandoning their respective bases of operation. Handing the reigns to their subordinates would be unacceptable. This would inevitably push them out and sever their business interests for good. It was intolerable and the money presented was only a fraction of what they were worth.

"Who do you think you are?" said Domingo Martinez in a calm and controlled tone. A mathematician and professor at UCLA, he portrayed himself as the trim and proper citizen by day. Teaching fresh young minds was his façade while he managed the largest cocaine and marijuana distribution network in the southwestern United States. "I have been in the U.S. for nearly nine years. My reputation and operation are on solid ground. You can keep your money. I am not going anywhere."

"Our situation is dire," Juan Pablo said. "The excellent work you have done to build your operations from the ground up have provided years of prosperity. The code we have clung to ensures that we do not take unnecessary risks. We have always dealt with our issues swiftly and discreetly and kept our identities anonymous."

"That is no longer the case," Ed said. "Your identities and teams are all compromised."

"So what?" Ben Smith said. He was a six foot three white man educated at Oxford. He practiced criminal law in Massachusetts. For nearly two decades, he had controlled the drug distribution in the northeastern region. "Who cares if they know our identities? I think you already know we will push back. What do you have that will convince us we have no choice but to do as you propose?"

"Along with the money, I provided a copy of your FBI files," Ed said. "Before week's end, you will all be behind bars. The FBI has built a case on each of you. I can assure you that no one will see the light of day where you're going."

"Gents," Juan Pablo said. "Without stating the obvious, our leaders in Mexico, Venezuela, Panama, and Columbia do not wish any of you to be taken into custody. The trial will bring attention to our operation."

"And there it is," Domingo said. "Ben, does that sound like a threat to you?"

"I believe it does."

Ed watched the group argue and banter among themselves. The Band of Vipers are some of the richest men in North America, prominent individuals in their own right. They are educated and cunning, elites in their field of expertise. Heading for the doorway, the guard holding an M16 stopped Ed from leaving the salon.

"Ed, can you wait another five minutes?" Juan Pablo asked.

"I need to go," Ed said. "But five or ten minutes more won't make a difference." He scanned the room, looking at each face. "It seems everyone has made up their minds to take their chances with the law. I will leave the suitcase behind should anyone change their mind before the end of this cruise."

He walked back to the group and pointed at Hugo and Cecil. "The FBI does not have any information on these two."

"That's Hugo Perez from New Mexico and Cecil Longhorn based out of Virginia," Juan Pablo said. "They don't know it yet, but they will run our operations. For the interim, Hugo will oversee the west and Cecil will manage our business in the east."

"They need to come with me," Ed said. "We can't afford to have anyone identify them. Can the staff be trusted?"

"Don't worry about the staff," Juan Pablo said. "They are all handpicked."

"That may be so," Ed said. "We need absolute secrecy. Otherwise, this is all for nothing."

Juan Pablo gestured at Hugo and Cecil to leave.

"I don't want to go," Hugo said.

"You must and you will," Juan Pablo said. "Special Agent Stone has been on our payroll for years. He will serve in my stead until we select a permanent liaison. Ed will advise when it is safe to return and I'm not naive to think it will occur any time soon. Until then, shut up and do as you are told!"

"Hurry, men," Ed said. "We need to leave for the mainland now."

Cecil inched forward to join Hugo next to Ed. He tried not to show his excitement at getting off the ship.

"Can you pick up the pace?" Ed said. "The helicopter is burning up fuel we need to get out of here."

"Then what the fuck are you waiting for? Lead the way," Hugo barked.

Ed noticed Juan Pablo handling the metal suitcase. It had a unique construction, without buttons or visible release latches. Spinning the case around, he searched all sides for the locking mechanism to split the case open.

"Well?" Hugo said. "Are we going?"

Ed swung his arm to nudge Hugo to one side. "Juan," he called. "You'll need a key to open it." He had intentionally left the key at the helicopter and theatrically searched for it on his person. Using the palm of his hands, he patted his pockets. "The key is at the helicopter. I'll take these two down and return with it."

Juan Pablo nodded. "No one is leaving this room until we come up with a resolution," he said to his group.

The three hurried down the ladder. On the main deck, Cecil and Ed jogged to the stern while Hugo walked briskly to keep up.

Ed got in the pilot's seat and put Cecil in the passenger seat.

"Where am I going to sit?" Hugo shouted, drowned out by the noise of the engine and spinning blades.

"Wait!" Ed shouted. "Wait here!" He moved around the front of the Huey, keeping himself in Paulo's view.

"You sure took your time!" Paulo yelled. "I don't have all day to baby sit your bird."

"The Band of Vipers is a stubborn bunch," Ed replied.

"Don't I know it," Paulo said, exiting the Huey.

Cecil watched Ed reach underneath the pilot's seat to pull out a small metallic box that held two similar keys. He selected the key with the pointed tip and handled it to Paulo.

"Take this key to your uncle right away," Ed said. "He is expecting you. Hurry!"

Paulo left the helipad and entered the ship's cabin. Cecil also noticed Ed dismiss the ground crew and then circle back around to the passenger side. He unzipped his flight jumpsuit to reach for the Walther PPK pistol hanging from his neck. Tugging on the small handgun broke it free from the ball chain necklace. He pointed it at the Cuban.

Hugo held his hands in the air. Cecil could not make out the discussion. Ed pressed the gun's barrel against the Hugo's head, leading him to the edge of the helipad, overhanging the water. A single shot fired and Cecil watched Hugo drop like a rag doll into the ocean.

Paulo rushed into the salon, flashing the key to his uncle. "I guess you were expecting this?"

"Where's Ed?" Juan Pablo asked. "I expected him to return with the key."

"Uncle, he barely has enough fuel to get back to the mainland," the nephew replied.

"Give me that," Ben said, snatching the key out of Paulo's grip. "I am dying to know what the feds have on me." He strolled to the end of the table where the metal suitcase sat. "I will show you all we have nothing to fear."

Juan Pablo walked to the cabin window to watch the blue helicopter fly away. He wondered by Ed chose to fly on a southeasterly heading when the mainland was west.

"This is an FBI standard issued case," one Viper laughed. "Apply stupid American logic and try unlocking each keyhole in sequence. Insert and unlock the keyhole labeled number one, then number two."

"That's idiotic," Ben said, thinking the mechanism would not be that sophisticated for a mere metal suitcase.

"That's American logic for you."

"The key is not working," Ben said.

"Try turning it counter-clockwise," another suggested.

He did and a pronounced click sounded. The Band of Vipers smiled at one another.

The ship's crew filed into the salon.

"Why are you all here?" Juan Pablo asked.

"Mister Berra, you asked for our immediate presence in the salon," the lead crewmember said.

"By whom?" Juan Pablo asked.

"The FBI agent who came out of this stateroom."

Ben inserted the key into the second keyhole and forced it counter clockwise. "Gents, regardless what we decide to do, the Federal Bureau of Investigation will be out one hundred million dollars."

The Band of Vipers laughed. They watched Ben lift the top half of the suitcase.

"Mister Berra, have we misunderstood your instructions?" The Lead Crew member asked.

Juan Pablo glanced out the window and noticed the helicopter stopped and was facing back at the ship. A feeling of dread rushed over him. "Don't!"

The suitcase fully opened had exposed numerous brick-shaped packages wrapped in brown wax paper. They were all connected with red and blue wires. A display in the center of the case flashed. "Oh shit," Ben said.

The shock wave rocked the helicopter and the explosion shot debris in all directions. The ship's fuel tanks, holding ten thousand gallons of gasoline, ignited a secondary explosion, demolished a third of the ship's aft section. It quickly took on water.

Cecil remained silent as the devastating display unfolded before his eyes. He felt no remorse or empathy toward the lives lost in the explosion. Not knowing what his future had in store for him, he feared nothing.

Ed selected the intercom switch and spoke into his microphone. "You're awfully quiet."

"Just enjoying the show," Cecil murmured.

"I thought you be the type to plead for your life. Your silence is surprising." He shifted in his seat to look at his passenger. "You're not in shock, are you?" He smiled.

"I am here because you, or should I say the bureau, needs me."

The bow of the ship was nearly vertical, slowly sinking below the waterline and Ed steered the helicopter to the wreckage. As a precaution, he checked the area for any survivors. Satisfied the ocean was littered with debris, he glanced at the fuel gauge. "We will be on fumes by the time we reach shore," Ed said.

"Look!" Cecil pointed to the ship. "Someone is climbing on the bow."

"Do you recognize him?"

Cecil squinted. "He is the one who stood up to Hugo Lopez."

"He's either courageous or stupid to go up against Psycho-pez," Ed replied, while approaching the ship. Circling around the bow, the last surviving crewmember is now slumped over the bow's lifeline, bloodied and motionless. "He's not going anywhere."

# CHAPTER 31

**SPECIAL AGENT STONE'S** footsteps echo through the hallway of an abandoned shipyard. He approached a locked door guarded by two armed FBI contractors dressed in black military fatigues, bullet proof vests, and ski masks to preserve anonymity. "It's feeding time, boys," he said, holding up the food tray.

"New York striploin, vegetables, dinner rolls, and a glass of red wine," one of the guards said. "He's treated so well, he must be important."

"If he's that important, the bureau would have put him up at the Fontainebleau," the other guard said.

"Just open the door," Ed said. He noticed Cecil Longhorn seated by the barred window reading a magazine. "I brought you dinner."

Cecil dropped the magazine on the table. He crossed his legs. "When will I be released?"

"You should eat." Ed placed the food tray on the table. "Starving yourself will not get you out any quicker."

"When will I be released?"

"You're so exhausting," Ed said. He picked up the glass of wine. "For the last three days, you have offered no information on where Juan Pablo's investments and liquid funds are located, and yet you have the nerve to ask the same question every time we meet." He took a sip of the wine and returned the glass to the table. "Tell us what we want to know and you will be on your way."

"If I give up that information," Cecil said, stepping to the door, "I will exit this place in a pine box." He turned the knob and as suspected, confirmed it was locked. "We both know if my detainment is on the up and up I would have been arrested. Instead, I'm barricaded here, still alive because I haven't relinquished my only leverage."

Ed cut the steak into small strips and ate one portion. He also tried the vegetables. "There, I have just proven we haven't poisoned your food. Now sit down and eat."

"The steak is overcooked," Cecil said, pushing the plate away. Instead, he drank the wine.

The door creaked open and a guard stepped through. He left the door wide open as he walked to the center of the room. Standing with his feet slightly apart, his hands were behind his back.

Cecil turned his gaze to Ed. "Your escort has arrived. Now go back to your superiors and tell them to find another stooge." He lifted the napkin off his lap and tossed it on the table. "I'm an American citizen, for Christ's sake, and unlike those you sent down to the bottom of the ocean, I know my rights."

Ed ignored him and joined the guard. "Good you made it," he said. "Let's get started."

The guard pulled up a chair and took a seat facing Cecil. He reached into his pocket and pulled out a piece of paper and a 38 caliber Smith and Wesson. Cecil tried to stand and Ed pushed him back down.

"I will ask you several questions," the guard said as he screwed the silencer into the barrel. "For every question you refuse to answer, I will put a bullet in you."

"Your scare tactics won't work on me," Cecil said. "When I'm finished suing the FBI, you my friend will be in for a world of hurt."

The guard fired a shot in the ceiling. "That was a gimme. I will start putting holes in you if you continue to test me."

"I know what the problem is," Ed said. "Perhaps he could hear you better if you remove your mask."

"You think that's the problem?" the guard asked. "This mask is the reason he is being such a fucking dick."

"Yeah," Ed replied with a grin. He stepped away from behind the chair to watch Cecil's expression.

The guard grabbed the mask at the crown of his head and pulled it off in one swoop.

Cecil didn't react. Nothing! It's as if he knew who the guard was all along.

"Oh, it's you," Cecil said.

"You're such a fucking asshole," Thomas said, articulating each word. "I can see your predicament has permanently wiped the smirk off your face. That's a good thing. If I had known, I would have asked the FBI to detain you sooner."

"There you have it," Ed said. "The introduction was very touching." He dragged a chair across the floor and joined the two men. "We'll need to get started and before anyone says anything meaningful again, we don't have much time."

"You're wasting your time," Cecil said. "If I give you what you want, I'd be signing my death warrant. I thought I made this point crystal clear." He looked at the furnished room with freshly painted walls and varnished floors covered in area rugs.

"There may be another possibility. I won't be leaving here anytime soon. If that is the case, then why should I bother telling the bureau where the cartel's money is hidden?"

"Ed, what did I tell you?" Thomas said, "This man has no sense of decency. It is all about him. Just look at him, he has no remorse at all for the deaths of eighteen innocent people on flight 1001."

"I had nothing to do with crash and..."

"If you lie one more time, you'll be taking a bullet," Thomas said.

"Go ahead and make your idle threats," Cecil said. "Your team worked the aircraft the night before." He smirked. "Just face the facts that you are culpable. And you have the nerve to blame me!" He narrowed his eyes. "Who do you think you are?"

Thomas stared at Cecil's smug face and smiled. He pulled the hammer back on his .38 caliber gun and fired a shot through Cecil's left hand.

"Are you bloody mad?" Cecil yelled. He pulled the napkin from the table and wrapped it around his bleeding hand. "You can't shoot me! I have rights!"

"Rights? When you put people in harm's way for profit, you forfeited your rights," Thomas said. "Michael Hall left me a note before he took his life. He provided incriminating evidence against you."

"They're all lies drummed up by a mentally deranged kid," Cecil said.

"Hang on," Thomas said. "It just so happens that this note mentions something about mental capacity, but not in the way you had suggested. Aiden's son, born with Down Syndrome, had figured out the micro-switch was incorrectly installed on the left hand T-Handle. You and your high IQ boys discounted it when the poor fool of a kid raised his concerns."

"You can't prove anything," Cecil said. "It will be my word against a dead man's fabricated story. Michael's termination from ASE provoked these trumped-up charges. It is nothing more than a disgruntled employee seeking imagined retribution."

Thomas fired a round into Cecil's right foot.

Cecil fell to the floor. He frantically removed his right shoe to expose his injured foot and applied pressure where his little toe once was.

"Get him a towel," Thomas said to Ed.

"I will have your head for this," Cecil whimpered. "You will not get away with this." He bandaged his foot with the towel. Ed reached for and lifted Cecil back on to his chair. He grimaced while settling into his seat. "Okay, I concede, I concede."

Thomas walked to the kitchen and poured himself a glass of water. "You will provide Ed the information he needs?"

Cecil eyed Ed. "No, I can't do that, but I will give you as much as you want. I know you hold me responsible..." He paused. "I mean, I know you feel I could have prevented the crash. Knowing what I know now, it is true, I could have prevented eighteen senseless deaths."

Thomas turned off the tap and guzzled a second glass of water. He picked up the gun from the kitchen counter and stepped back into the living room. He dabbed his lips dry with his handkerchief and stuffed it in his back pocket. He spun the chair around and straddled it, leaning forward with his arms crossed on the backrest. "I have thought a lot about aircraft 641, especially the passengers and the crew members. Their demise was set in motion in 1963 when Alexander announced he would start an airline. He gave you the Fairlane retrofit program, which he felt obligated to do after you helped him raise the start-up funds."

"Thomas," Ed said. "We'll need to hurry up."

Thomas nodded and focused his attention on Cecil. "You cut corners to make deadlines and Alexander knew it. His airline suffered for it and would have canceled your contract if it wasn't for the board insisting on giving ASE one more chance. That was your motive, to hide the quality issue on the engine's fire protection panel. You used Michael Hall to secretly fix the units installed on the aircraft."

"If you have it all figured out," Cecil said, "what's the point in rehashing it? I have already admitted I am at fault."

"I will get to that," Thomas replied.

"Losing the Virginia Airlines contract was not the concern," said Ed. "It was losing the unrestricted access to aircraft. It would have stopped your cartel's cocaine smuggling ring. Hiding kilos of cocaine in tire assemblies was truly innovative."

"That's right," Thomas agreed. "No one federal agency would ever suspect honorable aerospace engineers and technicians to traffic drugs. Aviation breeds an inherent code of ethics to champion the skies safely." He rose from his seat and looked out the window at a cruise ship passing in the distance. "This became your guarantee for your cocaine's safe passage across our nation."

"Okay, I appreciate the insight. Now how much will it take to set me free?" Cecil asked.

"Did you put a contract out on Aiden's son?" Ed asked.

Cecil sighed. "What does this have to do with what we're discussing?"

Thomas returned to his seat. "I served in the Korean War..."

"So have I," Cecil said.

"I know. My point is," Thomas continued, "I killed no one during the war. I did not even point a gun at someone. I have however, killed two men stateside. The first man I shot raped Ed's mother. The second was the sheriff in Mariana, Florida, who stood by and allowed a mob to hang my father. Both occurred before I turned nineteen years old."

He took a deep breath. "When we ask a question, just answer it. Did you put out a contract on Aiden's son?"

Cecil's eyes welled up. Tears twinkled down his cheeks. He sobbed quietly and simply nodded.

Cecil felt a barrel at the back of his head and another at his left temple briefly until Ed and Thomas pulled the trigger. Two bullets entered his head, spattering blood against a nearby wall and on the rug. The body fell to the floor.

Thomas holstered his gun while he glanced at Cecil and noticed the arrogant smirk was no more.

"It's too bad we didn't get the banking information from him," Ed said. "It would have put a dent in the cartel's finances."

Thomas handed him the note left behind by an aircraft technician.

"What's this?"

"All the banking information, courtesy of Michael Hall."

"If you had this, what took you so long to take him out?"

"I promised someone I wouldn't go through with it unless I was absolutely sure." He looked at Cecil's body one last time. "Now I'm sure."

* * *

Emma shouted Thomas's name as she searched through his house. Standing in his bedroom, she noticed the Morgan roadster parked by the barn through the partially opened blind slats. She spread two slats apart with her fingers and saw the barn door slightly opened.

"So here you are," Emma said, in her stone cold demeanor. "I spent the last couple of days searching for you. No one knew where you were." She slowly entered the barn. "Where have you been?"

Crouched beside a 1942 Harley-Davidson Flathead motorcycle, Thomas finished the meticulous task of cleaning and waxing every square inch. Minor paint scratches polished away and he had restored the chrome to a mirror finish.

"Are you going to let me in?" He placed the rag in his back pocket and received Emma in his arms. They held each other tight as they kissed.

She pushed him away. "Where the hell were you?"

"I left a note for you on the kitchen table," he said calmly and expressionless.

"I suppose your telephone was out of order? Instead of spending your time waxing your motorcycle, why didn't you ride it over to see me..." She paused when she recognized the old but immaculate Harley-Davidson. Emma ran her fingers along the seat, the gas tank and then along the handle bar. She moved slowly toward Thomas and embraced him. "I'm so sorry," she whispered.

"I cleaned her up for you. She's yours."

She motioned no. "It belonged to Philip. He left it to you and that's how it should remain."

"I already have a bike. Anyway, I'm certain he would approve."

While they kissed, Emma unbuttoned her blouse and Thomas did the same. They laid on bales of hay. She rolled on to him and grasped his head with both hands. "Have I lost you again?" She said, looking into his eyes.

He clasped his hands behind his head. "No."

"Look at me when you answer."

"Emma, I'm not going anywhere. You haven't lost me."

"So where have you been?" She asked. "Don't roll your eyes at me, just answer the question."

"I just needed to take care of a personal matter," he sighed. "You need to trust me when I say I can't tell you."

"And why not?"

"Because you love me and you have all the faith in the world to respect my wishes."

Emma stared at him for a moment then slapped him across his face. "You don't deserve me."

He rubbed his cheek in a circular motion. "That hurt."

"Good. It's supposed to hurt." She gave him a peck on the cheek and another. "You had me worried."

Thomas rolled Emma on her back. "I'll promise that won't happen again." He kissed her on the neck.

"Thomas."

"Mm-hmm."

"Do you really want me to have the bike?"

"Mm-hmm."

"It doesn't feel right," Emma said. She put her finger over his mouth. "Hear me out. Let's say it's on loan to me. I wouldn't have it any other way." She kissed him on the lips and they made love.

*\*\**

Nicolas Diaz, ASE's general manager has twenty-three employee files scattered on his desk. Rummaging through their information a pattern formed connecting similar heritage, race and ethnicity. He dealt with his staff daily so this was no revelation. They all immigrated from Columbia and proven to be hard workers.

"Natalia, do you have those other files I've asked for?" Nicolas shouted.

"I'm still working on it," Natalia said, from her desk outside the office.

"Any luck on getting a hold of Cecil? I really need to speak to him."

"I've been trying for the last two days. I tried his office, home, and the country club." She stepped into the office. "I also spoke to his bodyguard."

"How did you manage to get a hold of him?"

"I didn't, he called here," she said, placing the remaining two folders on his desk.

"Cecil never goes anywhere without Sullivan."

"Sullivan?"

"Yeah, his bodyguard."

She stepped around the desk and glanced at his note pad. "Is this accurate? Two dozen people living at three separate addresses."

"That's not uncommon, they don't make enough money to get a place of their own," Nicolas said, while he collected the folders and set them in a neat pile. "But not one of them have a valid social security number."

"You're thinking they're illegal aliens?"

"I'm not sure what to make of it," Nicolas said. "For whatever reason, something had spooked all twenty-five employees to stop reporting into work."

A knock caught their attention. Nicolas rose from his seat and rushed to the door. "Aiden," he said with an extended hand. "I'm glad you made it."

"Any word from Cecil?" Aiden asked.

"Not yet however everyone we called, they too are asking the same question. Natalie, can you please get us coffee."

"Of course," Natalie said. She left the office and closed the door behind her. Pressing her hear against the oak door, the voices were barely audible.

Aiden placed his leather attaché on the floor next to a chair. Seated and with clasped hands, he rested his arms on his knees. "I hired a local private eye to look into the walk out. He's quite good. It only took him a mere four hours to report back to me." He planted his head into his hands.

There was a long stretch of silence. Nicolas respectfully gave his employer the time to formulate his words. Each passing second felt like another brick laid on his chest. Breathing became difficult in the five second lull and he couldn't restrain himself. "How bad is it?"

Aiden straightened his posture. "Well, Nicolas, I thought twenty-five percent of our staff walked out to demand more wages. It seems they all left the country. They had gone back home where Cecil had rounded them up to begin with." He tapped the armrests gently with the palms of his hands. "It looks as if we're going legit."

"We're no longer moving the merchandise?" Nicolas said. "Aiden, you have no idea how much of a burden you just lifted off my chest." He smiled. "No disrespect but I don't understand why you look so grim. Whatever the reason for them to pull out, I see it as a win-win. We're free and we can get back to doing what ASE does best."

"You don't find it odd that Cecil," Aiden began in a soft and methodical tone. "Our liaison with the cartel is missing just as our Columbian workforce stopped coming in without saying a word?" He stood in the center of the room. "It's too coincidental and I'm certain that this is only the beginning."

Nicolas approached and placed his hand on Aiden. "Cecil always had an inkling this whole operation may fall through the cracks."

Aiden gestured his concurrence. "I remember him sharing that sentiment with me on more than one occasion." He held his head up and proudly said, "He made sure to keep us at a distance. I've always admired that that he wanted to shield us from any repercussions."

Nicolas put his fist up to his mouth to conceal his grin then cleared his throat. "Aiden, I know you hold Cecil in high regards for helping your business get off the ground and all. No disrespect, but he isn't the person you think he is. Keeping us at a distant is merely to manipulate and pull all the strings without interference."

"Well, whatever his motives were..." Aiden was interrupted by the noise erupting outside his office. The door swung open by FBI agents lead by Special Agent Reese. "Mister Lynch?"

"Yes," Aiden said, looking through the opened door. He saw FBI agents emptying ASE's filing cabinets into cardboard boxes. "What's the meaning of this?"

"I have a search and seizure warrant," Special Agent Reese began, "And you two are under arrest."

"On what charge?" Nicolas said.

"For starters, drug smuggling," Special Agent Reese said, as he handcuffed Nicolas.

"That's absurd!" Aiden declared.

Special Agent Reese stood toe-to-toe with Aiden. "We have twenty-five of your employees that say otherwise."

# CHAPTER 32

**AT THE ONSET,** the NTSB's accident investigation into flight 1001 had concerned Olivia. Alarmed by the media's fixation to the bird strike speculation had rendered both engines inoperable. Unsettled by the false information leaked to the Washington Post, at first, she did not react. There was no need to address the unknown source, who claimed to belong to a federal agency.

A week into the investigation, the headlines changed and alluded to pilot error or maintenance induced, and then implied aircraft design flaws. Olivia could no longer look the other way. Yielding to her legal counsel's advice, she did not engage the press. Instead, she pressured the federal agencies to denounce the media's hypothetical claims on their investigation.

While Olivia anxiously waited for the NTSB to publish their report on the accident, she called in favors from five of Virginia's eleven state representatives and two state senators. She needed help to persuade Charlottesville's airport management and the local FAA office to join forces with her airline. Collectively, they would take the lead and impose mitigating measures to instill air travel confidence.

They established the Avian Control Committee consisted of specialists in aeronautics, agricultural, environmental, federal air rules, biology, and ornithology. These specialists elected Jean Martin,

Virginia Airlines' first officer, who planted the seed for such a committee. The committee members elected Jean to serve as the chairperson after they had witnessed his drive, enthusiasm, and knowledge on the subject matter.

The committee's purpose and objective, when cast in stone, was to impose bird deterrent measures in a safe and humane manner. Titled appropriately as the Avian-Airport Project, there was no intent to reinvent the wheel. Instead, they're tasked to examine all available data and to immediately apply proven methods to address the airport hazards. The project encouraged universities to take part and expand the current knowledge base quickly on all wildlife threats occupying at or near the airport.

It's September 27, forty-one days following the crash and a month after forming the Avian Control Committee. A large white banner hung across the entrance over the road leading into Charlottesville Airport. It read, 'Students Cutting Class' in bold red lettering with 'An Avian-Airport Project' written below in blue. Air travelers notice the flurry of activity throughout the airport grounds. They watched university faculty members and their students answer the call to improve flight safety by setting up their bird deterrent solution.

Each group of students assembled at Charlottesville Airport worked diligently in their assigned twenty-acre parcel of land. They set up their version of a bird deterrent contraption and once deployed, they would return to the airport regularly to collect data on its effectiveness. They would make adjustments throughout their senior year, gauging their success or failure by the bird population in their respective area.

In all this activity, the Virginia Airlines board members strolled through the airport grounds, stopping occasionally to speak to the students and learn what part in the avian-airport project they have undertaken. They watched with great interest to Virginia Tech's use of multi-colored balloons launched into the sky. The black painted eye with attached ribbons worked similarly to a premise of a scarecrow, but with greater effectiveness. Tethered to a ten-foot carousel ensured its unpredictable movement while floating fifty feet in the air.

"I can't believe how everyone has come together," Olivia Cooper commented to the board. "Remember this spectacle, guys. This is a rarity. The community pulling together to ensure we have no repeat of 641's tragic accident. Look at them. They all want to be active participants to improve airport safety."

"I hope it's not all for nothing," Betty Windsfield said. "It would be a shame should the NTSB decide it was something other than a bird strike."

"I don't think it would matter," Anthony Peters said. "Everyone we spoke to realizes the bird strike played a part but are aware the risk of a repeat event is unlikely but not impossible. Keeping birds away from the airport is the right thing to do to lessen aircraft damage and it benefits everyone."

"I hope the press is here today," Sean Hopkins, Virginia Airlines board member and Hollywood producer, said. "It would be a nice change to see them report factual information instead of the rubbish they had been printing."

"Don't hold your breath," Betty sighed. "The media are nothing more than bloodsucking turkey vultures. They knowingly sensationalize Virginia Airlines crash to sell newspapers."

"It was disappointing," Olivia said, "To suggest technological advancements we made on the Fairlane turboprops was the catalyst for both engines to stop working that morning." She glanced at Sean, Cecil's strongest ally and collaborator. "They implied the new design concept we introduced to heighten aircraft reliability and safety may have overwhelmed the pilots."

"I knew it was a matter of time for someone to throw that in my face," Sean said.

"And why would that be?" Olivia said, mindful Sean put up a fierce argument against the costly Fairlane retrofit.

Sean flashed a grin. "Let me see, it's a feeling I have because of my opposition ten years ago is still spoken today. Oddly, everyone has forgotten I admitted publicly I was wrong. The modifications have exceeded our expectations."

"We know it wasn't you," Olivia said. "And whomever went to the press merely regurgitated your concerns." Turning to face the group, she continued. "And I'm not suggesting it was one of us. If it's any comfort, the unknown source claimed he or she is a government employee."

"It's no secret we rarely agree and have said inappropriate comments at one another," Betty said. "But none of you have given me a reason to suspect our discussions did not remain confidential. We may be dumb, but we're not stupid."

"The Fairlane program has employed a lot of people in this area," Olivia said with pride. She crossed her arms and focused her attention to the airport's activity. "My father did a good thing to start up an airline in his hometown. It gave the economy the needed booster shot in Albemarle County."

"They are good decent people," Betty said. "They became fact checkers and took the press to task."

"Yup," Olivia agreed.

"The best part," Sean said, "is watching the media criticize one another."

"The pot calling the kettle black," Betty said, shaking her head. "It's unfortunate the FAA and NTSB took as long as they did to set the record straight. Information leaked to the press was bullshit and shamed the media back into reality."

"Look at that." Anthony pointed to the falcon flying above the treetops, weaving side to side until it struck a kite resembling a waterfowl. With balled up talons, the falcon punctured a hole through the wax paper wings. The predatory bird tumbled as it pressed through the ruptured kite and regained flight control just above the treetops.

While holding out her left hand, Emma blew three spurts into the whistle. She watched her falcon, Scarecrow return, descending in a slow approach. It landed on her left hand and plunged her beak into Emma's palm, searching for her reward.

"Scarecrow," Emma said, pulling the predator closer to her face. She eyed the bird. With a stern tone said, "What the hell has gotten into you? You could have hurt yourself, smashing down on that kite."

"Not to worry," Todd Bailey said. "She loved every minute of it. That kite is three times her size and that did not stop her at all." Watching Emma stroke Scarecrow's breast feathers, he saw similarities between the two. They were cut from the same cloth; tender creatures with strong constitutions.

"I suppose," Emma replied. She reached into her side pouch to retrieve another treat for Scarecrow. "That was a foolish stunt. I can't bear to see her get hurt."

Todd put the hood on Thunder's head to calm his bird's anxious behavior. "I think it is best I put him away," he said. "I believe the crowd is a little too much for him."

"He is acting a little jumpy," Emma said. "I've noticed Thunder is behaving that way when separated from Scarecrow. I have an idea." She headed toward her pickup truck to get the falcon cadge.

Scarecrow and Thunder perched together on the cadge, both tethered. Todd carefully removed Thunder's hood and his bird flapped his wings frantically while getting his bearings. Thunder then moved immediately beside and settled next to Scarecrow. He nibbled at her talons and the crowd watched in awe at the sign of displayed affection.

Emma witnessed the crowd's intrigue with the two apex predators. Within a few feet, they watched these majestic animals, outside a barrier and the confines of a cage. The public's electrifying experience gave her the idea to generate revenue on Todd's behalf. She sent Debbie Bailey to fetch her Polaroid camera from her truck. Debbie returned with the camera and Emma sent her off to town with twenty-five dollars to purchase three more film packs.

The crowd grew larger and questions were posed about the raptors. They ignore Todd and it's a damn pity, Emma thought. If they can only see beyond his missing legs, wheelchair, and crusty behavior, they would learn he has much to offer.

"Ladies and gentlemen, may I please have a minute of your time," she shouted to get the crowd's attention. The chatter softened. "Quiet please," she said, giving the group a few seconds to comply. She removed her jean jacket and laid it on the ground by her feet. "You're looking at a pair of peregrine falcons, the fastest animals on earth."

"Faster than a cheetah?" a twelve-year-old boy asked.

Emma smiled. "The cheetah is the fastest land animal at seventy-one miles per hour, but it does not compare to speeds of over two-hundred miles an hour." She walked over to the boy. "Do you still have any doubts?"

The boy did not say a word and merely shook his head no.

"Do you want your photo taken with a falcon?" Emma asked.

"Yes, please!"

"What is your name?"

"Eric."

"Ladies and gentlemen," Emma said, "While I get Eric ready to be photographed with the falcons, let me introduce you to Todd Bailey. He is the master falconer and I am his apprentice."

Emma noticed the crowds eerie glances shot at Todd. An elderly woman, gray haired and petit, leaning on her wooden cane, caught Emma's attention. The woman displayed the most sympathetic facial expression. That did not sit well with the apprenticing falconer.

"Before Mister Bailey became a master falconer, he used to handle alligators," Emma said, then pointed to his missing legs. "As you can tell, he wasn't good at it."

The crowd laughed.

"Working with falcons," Emma continued, "is less of an occupational safety hazard."

The crowd laughed a little louder.

An eight-year-old girl ran up to Todd on the verge of tears. She took Emma's comments literally "Why did the bad alligator eat your legs?"

"Because I'm a slow learner," Todd responded.

The crowd's laughter intensified.

"No," the little girl cried.

Todd lifted the girl and placed her on his lap. "We're only joking, honey." He hugged her and smiled when she reciprocated.

A second or two lapsed when the girl released her embrace and asked, "What really happened?" She rubbed her eyes, wiping away her tears. "Was it an accident?"

"You are a smart little girl," Todd replied. "Yes, I had an accident far faraway."

Emma moved in and took the girl in her arms, "Would you like a picture taken with the falcons?"

She nodded.

Emma whispered in Todd's ear, "You have their attention. Educate the crowd on falconry and the role it will play in the Avian-Airport Project." She faced the onlookers. "If anyone else wants their photo taken with the birds, it's only five dollars."

An elderly man approached dressed in tattered coveralls, worn out boots laced with string, different colored socks, and a new white shirt that stood out of place. He had an excessive amount of Brylcreem applied to his parted hair and Emma guessed he was a farmer. Flashing his folded money, he said, "I only have two dollars." He glanced at the two falcons. "Would that be enough to have a bird sit on my hand for a spell?"

Emma put the money in her shirt pocket. "Thank you for the ten dollars sir," she said, raising her voice. "After I'm done with the kids, I'll take the photo of you holding a falcon."

"You're mighty kind, ma'am," the farmer said.

The marketing scheme worked. Others lined up, now eager to pay ten dollars for a photo op with a raptor perched on their hand. Emma dealt with the photo shoot, while Todd chatted with the on lookers.

A reporter and his photographer moved through the crowd. They overheard Todd say, "Before the dawn of aviation, our feathered friends had the skies all to themselves."

"With the advent of airplanes," the reporter blurted, "the skies are now shared. Why don't birds move out of the way of oncoming airplanes?"

"Within a planes' flight path, birds have as much of a chance to evade a collision as you would from a sniper's bullet." The crowd chuckled. "It's hard to stay clear from an object you don't see coming your way."

"Touché," the reporter smiled. Pointing to the falcons he said, "I suppose they will keep the flight path clear of birds?"

Todd gently nodded. "The falcons will serve as the airport's guardian similar to a school crossing guard."

"A crossing guard?" The reporter questioned looking up from his notebook.

"School crossing guards provide a safe passage for our children to cross a busy street. Scarecrow and Thunder will do the same for the arriving and departing airplanes."

The photographer held a large camera up to his eye. "Look this way, sir."

Todd turned his head and saw a bright flash.

CPSIA information can be obtained
at www.ICGtesting.com
Printed in the USA
LVOW08s0303200517
535205LV00001B/1/P

9 781525 501418